The
Last
Trail
West

The
Last
Trail
West

A Western
Quest Series
Novel

Stephen L. Turner

SUNSTONE
PRESS

SANTA FE

Sunstone books may be purchased for educational, business, or sales promotional use.
For information please write: Special Markets Department, Sunstone Press,
P.O. Box 2321, Santa Fe, New Mexico 87504-2321.

Book and Cover design › Vicki Ahl
Body typeface › Book Antiqua
Printed on acid-free paper
⊗
eBook 978-1-61139-292-0

Library of Congress Cataloging-in-Publication Data

Turner, Stephen L., 1957- author.
   The last trail west : a western quest series / by Stephen L. Turner.
      pages cm. -- (Western quest ; 8)
   ISBN 978-1-63293-010-1 (softcover : alk. paper)
   1. Cattle trails--West (U.S.)--Fiction. 2. Texas--History--20th century--Fiction. 3.
Western Stories. 4. Historical fiction. I. Title.
   PS3620.U76596L37 2014
   813'.6--dc23
                              2014019839

WWW.SUNSTONEPRESS.COM
SUNSTONE PRESS / POST OFFICE BOX 2321 / SANTA FE, NM 87504-2321 /USA
(505) 988-4418 / ORDERS ONLY (800) 243-5644 / FAX (505) 988-1025

Dedication

THIS BOOK, ALONG WITH *On the Road to Glory, Up from the Ashes, and On the Western Trail* is dedicated to Aaron Lloyd Turner. It is also dedicated to Ilene Hairston, the daughter of Bill Turner, and to my uncle, John K. Turner, Jr. These grandchildren of Aaron Lloyd and Ella Turner left this life during the writing of this book.

Acknowledgements

THANKS ARE DUE TO MY COUSINS Ella Turner Bullard of Albany, and Glynna Turner Critz of Sweetwater who shared many family photos passed down to her by her mother, Ruby Carson Turner. They have been fountains of family information especially pertaining to this last book. Thanks to my friends Jim Ainsworth and Harlan Hague for reading and evaluating my manuscript, and to my parents Aaron Lynn and Alene Turner for their patient proofreading. I must mention the tireless encouragement of my wife, Roberta. Without her encouragement, this series would have never come into existence.

Part One

Paradise Lost

1

Humble Beginnings

April, 1883
Belle Plain, Callahan County, Texas

"GIT OFFA HIM, SAM!" THE LONG black bullwhip cracked loudly over the big mule's left ear. He recognized his name and the meaning of the lash, instantly straightening out his gait and ceasing to lean on the right lead mule's shoulder. "All of ya worthless coyote bait, git up!" The whip popped over their broad bay backs. They surged into their collars with a will. Sometimes they had to be reminded of their duty. The four matched bay draft mules were tall, thick and muscular, just like the ones pulling the two wagons behind me. These twelve mules were as good as any west of the Brazos.

The wagons were freshly painted Studebaker heavy-duty freight haulers, the best money could buy. The harness was well-oiled and in good repair, with polished brass hames and buckles. The dust rose in thin red clouds over the following wagons, driven by Kirby and Keenan Nixon. They had worked for me since they were just kids as we drove wagon loads of buffalo hides and thousands of cattle up the Western Trail to Dodge City, returning with loads of freight, trade goods and barbed wire. The arrival of the Texas Pacific Railroad to Callahan County had eliminated the need for long cattle drives, and freight arrived by boxcar to the depots in Baird and Clyde.

Kirby was twenty, six foot two and thin as a coach whip snake. He had dark red hair, bright blue eyes and so many freckles there was hardly any room for his big smile. Keenan was eighteen with darker hair and eyes. He was about six feet tall with shoulders as broad as an axe handle. What he lacked in freckles, he made up in pure sass. We had been together since 1876 and they had become like brothers to me.

The freight business was doing well. We had won the bid on the contract to haul the Callahan County wooden courthouse and limestone jail from Belle Plain to the new county seat in Baird. The railroad had gone six miles north of Belle Plain, spelling the beginning of the end for another small town.

The wagons rolled up to the newly completed foundations in Baird. The foreman put all his men unloading the wagons. The mules were unhitched, watered and allowed to loaf in the shade of a big elm tree. In half an hour, we were heading south with empty wagons, except for one sack of mail and two crates of groceries for the little Belle Plain store. We repeated the process from first light until dusk six days a week; a few more days would see the job finished.

———

Camp was set up behind Matt Dawson's house and blacksmith shop. There was a five acre trap with good grass and fresh windmill water. It took a while to rub down and curry all twelve mules and check the harness. We gave the stock three pounds of oats and two pounds of corn morning and night.

Matt came out to sit by the fire, drink coffee and swap a few lies after supper. He brought his curly headed little boy, Travis, with him.

"Boy, what are you carryin' that big ol' stick for?"

"I gonna shoot a big ol' bear, Aaron."

"You reckon they's any around here, son?"

"I doan know. But if they is one, I'm gonna shoot it!"

"He's plenty punchy, Matt. Seems like I remember when you were pretty full of vinegar, too."

"I calmed down a little since then, ol' timer." He cut his gray-blue eyes at me and grinned.

"Who are you callin' old? I think you're about twenty-nine, and I'm only thirty-three!"

"Aaron, looks like you forgot. I'm thirty-three same as you. You just act like an ol' man!"

"What year was you born?"

"I was born in 1850, same as you. I didn't grow much 'til I was about seventeen."

"You and your little brother, Jake, went up the trail with me to Sedalia in '66. That was seventeen years ago. I guess you have grown up some. We had some times in Abilene, Caldwell, and especially, Dodge City. Lord, it's a wonder you and ol' Pecos didn't git shot or thrown in jail."

I fired up my pipe and passed around a jug of scamper juice. We reminisced about the friends we had known so well that had gone from this life.

"I enlisted in the Confederate army as a twelve year old messenger boy with my brothers, David, and Noah. David died at Camp Stephen Douglas in Chicago, but me and Noah got outta there alive. Last time I seen Noah was in '72. I figure his bones are restin' up on the Plains somewhere."

Passing the jug, Keenan stared into the fire. "Me and Kirby was both there when Pecos got kilt. I won't ever forget him if I live to be a hundred."

"Yeah. He survived the war, stampedes, storms, Injuns and outlaws, but a dang bronc killed the best horseman I ever knew."

The reminiscing settled over us like a dark cloud. We had seen plenty together, but we had lost a part of ourselves we could never replace. Matt gathered up Travis, who had fallen asleep, and headed for the house.

"Night, Aaron. Boys."

When sleep came over me, I dreamed of those days when we were young and brave on the trail and of those we had left behind along the way. Their spirits hovered near through the night.

———

Ella Fisher was the most wonderful woman I had ever met. She wasn't the kind of woman who would attract the attention of other men, for to see her true beauty you had to know her. She knew when to speak to me and what words to say. She knew when to leave me alone. She was warm, kind, giving, and generous to others. But she had a feisty side that any woman would need to stay married to a man like me. She didn't take herself too seriously, she loved to laugh, and she accepted me for who I was. Ella brought out the best in me, made me want to do better, reach higher and be a better man. She blessed our home with a forgiving spirit.

For all her qualities, Ella was afraid of mice. I had thought it would be funny to put a dead mouse next to the basin on her dresser. She had screamed like the house was on fire, then seeing how hard I laughed, she whacked me on top of the head with the basin. It was worth the bump on my head for the laugh I briefly enjoyed. In Ella, I had met my match.

She had borne us a son, Aaron Allinson, in 1880; everyone just called him Al. Folks seemed to love the little stinker with the auburn hair, bright blue eyes and big smile. The kid never met a stranger. He would talk to anyone, even the livestock. Riding the freight wagon with me or the Nixon brothers, or riding his Welsh pony with us to check the cattle, were favorite activities. He would give every day all he had until he fell asleep still in his clothes.

By homestead and purchase we had come to own sixteen sections of the best cattle country in Callahan County, and had inherited another four adjoining sections when Pecos was killed. Our little corner of the world was about a hundred miles east of the breaks that began the approaches to the Southern Plains, and about a hundred miles south of the Red River. The wind rippled through the beautiful native grasses that clothed the gently rolling plains. The breeze carried whispers of promise and the scent of success blended with the smell of fresh grass.

The perimeter was a tight five wire fence, and the land was fenced into four section pastures, each with its own windmill. The ranch would easily carry our six hundred cows and their calves, with plenty extra to grow out each year's calf crop another summer to sell as long yearlings. We had started the herd with maverick longhorn cows we had roped out of the river bottoms and cane brakes, keeping the best heifers for cows. But I had bought English bulls, first Red Devon, then a few years ago, Herefords, to improve the herd. Each year we selected the top twenty percent of the heifers to add to the herd. Once we reached our carrying capacity of six hundred pairs, the bottom twenty percent of the cows was culled. It had brought up the quality quickly. Now we were holding back some of the bull calves that were at least three-quarters Hereford for replacement bulls, but they had to be exceptional animals.

Besides the herd, there were the dozen prime draft mules, a good Guernsey milk cow, several Tamworth hogs, and a mixed flock of laying hens. Along the creek, there were native pecan trees, a large fruit orchard, and Ella's big garden with a tall deer-proof fence.

A white Sears and Roebuck catalogue house built from a kit was the crowning glory of the ranch. I had built a house; Ella had made it a home. It was all ours; we didn't owe a dime to anybody. From either front or back porch, we would sit in the evening, where on still days we could hear the laughter of the water in the stream. The wind rustled the leaves and branches of the ancient pecan, cottonwood and elm trees along the creek. Life on our piece of Paradise on Pecan Bayou was good, very good, filled with peace and joy. I knew we had been abundantly blessed.

2

Cure for Coyotes

June, 1883
Turner Ranch, Callahan County, Texas

THE BIG RED DUN MARE SIDE stepped suddenly and stopped dead in her tracks. Her ears pointed to the left as she rolled a deep snort through her nostrils.

"Easy, Moon. What's got you boogered? Let's ease up and have a look." I patted her thick, muscular neck and clicked to her, taking a deep seat in the saddle, just in case she blew up under me.

In the tall grass lay the partially eaten carcass of a white-faced cow. Protruding from her reproductive tract was the gnawed skull of a calf. Fresh coyote droppings mixed with red hair left little doubt as to the cause. Apparently, she had delivery problems and the predators had seized the opportunity to attack her.

"Moon, there's plenty left to eat. Those coyotes will be back tonight. We'll be waitin'."

Riding down about an hour before sunset, I left Moon at the bunkhouse corral and walked south toward the kill site. The water in Pecan Bayou was low enough I was able to jump across without getting my boots wet. Scrambling up a big cottonwood tree, I eased out onto a stout branch and leaned against the smooth trunk. It was about seventy feet to the flattened grass where the carcass lay. The light breeze was blowing gently toward me, carrying my scent away to the north. Levering in a .44-40 cartridge, I settled down to wait.

Within twenty minutes, the coyotes began to yelp from various directions, calling the pack together. The closer they got to the fresh kill, the louder and more frantic they sang. Just as the sun disappeared and dusk descended, the tall grass came alive with half a dozen coyotes tearing into their feast.

I braced myself against the tree, held my breath and took a well aimed shot. The muzzle blast made an orange fireball in the fading light, but sent a coyote cart wheeling through the air to his death. I reflexively levered in and fired two more quick rounds. One coyote was slammed sideways by the heavy slug, as a third crawled on its front legs frantically trying to escape. I could see bushy tails jumping through the grass in three directions, but there was nothing to shoot.

Climbing down, I checked my rifle and slowly approached the crawling coyote. He snarled defiantly, but a bullet through the brain ended his misery. All three pelts had already started shedding the thick hair of winter, making them worthless as hides.

I walked back across the creek and up the gentle slope to the corral. Tightening Moon's cinch, I mounted and headed home in the cool darkness. "Moon, ol' girl, this ain't over by a long shot."

Kirby, Keenan, Little Al and I made our regular freight run to Baird. The brakeman from the Texas Pacific stopped me on the loading dock.

"Aaron, while y'all was loadin' your freight, I heard you talkin' about the coyote trouble. When I was a boy, my daddy got to losin' calves to coyotes. He got him a pair of donkeys and never lost another calf."

"Well, you sure got my attention."

"There's a man near Mineral Wells that's shippin' a fine load of big Spanish jacks to a man out in El Paso. There was a little extra room in the boxcar, so he loaded a couple of jennies to see if they would sell. The jacks are bringin' $250 each, but jennies are $20 apiece. Wanna look at 'em?"

The dun jennies were fifteen to sixteen hands tall and thick. "I'll take 'em both!"

We got our deliveries made and even picked up a few new catalogue orders as the big eared donkeys trotted along behind. We got to the bunkhouse about four thirty and led the jennies down to the creek.

Soon, the ever curious cattle were wandering up to meet their strange looking new pasture mates. They had seen donkeys and mules before, so these pretty girls were welcomed without much ceremony.

We could hear coyotes in the distance. The jennies raised their long ears attentively. One jenny took off at a dead run. We saw a bushy tail stick up above the grass and wheel around in the opposite direction. She was on him before he could escape, felled by a smashing stroke of her hoof to his skull. She kept pawing him until there was nothing left but a bloody mess.

The other donkey raced off, braying as she ran. She plucked a fully grown coyote out of the grass at a gallop, slamming the predator into the ground until he was a mass of broken bones and bloody fur. We never lost another calf to a predator as long as we kept donkeys with the herd.

Al gave Ella an all too vivid version of the encounter. "Dem donkeys kicked and bited dem ol' coyotes 'til dem was dead! Dey ain't neber comin' back."

Resting her hand on her belly, Ella remarked "Well, Aaron, Al doesn't seem upset at all. Maybe our new arrival in January won't bother him too much, either."

My day just kept getting better and better!

––––––––––

The ranchers were hurt the summer of '83 by a lack of rain. Keenan claimed a frog could live its whole life without ever learning to swim. Pecan Bayou was a string of disconnected pools fed by underground springs. The meager two inches of rain that fell during the growing season was not enough to wake the sleeping grass from dormancy.

The cattle had eaten last year's surplus grass. It was dry, but still nutritious. We usually weaned the calves in early November, but we pulled them off their mothers in early September and drove them to Baird to sell as lightweights. The dry grass had not been especially good for making milk or fattening cows.

The official county weigher looked at me with sadness in his eyes. "Son, you usually sell big long yearlin's. These little guys only average three hundred and eighty pounds across the board, steers and heifers. I'm right sorry for you. I know what good stock you run."

I telegraphed the weight to the McCoy Cattle Company buyer in Fort Worth. His telegram chilled me. "Market flooded. Feed high. Ten cents per hundredweight. Sorry."

I responded "No rain. No grass. No choice. Must sell. Thanks."

We rode down the dusty main street of Baird to the bank. We waited in the lobby reading newspapers until the clerk signaled my draft had been deposited. "Boys, that's only $2250 for the year."

"Gosh, Boss. I remember you walkin' outta the bank in Dodge with a draft for fifty thousand dollars. Do me and Kirby still have jobs?"

"Now Keenan, that was sellin' way more full grown cattle in a good market. I doubt we ever see those kinda days again. But, yeah, you two knuckleheads still have jobs. We got cattle to tend and a freight business. We'll get by."

"Aaron, we ain't got the grass to get the momma cows through the winter. How are we gonna feed 'em?"

"I don't know yet. We'll figure somethin' out."

On the way back, we stopped in Belle Plain to make a delivery, then went by Matt Dawson's blacksmith shop. "When Jake and Dad bought that extra range, they planned to grow their own replacement stock. There's quite a bit of pasture that hasn't been grazed in two or three years. Jake's out back. Let's go talk to him."

"Heck, yeah, Aaron. I'd be glad for you to have it. I got way plenty for my stock and could use a little cash. Pasture usually rents for ten cents an acre. That seem fair?"

"Yeah. I need about 3000 acres. That would be $300. I can make that work."

We left the twenty bulls to clean up what sparse grass was left on my place. The Nixons, Al, and I drove the six hundred gentle cows the twelve miles to the Dawson Ranch. We would keep the freight business going and check on the stock; we had to pass right by Dawson's place on our route.

Very little rain or snow fell that winter. If spring rains didn't fall in abundance, we would be in trouble.

3

A Time to Weep, a Time to Mourn

January, 1884
Turner Ranch, Callahan County, Texas

"AARON! AARON, WAKE UP! SOMEthin's wrong with the baby!"

"What is it?" I was now fully awake and alarmed.

"The baby. Somethin's wrong. Get Robin Nixon quick."

I stepped out on the porch in my bare feet and long drawers and rang the bell, calling the boys from the bunkhouse a half mile away. I continued to pull the rope until I heard an answering ring from their bell. They would be here soon.

Running back into the house, I found Ella in a cold sweat. She looked more worried than I had ever seen her. "Bring me some towels; lots of towels. Light the stove and make sure the hot water tank is full."

I tossed kindling on the embers in the kitchen stove. When they began to blaze, I built up a good hot fire with dry wood. The water tank on the end of the stove was full, but I set a kettle of water on to boil for good measure. Remembering the towels, I ran to the bedroom and handed them to Ella. I pulled on my jeans and shirt. "Honey, what's goin' on?"

"I felt the baby kickin' and turnin' and kinda roll over. Then nothin'. It hasn't moved since then and I'm havin' contractions."

The slamming of the kitchen door announced the arrival of the Nixon boys. "Back here in the bedroom."

They took off their hats. "Miss Ella. Aaron. You need us?"

"There's trouble with the baby. Keenan, hitch two mules to the buggy and go get your mother. Use the whip." He was out the door without a word.

Kirby was good help in a medical emergency. The look on his face radiated worry.

Ella gasped. "Kirby, would you step into the kitchen for a minute, please?"

"Aaron, my water just broke." I raised up the sheet to see that the birth water was darkly stained greenish-black with thick sticky clumps. The baby had released its bowels in the womb. I knew that this was bad, really bad.

"Raise up just a little and let me get this wet towel out and put down a fresh one." I rolled up the soiled one and held it to my side.

"Aaron Turner, you show me that towel. I can tell from your face somethin's wrong." I opened the towel and showed it to her. "I've heard about this. It means the baby is in bad trouble."

"Yes. I think so, too. Robin will be here in a little bit. We'll take good care of you, I promise."

———————

Keenan's shouts brought the heaving mules to a sliding stop close to the porch. This time, it was Robin's voice I heard. "Go help your brother with the mules, then y'all get back here. Stay close."

Our friend of so many years appeared in the bedroom. Gray was streaking her red hair, but her blue eyes telegraphed trouble. "Hello, Aaron. Would you leave us girls alone for a minute?"

When she met me in the kitchen, the toughest woman I knew was clearly shaken. "Aaron, I don't hear a heartbeat at all. The baby isn't movin'. They release their bowels when there is serious trouble. I got a strong feelin' the baby has turned and somehow twisted the cord."

"You think the baby's dead?"

"I'm not gonna lie to you. Yes. I think it is. She's already dilatin' and havin' hard contractions. The closest doctor is thirty-four miles away. Even if we ruined the horses we couldn't get there in time. This is gonna be a hard night."

Robin tied cotton ropes to the footboard of the bed to help Ella when she pushed. Kirby and I ran things back and forth. All the commotion woke Al, but Keenan sat with him and read stories.

With the approach of daylight Ella's groans reached a new level. Robin urged her to push. There was a mighty scream and a limp, lifeless, blue baby girl was born. The cord was tightly wrapped around her neck. Wiping the baby off with a clean towel, I handed her to Ella's outstretched arms. "I'm so sorry, Darlin'."

She held the baby tightly against her chest and rocked and sobbed as I sat helplessly next to her in a chair. Robin said it looked like Ella was going to be fine.

Keenan stepped inside the bedroom door, wiping tears from his face. "I'll take Momma to town, but then I'll be back. Me and Kirby will take care of all your chores today."

Kirby rustled up some cornbread, scrambled eggs, bacon and a pot of coffee. He quietly entered the room. "Miss Ella, I brought you some coffee with a little milk and sugar just like you like it. Al already et a good breakfast. I'll get him dressed and try to keep him busy. The cow's been milked and the stock fed. Aaron, you want me to bring you some coffee and a plate of breakfast?"

"That sounds good, Kirby. Thanks."

Ella reached out for Kirby's hand and pulled him down to give him a kiss on the cheek. "Sweet friend. Thank you, Kirby. I'll take you up on the coffee."

Ella took my hands in hers. "Aaron, these things happen sometimes. I felt this baby growin' inside, and was so excited about her already. I feel sad and very disappointed. But I've got you and Al. We'll have more children. It'll take time, but we'll get over it. I love you." We sat together in silence and cried, holding hands. The tears I had held back all night came like a flood. I hurt for the loss of the baby; I hurt for Ella.

I ate my now cold breakfast, and heated up my coffee before I drank it. Kirby had started a pot of pinto beans cooking on the stove. I looked out the window and could see him pushing Al in the tree swing, as Al laughed as hard as he could in the cold January air. Beyond him, I could see Keenan digging a small grave in the pecan grove. Thank God, for friends like the Nixons. I stepped out in the back yard. "Hi, Pa! Me and Kirby been playin'." I scooped him up into my arms and hugged him tight.

Kirby walked toward me with an extended hand, but I grabbed him around the shoulders. "I'm so sorry, Aaron."

"Thank you, friend." Keenan walked up from the pecan orchard and handed me a flat limestone rock on which he had neatly scratched "Baby."

The women helped Ella pretty up and walk out to the pecan grove. Jake Dawson and Kirby tuned their fiddles, while Matt tightened his guitar strings. Keenan stepped out of the back door carrying a small bundle wrapped in a baby quilt, quiet tears rolling down his face. He gently laid the unnamed baby girl in the grave. *Shall We Gather at the River* played sweetly in the background, chilling me more than the winter breeze. It would take a long time for our hearts to heal, but our friends had already started the process.

————

February brought a heavy, wet, eight inch snow. March delivered a series of rains totaling eight inches. April arrived with even more rain. We drove the cows home from the Dawson place in time for calving season. The western wheat grass and annual rye came on strong. As the weather warmed, blue grama, sprangle top, little bluestem, side oats and buffalo began to grow. The huge disorganized flocks of slate gray sandhill cranes pushed northward after their winter stay along the coast. Pecan Bayou babbled in joy past the orchard where Ella's fruit trees were in full bloom and her garden was off to a good start.

The effects of the previous year's drought showed itself in our calf crop. Usually ninety percent of our cows had a calf. The stress of the drought dropped that figure to around seventy-five percent, as we had only four hundred fifty-two calves from six hundred cows. We culled the one hundred and forty-eight barren cows and drove them to Baird. Not only were they open, they were thin, weighing just under eight hundred pounds each. The cattle buyer was able to offer me $15 a head, but the $2200 wouldn't be enough to see us through another year, even with the freight business.

4

Frozen Hell and Echoes from the Past

November, 1884
Baird, Callahan County, Texas

THE POSTMASTER HANDED UP THE canvas satchel of mail I was to deliver, along with a huge smile on his face as he waved a newspaper. "Aaron, he won! Grover Cleveland beat that Republican. We're gonna have the first Democrat President in twenty-five years!"

"Let me see that paper. 'Grover Cleveland Soundly Defeats Republican James Blaine.' Ain't that somethin'! I'll spread the word on my deliveries."

The folks along my route and in the dwindling community of Belle Plain were excited. We had experienced nothing but Republican presidents since Abraham Lincoln had been elected in 1860. I wouldn't give you two bits for the hide and tallow off of any of them. It was time for a change. Maybe things would turn for the better.

Good rains fell through the summer of '84, growing enough grass to easily carry our cows and weaned calves through the winter. Maybe we could sell some long yearlings in the fall of '85. The cattle business had been thrown badly out of balance by the drought of 1883, and surplus cattle were still depressing prices.

Up on the Plains, the big ranches had gone into fencing in a big way. Unfortunately, some of them were fencing land that didn't belong to them by deed or lease, were keeping smaller ranchers away from water, and even building fences straight across public roads.

The small ranchers, farmers and settlers had responded by carrying fencing pliers and cutting offending fences, including much that was quite legally built. A war of sorts erupted that required the intervention of the Texas Rangers. New state law made fence cutting a felony. I didn't see the troubles spreading down our way, as most of our country had been fenced up for several years. But we were soon to have troubles enough of our own.

I still had a happy warm feeling in my heart over Cleveland's election and inauguration. The Nixons, Al and I rode out in late January of 1885 to check the stock. The sky was blue, but the wind had shifted to the north and had a raw edge to it.

"Look, Boss." Keenan pointed to the north. There was an enormous bluish-black wall cloud with rolled under edges stretching completely across the northern horizon.

"Boys, this thing looks bad. Get your stuff from the bunkhouse. You better stay with us until this is over. Get all the mules and horses, drive 'em over to the shed at the house. Come on with me, Al."

We penned the milk cow with her calf, unsaddled Moon and Al's pony then put them in the horse lot. Shutting the door on the hen house, we were just in time to let the Nixon boys through the gate. The freight mules and our saddle horses loped into the big pen. The shed was large enough to shelter all of them.

"We left the jennies with the cows."

"Let's gather enough firewood to completely fill the back porch." Ice pellets bounced off my hat and face. "It's here, boys!"

Sleet and freezing rain fell all night. The big feed store thermometer by the back door showed twenty-two degrees by supper time. We played checkers and tried to entertain Al. There were extra bunks in his room for the boys. I stepped out on the porch about ten to grab another armload of wood. It was down to sixteen degrees and sleeting hard.

In the gray light of a frozen dawn, the thermometer stood at a darn cold four degrees. Sledgehammers were needed to break the ice at the shed. We forked down a day's worth of redtop cane from the loft for the stock. Al carried a steaming teakettle of water to the chickens. He carefully gathered the eggs into his basket.

"Daddy, dem chickens broked all der eggs." We looked them over to find that they were all frozen solid as rocks and had cracked their shells. Ella washed and then boiled them. After a quick breakfast of boiled eggs, bacon and coffee, we headed over to the cows at the bunkhouse pasture.

We saddled the horses and bundled up against the cold and wind. The horses' shoes skidded on the hard ice. The only redeeming feature was that the sleet had left the surface slightly rough. "Let 'em pick their way, boys. Don't need a man or horse gettin' hurt."

It took all three of us to get the gate at the bunkhouse pasture open. It had frozen to the ground. We set about breaking the ice on the big tank with sledgehammers and used pitchforks to drag out the big pieces. It was frozen six inches thick. Once the cattle realized they could get a drink, they crowded around the tank. They had ice two inches thick on their backs, but looked like they were holding up pretty well.

We rode out to the big pasture that held the yearlings and bulls. It didn't take long to clear their tank of ice. The bulls seemed to be handling the cold weather fairly well, but the calves didn't have the layer of fat the mature cattle had. They were looking stressed.

"Boss, there must be four inches of ice on those yearlin's backs, and they got frozen snot hangin' down from their noses."

"Let's just hope it don't last too long. We ain't got any way to feed 'em."

After riding back to the bunkhouse, we built a hot fire in the potbelly stove and made coffee. The horses sheltered out of the wind in the shed. Once we could feel our fingers and toes again, we rode back home, slipping and sliding all the way.

"You boys notice it's cleared off and the wind laid? It's gonna git colder than rip tonight!"

Ella had a big pot of chili steaming on the stove with a fresh pan of corn bread and lots of hot coffee. We finished up a few chores, then settled in for another long, cold night.

The next morning, the temperature stood at twelve below zero. That was the coldest I could remember.

When we got to the cattle, they didn't look as good as the day before. "Their flanks is drawed. Some of 'em got frozen tails, ears and teats. I sure feel sorry for 'em. At least they got some cover in the trees along the creek."

The ice in the tank was eight inches thick. It was hard to break even with the sledgehammers. The yearlings looked worse than the cows. Some of them were starting to cough. I knew we would be seeing pneumonia soon.

With the clear skies, it got up to twenty-two degrees, but the lack of cloud cover saw temperatures plunge overnight to eighteen below zero. When we finally got to the bunkhouse the next day, the cattle were lowing pitifully. They were hungry and miserable. The sunshine had caused a little thawing, and many of the cattle had ice balls between their toes, making it painful for them to walk. The ice in the water tank was ten inches thick. We had to use a long spike and the sledgehammers to make cracks in the ice. It was back-breaking work.

"Boss, the yearlin's look like frozen skeletons. They got their heads hangin' down and coughin' out yeller snot."

"Kirby, I think we're gonna lose a lot of them before this is over."

During the night, I heard the tail of the windmill groan as it swung with the wind. I ran to the back door in my long drawers to look at the metal weathervane. The wind was coming out of the southwest! Warmer weather was on the way.

The next day, the temperature struggled up to thirty-eight degrees. Ice was melting everywhere. The cows' hooves broke through the slush to the muddy forage below. They shoved the ice aside with their noses and greedily ate as much as they could get. They ate through the night and into the next day, stopping long enough only to drink.

We carefully rode through the storm ravaged cattle on the second day of the thaw. Most of the ice was gone except in the shade. Two cows had broken legs and had to be shot.

"We gonna butcher them out, Boss?"

"No, they're fevered. The meat won't be fit to eat. If it was a fresh break, it would be fine to butcher them, but these have been sick for a few days."

All the bulls were fine, but the same could not be said for the yearlings. "They ain't gonna be hurt much missin' ears or a tail, but look at 'em. They got their heads hangin' down, they're hardly eatin' anythin'. Their ol' guts are drawed up clear to their backbone and they're coughin' up their lungs. We'll just have to see how many that green grass and sunshine can save, if they make it that long."

By the time the winter grasses were green and the wheatgrass in the draws had started to grow, we had lost one hundred and seven yearlings to pneumonia. The rest looked like twenty miles of hard road, but maybe they could stumble along for the twelve mile walk to the shipping pens at Baird by fall. For the first time, I felt the cold hand of doubt touch my shoulder. There was a hint of anxiety that the ranch could be slipping away from me.

In September, Keenan made the freight and mail run to Baird. He had hurried through his deliveries, and had even taken one new catalogue order on the way home. But from the lather on the mules, it was obvious he had come back in a hurry.

"Boss! Boss! I got somethin' important for you!"

I stepped from under the shed after putting new shoes on Al's pony. "You look like a Kiowa war band is on your back trail."

"No, sir! You got a letter from a bank in Omaha marked urgent and personal!"

"All right. Put your wagon up and cool those mules off and brush 'em out. Looks like you run ten pounds of fat off 'em gettin' here."

As I read, I got more excited than Keenan. "Ella! Ella!"

"What in the world is wrong with you, Aaron Turner?"

"A long time ago, Noah wrote that he had money in a bank in Omaha. The bank says since they haven't heard from him in ten years, they are to send the money to me. I got to send them a telegram with instructions of where to wire the money."

"How much is it?"

"Thirty-six hundred dollars. I've got an idea. You know Belle Plain has been dryin' up to nothin'. The storekeeper over there hardly sells anythin'. He offered to sell me the buildin' and all the goods for twelve hundred dollars. We could tear it down and haul it over here on the Abilene road right at the foot of Lytle's Gap. There's enough folks around here I already haul groceries for and a good bit of road traffic. I could keep runnin' the freight business and haulin' the mail."

"Well, if there's anybody that can make it work, it's you."

———————

The wire transfer arrived at the Baird bank, followed a couple of weeks later by a small box. There was a yellowed note from Noah inside.

Aaron,

If you are reading this, you know I have probably left this life. After Mary was killed, it took the heart out of me. Nothing was left but hate. I wanted revenge on the Comanche who had done it. I joined up as a scout with Colonel Mackenzie to hunt them down. When there weren't any more Comanche left to fight, I moved up into Nebraska to fight the Cheyenne and Arapaho. They're all on reservations now. There is no one left to hate but myself. I hope I can find peace before I leave this earth. The money may be of some help to you. I want you to have these spurs. You had them made for me in Abilene. I always loved you, little brother.

Noah

Feeling the spurs, holding the letter, hit me how much I missed Noah. Of course, we had fought like brothers will do, but nobody else had better lay a hand on me. We had been really close, especially during the time mother had been married to that horrible old drunk. Then we had gone off to war together. That had welded a bond even stronger than brotherhood. But Noah hadn't cared for the life of a rancher, and had taken a chance on the excitement and fast money to be made on the buffalo killing fields. It had cost him everything.

I grabbed my pipe and lit it as I headed down the slope to sit under a big tree on Pecan Bayou. As the fragrant smoke wreathed my head, I watched the clear water swirl past and thought of those who had been taken from us: Pecos, my mother, two brothers, and the two stillborn infants. I had Ella and Al, and a host of trusted friends. In that, we had been blessed. Life had been hard with these deaths, droughts and blizzards, but we would get along the best we could.

The Nixon boys and I stayed at their mother's house in Belle Plain for three days as we tore down the entire store and loaded all of its stock of goods. We carefully hauled it up and over Lytle's Gap. Another four days went into leveling and rebuilding, but the reassembled shelves were ready to stock. Our new little store had canned meat, sugar, syrup, cheese, coffee, tea, crackers, sardines, dried and canned fruit, and some hard candy. There was a mixed case of hard liquor, cartridges, patent medicines, quinine and calomel. We also had a small stock of pots, pans, utensils, needles and thread, and bolts of cloth. The catalogues held the key to anything a buyer could want. The sign over the store read: Turner Store, 1885; A.L. Turner, Proprietor.

5

Respite

July, 1885
Turner Ranch, Callahan County, Texas

THE RAINS HAD COME STEADILY
and the blessed native grass responded with strong, luxuriant growth.
Our cattle looked like they had been through a war. There were cattle
who would forever limp through life; cattle missing ears, tails and
teats. But their calves were fat and healthy. The yearlings could now
be called long yearlings. Some had survived in good health, some had
become "chronic lungers" who coughed and wheezed perpetually.

We stopped in to visit Matt Dawson at his smith, and deliver a
keg of horse shoe nails and three crates of horse shoes. "Dad says the
enrollment is way off at the college. He's gettin' ready to move back to
East Texas. They sold their place to my brother, Jake."

"I think he'll grow some feed on the crop land, or maybe some
wheat for pasture. He wanted their pasture land. It's fenced and fixed
up pretty nice like your place. The college said they was gonna offer
science and ag one more year, then see how the school is doin', but its
dryin' up just like Belle Plain. I aim to move my smith and house down
your way before too long."

"My little store is makin' it all right, but we'd have plumb starved
out if we hadn't had the freight business and mail contract."

"Yep. And you're gonna have another mouth to feed around
there pretty soon from what I hear."

"You gossip like an ol' woman! But Ella's due any day now. We're takin' Robin home with us. Ain't takin' any chances this time."

After breakfast on August 1, 1885, Ella's water broke while she was doing the dishes. Labor was coming on fast this time. Before noon, we had a pretty little brown haired baby girl we named Minnie. She was loud, healthy and hungry. Ella was fine and I was relieved.

That afternoon, right after Keenan got back from taking Robin home, it started to rain. It was a gentle, slow, soaking rain. It rained all afternoon and all night, and continued for four wonderful days. The rain gauge only held six inches, and it had overflowed on the third day. I sat on the porch, holding Al in my lap, as I smoked my pipe, and Ella rocked the baby. We watched and listened to the rain. Nobody rang the bell at the store to ask for groceries; the roads were too wet to travel. Pecan Bayou churned with red-tinged water and the land burst forth in a celebration of life. The grass, which had gone dormant with the heat of the summer, surged forward with new green growth. The native flowers that had bloomed weakly early in the summer turned the prairies into a carpet of color. The trees, which had looked tired and weary from the long summer heat, raised their branches in robes of deep green leaves. We remembered Minnie's birthday as "the time it rained so much."

"Aaron, folks who live in places where there's lots of rain and plenty of grass, don't know the joy of watching a slow soaking rain. There's no such thing as an unwelcome rain or newborn calf."

———

Come October, we drove the sorriest bunch of three hundred and forty-five yearlings I had ever sold to the railroad pens at Baird. They had been born in a dry year followed by the worst ice storm anyone could remember. Some limped, some coughed, but these were the survivors, the ones that had been too hardy to quit, too strong to give up and die. They were ugly, with missing ears and tails, but I was proud that these had made it to market. I telegraphed the buyer for the McCoy Cattle Company their break-down by weight, sex, and the number of chronics. He knew me well enough that I wouldn't cheat him. And I knew him well enough that he would give me a fair price. He offered six cents a pound for the steers and heifers, but only three cents a pound for the chronics. These long yearlings were eighteen months old; they had been born in the spring of 1884. Now they averaged only five hundred and eighty-three pounds. Our whole set brought just a hair over a thousand dollars. What was I going to do? I couldn't make it rain when the pastures needed it. I was powerless to stop the coldest weather we had ever known. I couldn't go out and raise up fat cattle to sell from the bones bleaching along the creek. I couldn't cause the market to move up or down a dollar. I could, and I would, try again. But the twinge of doubt I had felt before was growing stronger.

The remaining ranchers up on the Plains were mostly big operators with a handful of medium to small sized outfits thrown in the mix. The issue of fences there was not resolved. The big men still fenced across public roads, and jealously guarded water sources they needed, even on land they did not own. The state of Texas finally had enough. Any fence that crossed a public road had to have a gate. The public was not to be hindered from travelling these roads. They belonged to the people of Texas, and not the ranch they happened to cross. Every fence was to have a gate at least every three miles, whether there was a road or not, to facilitate gathering strayed livestock. Land leased from the public domain must allow any and all water resources to be shared by all who needed them. It was about time somebody did something.

6

Hotter than Hell's Hinges

June, 1886
Turner Ranch, Callahan County, Texas

OUR HERD WAS DOWN FROM THE ideal stocking rate of six hundred head to about four hundred and fifty, thanks to drought and blizzards. We had not had the replacement heifers to keep, and not enough grass to feed more head of cattle. But now the land had stabilized and rebounded from the battering it had received from nature. I was starting to think about selecting the best fifty heifers to add back to the herd. As the hot wind blew down through the cottonwood trees, the southwest wind seemed to carry a warning of worse things to come. Even in the heat, a cold hand clutched my heart.

The wind blew from the south, southwest or west every day. It was hot and dry like the doors of Hell had been left wide open. Usually, the wind would die down and cool off at night, but not this summer. The wind blew down from the Plains all day, all night, every day, week after scorching week. There was no breath of moisture in this cruel wind, no dew on the grass, no clouds in the piercing blue sky.

The native grasses never broke dormancy. The weeds sprouted and withered away. Except along the creek, the trees dropped their leaves, which promptly blew away.

Ella carefully watered her garden each day from the cool water of the discharge pipe on the house windmill. As the tender plants sprouted, the dust-laden hot wind cut them down again and again until she gave up. She concentrated her efforts on saving the orchard and her precious roses.

The cattle ate the surplus growth from the previous year's crop. It was dry and dusty, but it was all we had to offer.

Summer sizzled into fall, and still the drying wind blew each day. The wind sucked the life out of plants, beasts and men. The creek below the house was dry as a bone.

We weaned the calves in September, as we were running out of last year's grass. They looked better than last year's crop of yearlings, but the grass that had fed them and their mothers wasn't able to do much more than fill empty stomachs. The cows hadn't given much milk, and the calves hadn't eaten fresh green grass to fatten them. They were small and stunted. Perhaps they would grow out of it if they could be provided better groceries somewhere else.

We drove four hundred and forty-two steers and heifers the twelve dusty miles to Baird. The freight agent ran them in bunches across the scales at the railhead.

"Aaron, I hate to tell ya, but they only averaged three hundred and ten pounds."

"Boys, the drought has folks sellin' all classes of cattle everywhere. They're flooding the market. The best McCoy's could do was two cents a pound."

"Shoot, I remember selling big steers in Dodge for thirty-five dollars a head. And I heard Pecos say you sold some in Missouri for over forty."

"I know. Cattle were in big demand then and we had a world of grass to fatten 'em. Nobody wants these little knots we're tryin' to sell. But I took his price. I had to."

On returning to the ranch, we rode through the cattle, culling everything but the very best two hundred cows and the five best bulls. On arriving at the railroad, the cull cows only averaged seven hundred and thirteen pounds. They looked a lot better than some of the others we saw. The bulls, which normally would have weighed well over twelve hundred pounds, barely broke a thousand. Since the bulls and cows were big enough to slaughter without fattening, we got three and a half cents a pound. The bulls would have brought at least three times that price in a good year. This wasn't one of them. My ranch, which not so long ago held six hundred head of the best cattle and grass west of the Brazos, was a pitiful sight of dry dusty pastures. How could a man support a family on two hundred head? But I had started with nothing in 1865, and I wasn't licked yet.

The freight agent told me there was a farmer who had a huge barn in Baird stacked to the rafters with shocks of redtop cane. The boys and I found him at the hardware store. I recognized him from making freight and mail deliveries to his place.

"Afternoon. The drought hurtin' you like the rest of us?"

"Hello, Aaron. Yes, I haven't made any cotton to take to the gin in two years. The rain last fall came too late to help the cotton, but I did make a good crop of redtop cane. The bank is leanin' on me to make my payment, but all I've got is burned up fields, a few chickens and hogs and a milk cow."

"The freight agent said you might be willin' to sell some of your hay if you had plenty."

"I sure have got plenty. The barn on my place is full and oughta be enough for over a year. It's good hay; never got rained on and stored in a barn. You interested?"

"I might be. Could we look at it?"

The hay filled the barn literally to the rafters. It smelled fresh and clean, not moldy or dusty. The shocks were heavy and well-tied. I was definitely interested.

"Aaron, I know hay is mighty scarce around here. I don't want ya to think I'm tryin' to cheat ya. But I've got to have fifteen hundred dollars to pay the bank and another five hundred for us to live on. I guess I'll price it at two thousand dollars for the whole barn load, and you get to use the barn as long as you need it. Tell you what I'll do. I let you use my heavy hay wagon all winter and spring for nothin', as long as you bring it back to me the way you found it."

"All right. I know you're in a wreck same as us. No, I don't think you're cheatin' me. If I don't buy it, somebody else will. Will you guarantee me a few good rains in the bargain?"

"Neighbor, I think you need to be talkin' to somebody a lot more powerful than me."

We had twelve good mules, three drivers and four heavy wagons to haul hay from Baird to the ranch. We built wooden sideboards on the wagons six feet above the sides. We hitched the second wagon directly to the first, and repeated it with the other two. The harness, chains and double trees were arranged for six mules to pull each tandem wagon.

Little Al sat beside me on the wagon box. He was already tall and thin for a six year old, and had gradually obtained a mule-skinner's colorful vocabulary. "Git up there, you sorry, good for nothin' mules! Hup!" I cracked the whip over their broad bay backs. The six mules lurched the empty wagons forward on the dusty road followed by the Nixons. It took three hours to make the twelve miles to Baird. We could have made it sooner, but the mules had a hard pull ahead of them.

The barn had a huge loft and front and back doors so a team could drive straight through. Keenan and Kirby tossed the bundles down as I stacked them to get a maximum load in each wagon. When they were full, I tied a stout rope across the sideboards to keep them from spreading apart on the rough roads home. Once we were loaded, we unhitched the mules to let them water and loaf while we grabbed something to eat.

"Boss, can we go to that chili parlor I like so much?"

"Keenan, you know how bad that chili tears you up."

"I know, but I wanna aggravate Kirby on the way home."

We loaded up on pretty good, but greasy, spicy chili and plenty of cornbread. Even Al ate a bowl. "Papa, that shore was good chili. I couldn't eat all of mine. Do you want it?"

"No, offer it to Keenan."

"You want it Keyman?" He raked it into his third bowl and lapped it up.

"Papa. Somethin' stinks."

"Hush, Al."

"No, Papa. Somethin' stinks real bad!"

"Hush, Al!" By now, Kirby and I were red in the face from trying not to laugh. This time, Keenan added sound effects to the aroma.

"Papa! Keyman tooted really loud, and it stinks, too!"

The cook came out frowning. "Son, you are bad for business!" and opened all the windows.

"Papa, I'm gonna tell Miss Wobin what Keyman done!" We all fell out laughing. Fortunately, we were the only customers at the time.

"I swear, Keenan, you'll colic the mules!"

The return trip was complicated by Lytle's Gap. The grade of the hill and the weight of the load proved too much even for these big mules. We hitched all twelve mules onto the first tandem wagons, with Kirby and Keenan holding the lead mules by their halters. When we reached the top, I moved the boys into the wagons. "When we start goin' down, you ease on the brakes. When I holler, you put everythin' you got into those brakes, or we ain't stoppin' 'til we hit Pecan Bayou."

As the boys applied the brakes, the wood and metal groaned loudly. As they pressed harder, I could smell smoke coming from the oak pads. The wheel mules began to dig in their heels as they had been trained. The metal cleats on their shoes left freshly gouged dirt in the road. But the brakes and mules held, and we were home free. We unhitched the first two wagons and repeated the process with the second set. We had all the hay tightly packed in the loft at the house and the big shed at the bunkhouse corrals in time for supper.

I had noticed the livestock had grown their winter coats earlier and thicker than I had even seen. The sandhill cranes were heading south by the end of September in large flights, followed by great flocks of ducks and geese. In my thirty-six years, I couldn't remember them coming so early.

Because of the hot dry, summer, the earth had not yielded its bounty, but Ella had proven to be fruitful. She went into labor October the third while doing the lunch dishes. I sent Keenan to get his mother, but this baby wasn't waiting, it was already crowning by the time Ella got settled into the bed. She grabbed the soft cotton ropes tied to the bedposts, and began to push with each contraction, while I supported her under the back and shoulders. After only a few minutes of hard pushing, a blonde-headed little girl slid onto the cotton towels laid on the bed. I cleaned her with a dry towel, and she began to loudly exercise her strong lungs. We had silk thread to tie off the cord, which I treated with iodine. Robin arrived just as I was finishing.

"Got in a little hurry, did ya, Ella? Couldn't you find any better help than this old cowboy you married? Let me check and see how big a mess he made. All the men folk to the kitchen and leave us girls alone, please."

"Well, for a beginner, you did real good, Aaron. Course I figure Ella told you what to do." A blonde, blue-eyed wrinkled baby girl was noisily getting her first meal. "What's her name?"

"I want to call her Lela Mae, if that's all right with you, Aaron."

"Seems to suit her. Come over here and see your baby sister, Al."

"Another gurl? Why can't I have a brother?"

"Maybe next time, son."

"Oh, Miss Wobin, I gotta tell you what Keyman done in Baird..."

7

Blue Norther

November, 1886
Turner Ranch, Callahan County, Texas

MATT DAWSON HAD ALREADY gotten busy at his relocated blacksmith shop next to the store. Their house stood neat and tidy next door to it on the red dusty Abilene road. Robin had us disassemble her house, move it from Belle Plain, and rebuild it next to Matt's house. Ella and I were glad to have Robin close at hand. She agreed to run the little store for us.

One Sunday at the dwindling church in Belle Plain, I sent Al to give a nickel to the preacher. "Thank you, Al. Do you want me to put it in the offering plate?"

"Nah. Pa sent it to you. Said to say you were the poorest preacher he knew." I laughed out loud, but caught a sharp elbow from Ella.

In the middle of November, we awoke before dawn to a screaming blue norther. The temperature at supper had been a pleasant fifty-two degrees; the thermometer on the back porch now read eight degrees! The wind had an edge to it like a knife.

"It's sure enough the real deal. Go on back to bed; I'll get the stove going."

"If you're gonna be up and out in this, you need some hot coffee and a good breakfast. You get both stoves goin', and I'll stir up somethin' to eat. I can't sleep with the wind bangin' branches into the house, anyway."

As I stepped off the protected back porch, the north wind

slammed into me like a freight train. My hat went sailing away, only to be saved by a rosebush. I rescued it and ran back to the house. "I'm not wearing enough clothes!"

I pulled on my scratchy wool winter drawers, two heavy shirts, a pair of overalls on top of my jeans and shirts, and my heaviest jacket topped off with a wool cap and a pair of leather gloves. Now, better equipped for the weather, I made it to the wood pile. I got the kitchen stove going for Ella, then lit the pot-belly stove that heated the rest of the house. It was cold enough in the den to see my breath. I stepped into the kids' room and pulled another quilt over Al and Minnie. Baby Lela was happy as a clam having our bed all to herself.

I filled the back porch with wood and stepped out to check on the milk cow, horses and mules. A fine dry snow was falling, but the wind carried it away parallel to the ground until something slowed it down enough to drift to the earth. I fed all the stock before running back for the warmth of the house.

"Strong and black, just like you like it."

"Thanks. That sure smells good." In a few minutes, Ella set a pan of biscuits and a plate of bacon and eggs on the table with butter and plum jelly.

I harnessed a pair of mules, riding one bareback and leading the other, to the bunkhouse. I saw smoke coming from the stovepipe, so I knew the Nixon boys were up. I turned the mules loose under the shed and rain for the dugout. "Hey, boys! Got some coffee for a frozen man?"

"Mornin', Boss. Yessir. It's just been made."

"Y'all put on your warmest clothes. It's really bad out there today. I saw you already have the sled ready."

Once the wooden sled with its oak skids was pulled into place, we filled it to the top with shocks of redtop cane. Kirby ran ahead to open the gate, but hit an icy spot and went sprawling across the frozen ground. The coming gray dawn revealed that the tiny dry flakes of the night had changed to huge, fat flakes blowing horizontally across the dreary sky. In this short time, it had already piled up two inches deep on the flat grassy areas, with drifts up to eighteen inches deep in sheltered places. I had never seen it snow so hard.

"Boys, looks like we're in for it now!"

The homemade sled inched along as the mules carefully picked their footing. The cows saw us coming and started up the slope from the creek. We tossed out bundles about ten yards apart until we had a long line stretching away until it disappeared into the blinding whiteness behind us. The sheaves were far enough apart that all of the cows could eat at once. We saved a final bundle for the bulls that we threw across the fence into their pasture. When we got back to the bunkhouse, we found that the water tanks were starting to freeze. The ice wasn't too thick or hard to clear.

We left Kirby at the bunkhouse; Keenan took me back home in the sled. It was too windy to even shout to each other. When we got to the house I gave him his instructions.

"Here's some extra coffee. Y'all got plenty of grub and firewood?"

"Yessir."

"If it's still like this tomorrow, put out hay again and break the ice. I'll take care of things here. I want to hear you ring the bell mornin' and night so I'll know you're all right. Keep ringin' 'til you hear me answer. This is the first time I've left you there, but it'll take all day for us to make the trip back and forth. You're both grown; I shouldn't even worry about you knuckleheads."

"Heck, Boss. We'll be fine."

Keenan and the mules vanished into the blizzard before they had gone fifty yards. This was going to be bad; Old Testament, plagues of Egypt bad.

———

After supper, we made pallets in the den for Al and Minnie. In weather like this, it was hard to keep their bedroom warm. We closed all the doors off the den except the one to our bedroom. Ella put more quilts on the bed and another on the kids. Baby Lela would sleep between us, as usual. I had to get up twice during the night to add wood to the pot-belly stove. When I opened the door into the kitchen, my breath hung like frost in the air. A pitcher of water we had left on the kitchen table was frozen solid. I had often cussed and complained about the stove keeping the house too hot; tonight, it was keeping us alive.

In the morning, the snow was eighteen inches deep on flat ground with drifts four or five feet deep; only the top wire of the north fence showed above the snow. The wind still howled around our ears, while the snow flew in blinding whiteness. The thermometer on the back porch had frozen, leaving a thin red icicle. As I surveyed the frozen landscape, I heard the bell from the bunkhouse above the roar of the wind. Pulling the frozen rope, I rang out a reply.

By afternoon, the wind died down enough to allow the snow to fall at a forty-five degree angle. The flakes were smaller, and visibility improved. We had survived the worst.

That night the wind finally laid. The snow fell straight down and the smoke rose straight from the chimney. After two days of howling wind, the quiet was eerie. Fully two feet of snow had fallen. The drifts reached the eaves of the house and barn. Even with all the inconvenience of the ice and snow, the moisture was a blessing.

Dawn broke through thinning clouds, the first sunlight we had seen in three days reflected from the snow that blanketed everything in sight. As the day warmed, water began to drip off the eaves and the ground became slushy. The wind shifted to a gentle dry southwest breeze, hastening the thaw. Rivulets of runoff trickled into Pecan Bayou. By afternoon, wheelbarrows and odds and ends of tools could be seen poking through the melting snow.

I saddled up Uncle Joe, my bay gelding, and sloshed over to the bunkhouse. The boys had survived no worse for wear. We loaded the hay sled and let the mules slog through the mud and slush to feed the cattle. Only a hundred and seventy-eight head came up to eat. They limped slowly up the slope with painful balls of ice between their toes. Several had frozen ears, tails and teats. Two had frozen their feet so badly, their hooves had fallen off, leaving them crippling along on frozen, bloody stumps. I shot them both in the head with my pistol. We left the sled and walked down the draw to find twenty-two cows had frozen to death.

"Want us to skin 'em out to sell them hides?"

"Nah. They won't bring six bits a-piece. Y'all can butcher out as much meat as you and your mother can use. I don't think I can eat it. This whole thing makes me sick."

Once the roads had dried, we made the trip to Baird to refill our hay barn. It would take two trips, so we got a very early start. We stopped at the chili parlor again for lunch.

"Oh. It's you again. I'll go open a winder. Mr. Turner, did y'all get hit pretty hard at your place?"

"We lost over twenty cows that froze to death, and I had to shoot two more that lost their feet. It woulda been worse if we hadn't had the extra hay."

"Guess you ain't heard yet about up on the Plains. They had ninety percent death losses. The cattle turned their tails into the north wind and kept walkin' south lookin' for shelter. They hit those drift fences and stood there 'til they froze to death. Paper says most of the big outfits are broke."

I sat back and stared at the cook. "Ninety percent losses; I guess I oughta feel grateful."

While we were eating, a man came in with an Abilene newspaper. "Look at that picture from north of Lubbock." There were hundreds of cattle stacked up as high as the fences that stopped them. I felt a cold sweat break out. This winter wasn't over yet.

In January, 1887, the cattle were still weakened from the November blizzard, when another just like it hit us right between the eyes. We fed all the hay in the shed and counted our losses: another twenty-one head had died.

We refilled the shed with redtop cane again. And in February, another storm hit. This time, it was more sleet than snow, but was just as hard on the surviving cattle; another twenty-seven head had frozen to death. Each storm pushed the herd closer to the edge, and the ranch sank into deeper trouble.

We used up the last bundle of feed to try to get the remnant of the herd through the winter. At least there were fewer head to feed, as nearly half the cattle lay in various stages of decay in the pasture. The tough little donkeys seemed unfazed by it all, and the five bulls, although thinner, had fared well.

The spring of 1887 brought abundant warm rains and ideal weather. The cattle started to fatten on the new spring growth. But the three blizzards had worked an undiscovered loss on the battered cows. Of the surviving one hundred and twenty-eight cows, only seventy-five had calves.

At weaning time in the fall, I picked through the cattle and calves. There were thirteen that had suffered so much from the freeze they had raised stunted calves, even during an ideal summer. They were destined for the railhead at Baird. I picked the twenty best heifers to hold back to grow into replacement cows. The rest of the heifers, all the steers and the cull cows went to town. The weights were low; the prices even lower. I went to the bank with a check for two hundred and twenty-five dollars; a year's worth of work and grief for almost nothing. The herd of six hundred of the finest cattle around was reduced to one hundred and fifteen cows, twenty weaned heifers, and five bulls. The little store made enough to pay Robin and return a small profit. Of course, we were able to buy our groceries wholesale. The freight and postal business declined as more people moved away. I had not felt this discouraged since the dark days after the war.

8

Hinnies at the Home Place: Honey, Punkin, and Al

Spring, 1888
Turner Ranch, Callahan County, Texas

THE BUNKHOUSE BELL RANG URgently in the frosty March air. "Guess we better go see what's up, Al. Ring 'em back, son." He stepped out onto the kitchen porch and rode the rope up and down until the bell at the bunkhouse stopped.

Al was nearly eight, and big enough to saddle his own pony. We loped the half mile to the bunkhouse. Something had the Nixon brothers riled up.

"Come see what's in the corral!"

Kirby took the horses while Keenan led the way, chaps flapping in the wind. "I thought them donkeys was just gettin' a grass belly, but look here!"

Two line-back dun foals stood wobbling next to the guard donkeys. "I guess ol' Sam Houston ain't as picky a stud horse as I thought. That's the only hinnies I ever seen. Don't get too close, Al, 'til I see how the mommas feel about us bein' here."

"Easy, little momma. We just wanna see your baby."

She eyed me carefully. I patted her neck and reached forward to stroke the foal swaying at her side. At the touch of my hand, she shied away and hid under her mother. The jenny nuzzled my face, giving her blessing to my approach. I squatted down and held out my hand. The momma gently nudged the foal closer to me. "That's it, little girl. Let me pet ya."

I stroked her velvet soft black nose and she nibbled my finger. Soon, I was able to run my hand along her back, up and down her legs and over her ears. She stood quietly, keeping an eye on her mother. Finally, I cupped her soft nose in my hands and slowly exhaled into her nostrils.

"Okay, Al. Go easy. I think she's ready to let you love on her. I'm gonna go check out her sister."

The other filly was just like her sister in size, color and temperament. The jenny stood quietly as the baby and I got acquainted. I heard giggling and looked up to see the first foal licking Al's face.

"That tickles!"

"Kirby, bring that bottle of iodine from the shed. We need to paint it on their navels."

"Hey, Boss. I don't see any afterbirth, but the ground over here is wet and kinda bloody."

"I reckon they both ate it, Keenan. It hides the scent from predators."

"Pa, I'm namin' this 'un 'Honey' and her sister is 'Punkin'."

Kirby dabbed the iodine on the wet umbilical stumps. "Why did you breathe into their noses like that?"

"So they will always recognize my scent as somethin' safe. It seems to work."

By the end of the week, the boys had made little halters and taught both the babies to lead. They got plenty of attention and were about spoiled rotten. Al and the boys always brought them a little nibble of oats or a piece of apple. Al spent every spare minute with them.

We finally turned them out into the pasture. Al would ride his pony right up to them and the babies would come running straight to him. It was the first time that I realized Al had a special gift with animals.

The spring rains were better than we had dared to hope, the weather was gentle and mild. The native grasses greened up early and grew thick and fast. The depleted herd produced as nice a set of calves as had been born on the place. Although I had warned him not to do it, Al would walk up and pet the baby calves. There were several that would walk up and follow him like sheep following a shepherd. Of course, the two hinnies were right with him all the time. He talked to the foals and calves, and had names for his favorites.

One afternoon, I noticed Al's pony grazing with the reins tied to the saddle horn. Al was nowhere to be seen. My paternal instincts quickly brought several dire scenarios to my mind: rattlesnake, injury, and a cascade of others. But there was something strange going on in the pasture. There was a knot of calves loafing in the thick grass, some standing switching flies, others bedded down. There were two pairs of extra long tan ears poking above the rest. I quietly walked up to find the answer. Al was fast asleep with his head resting on the flank of a calf, with his four legged friends gathered around him.

With the closing of Belle Plain College, they sold off furniture and books. There was a set of reading and math primers. I bought a full set of these with the idea that Al and the other children would eventually need some schooling. There were some nice desks, a chalk board, globe and a big dictionary that were too cheap to pass up. There were good books by well-known authors, history, geography and other more advanced textbooks, including agriculture and animal husbandry.

Robin Nixon set up a school in the front room of her house, charging ten cents a day per student. Al had to call her "Mrs. Nixon" at school, but outside of there, it was just "Miss Robin." He attended with Travis Dawson. Robin was still able to run the store next door.

November of 1888 brought a hard political disappointment. Grover Cleveland had been the first Democrat President since before the War of Northern Aggression. He had been a good President who had worked hard to swing government back to fairness for the "little man." He had won re-election with the popular vote, but not the Electoral College. Benjamin Harrison, another Republican, would be our next president. I had never met a Republican I liked since that scalawag Governor Edmund J. Davis and his band of thieves had taken over Texas during Reconstruction. Well, we had lived through that, I guess we would survive this, too.

Better news graced our home when Ella gave birth to a baby boy, December 12, 1888.

"He looks just like Al," Robin had decided. "Boy, you finally got you a brother!"

"Thank you, Miss Robin. I just don't think I could stand no more hair pullin', whinin' girls!"

He was a fine looking baby with dark red hair and blue eyes. Ella named him Ed S Turner. "What's the S for?"

"Ed sounds kinda lonely by itself, so I added an S on to it; just the initial S. It doesn't stand for anything, I guess."

"Well, if it suits you, it's fine with me. Ed S it is."

The winter of 1888-89 was pretty normal. There was some snow and rain, but nothing too bad. We carried the calves born in '88 over on the surplus grass. I held back the twenty best heifers again. Come the fall of '89, we sold the rest of the long-yearling heifers and steers. They weighed up as heavy as any I had sold at just over seven hundred pounds, and brought eighteen dollars a head. We weren't going to get rich, but we wouldn't starve either. The freight business, mail route and store made a little more money than usual. Things were looking better.

9

Ghost Riding

Summer, 1889
Turner Ranch, Callahan County, Texas

THE SPRING OF 1889 WAS AGAIN A kind year to the fragile earth. The grass sprang from the ground. Blue grama, side oats, sprangle top, little bluestem, and curly buffalo grass grew thick and lush. The cows quickly recovered from the delivery of a fine crop of calves and gained weight like corn-fed steers and gave plenty of milk. The calves responded by growing taller, heavier, and butter-ball fat on the good grass and rich milk. The water of Pecan Bayou surged strong and clear across our pastures. Most of the white-tail doe were seen with twin fawns following them. The turkey and quail hatched large clutches of chicks to make up from those lost from drought and blizzard. The land was as alive as I had ever seen it.

On a freight run into Baird, I stopped to get a much needed hair-cut. A recent copy of the Ft. Worth Star-Telegram lay in an empty chair. As I waited, I thumbed through the paper.

ATTENTION ALL CONFEDERATE VETERANS:

A Reunion of all Confederate Veterans from all branches of duty and all fields of service will be held at Mexia, Limestone County, July 31 through August 2. Activities for all ages. Dances, bands, speeches, barbeques, inexpensive meals. Rejoin your brothers in arms. A special train will run twice daily from Dallas to Mexia. Free station service to campgrounds.

I showed the article to the other men in the barber shop. "Boys, I think I'm gonna take Ella and the kids. It sounds fun."

The owner of the chili parlor was there. "Aaron, why do you want to go all that way to sleep on the ground? Ain't you done enough of that in the war and on the cattle trails?"

The barber sniffed his disinterest. "Some of us gotta stay here and work for a livin'. Why do you want to go, anyway?"

"Well, I can't rightly say. As far as I know, I'm the only one left alive from Company F, but there'll be people there that I know."

The barber stopped the haircut he was giving. "Well, ever since the war was over, we've had nothin' but trouble from Washington. I had a belly full of all that during the war. I'm stayin' home."

The cook looked out-numbered. "I was too young to fight, so there's no point in me goin'."

As I took my turn in the barber's chair, I began to wonder why I wanted to go. One hundred and twenty-four of us left Texas in 1862. Only six of us returned in 1865. Now, I was the only one left. Memories flooded my mind. I wondered if any of my family in Limestone County was still alive.

"Aaron, you still with us? Your mind wandered off somewhere for a while."

"Sorry. I was doing a little ghost ridin', thinkin' about those we've lost along the way." My mind was made up. We were going to Mexia.

───────

"Aaron, both my parents are dead and buried. We don't know anybody there anymore. Is it important for the children and me to go with you?"

"It's important for me to go, but I can't quite figure out why. I'd like it better if you'd go with me, but I'll go by myself if you don't want to go. The Nixon brothers can cover the ranch and freight business. Robin can handle the store."

"You always could talk me into about anything with those blue eyes and dimples. All right, we'll go!"

Keenan brought up the spring wagon hitched to a matched pair of bay mules.

"You remember what you and Kirby are supposed to do?"

"Yessir, Boss. We got it all memorized and wrote down, too, in case we forget."

"All right. Help me with the suitcases. Al, you catch Minnie and Lela and put 'em in the wagon. Y'all sit down, and no fussin'!" Keenan helped Ella into the wagon.

"Boss, ain't you gonna take this big ol' canvas tent you borrowed?"

"Shoot. I'll have to help you. It's heavy." We hoisted the canvas bundle into the wagon. "I know there's somethin' else. The crate of pots, pans and food is sittin' on the porch!"

"Honey, I believe we have forgotten Baby Ed. He's asleep on a quilt on the kitchen floor."

"Good grief. I'll get him."

"Daddy, I gotta pee." Minnie complained.

"Me, too." Lela added.

"Al, take your sisters to the outhouse." With the girls occupying both seats, Al let fly on the wagon wheel.

I counted heads and slapped the reins on the mules. We took the hard dirt road at a trot until we reached Lytle's Gap. The two mules strained to get the overloaded wagon up the slope, but had to use their breeching to hold the wagon back on the way down. The road passed what was left of Belle Plain, the three story limestone college standing alone in a pasture. It was only six more miles to Baird. I set the mules to their paces. Ella held on to the wagon seat for dear life, as the children held each other in the wagon bed. We rolled up to the station in a cloud of dust at seven forty-five.

"Mornin', Aaron. There weren't no need to hurry. Train's runnin' late. She ain't even left Clyde yet. That's a mighty lot of stuff! Let's see you need two adult and one child's ticket round trip to Dallas. No charge for the little ones."

"Papa, me and Lela gotta pee!"

"Al, would you please take the girls to the outhouse behind the station?"

"Oh, Pa. Do I have to?"

"Yes, son. Now go get it tended to."

At eight forty-five, the big locomotive came smoking in from the west, blowing off steam with the brakes screaming. Ella, Baby Ed and I sat in a seat facing Al and his adoring sisters.

The children delighted in pointing out anything of interest along the way. The train stopped in every town with a station. The weather was fair, and the breeze from the open top windows felt nice. We saw farms and ranches of all sizes and levels of prosperity. Ella served out a little lunch she had packed for us, and we took turns drinking from a quart mason jar. Minnie and Lela were fascinated with the toilet inside the passenger car and begged to go a little too often. Feeling sorry for their long-suffering big brother, Ella handed Ed to me and took the girls. As the afternoon warmed the passenger car, the motion of the train lulled all three kids and the baby to sleep.

We finally pulled into Dallas, and were directed to the south-bound train that would take us to Mexia. I hired a porter to move all the bags, tent and crate of food for us. Three passenger cars and two freight cars pulled out at seven fifteen.

When we arrived, a middle age man in an old Confederate uniform met us at the Mexia station. "Y'all headed to the reunion grounds?"

"Yes. I'm Aaron Turner and this is my family."

"Yep. You're on the list. Name's Daniel Tucker. Anyone calls me Ol' Dan Tucker can walk." We all turned and stared at Al.

"What's your name, boy?"

"Al Turner."

"You know anything about drivin' a wagon, son? Good. You can sit up front with me and cuss the mules if they're goin' too slow."

Three wagons were hitched together with six stout mules up front. The first two wagons had double rows of padded seats and the third was loaded with our baggage. The wagons were full to over-flowing when we heard a whip crack and Al cut loose cussin' like a teamster with a toothache. Mr. Tucker turned and grinned. "Bet he didn't learn that in Sunday school!" Ella turned red, but I couldn't help but laugh. Finally, the wagons lurched across a ford of the Navasota River into a campground that looked like it had been laid out by a Yankee Engineer Company. There were wide lanes between the neat rows of tents, and bedrolls were laid out neatly under enormous burr oaks. Children laughed while they played and the trees were alive with song birds.

There was a huge tent pavilion with a swept dirt floor where a dozen couples danced to the music of a small band. There was another large tent pavilion with rows and rows of tables and benches, with a bar set up at the far end, and a huge kitchen and serving tables set up under an awning down one side. There were plenty of newly built outhouses set a respectable distance from the tents with cleared paths leading to each one.

In the middle of the camp was a central "town square" with a wooden bandstand, flag poles flying the old "Stars and Bars" and the Texas flag. Between the flags, stood a cannon with a sign reading "Old Valverde."

Some of the men who were camped next to us came over and introduced themselves and helped me unload our things and set up the big tent. Soon, the women folk were giving directions and introductions to Ella. Al and the little girls were played out. We put them down in the tent to sleep. There was a pleasant breeze blowing across the Navasota, so we rolled up the canvas sides. Ella and I walked hand in hand, taking turns holding the sleeping baby as we explored the camp a little more. Some folks were playing dominoes or checkers by lantern light, while other folks were just enjoying the nice night like we were. We didn't quite know what to make of it all, but it was good to be away from the ranch for a while.

The soft morning dew-laden summer air was thrust into immediate alertness as a bugler played reveille. I hadn't heard that in twenty-five years, and hadn't missed it. I immediately dressed, as the bugler announced in a booming voice that breakfast of pancakes, bacon and coffee would be served at seven for ten cents a head; children eat free. Ella grinned at me. "It's hard to feed five of us for twenty cents. Think you can spare it?"

"Oh, if I dig deep enough, I think we can afford it."

"Well, Private Turner, the trip out here wore me out. But I slept like a log. It's so nice to be back in Limestone County with somebody else cookin' my breakfast!"

"Hope I didn't snore. I haven't slept on the ground since we quit drivin' cattle to Kansas. I believe I like a bed better. Looks like Ed S is already awake. I'll get the kids up and dressed and we'll go eat."

"Pa, I heard the bugle. Do we get to eat in the soldiers' tent?"

"Yep, son, we sure do. Get dressed and run to the outhouse while I get your sisters ready."

When I stepped outside, there was Al, relieving himself on a tree. "Al Turner, we ain't at home. Use the outhouse."

"There was a line and I couldn't wait."

Breakfast was fun and worth the money. The food was good and all you could eat. They served locally made ribbon cane syrup. I sure got my dime's worth. I found some men I remembered from the Fifteenth Regiment. I recognized them, but they didn't know me until I told them I had been the courier.

As the day got organized, they divided by groups. The Fifteenth had spent most of the war as part of the Army of Tennessee. There were actually twenty-one men who had served in the Fifteenth, eleven who had been in Granbury's Brigade. I knew a few, and vaguely recognized the rest. You can't spend three years with the same group of men without getting to know them. I was remembered and introduced as "the skinny red-headed messenger boy from Texas, the one who brought reinforcements at Picket's Mill."

There were elections for representatives for each regiment present. All morning, delicious aromas had drifted over the group. At noon, a huge barbeque lunch was laid out. Beef had been cooked all night until it was succulent and tender. The tables groaned under the weight of the meat, pinto beans and corn bread. There was coffee, water and milk, with blackberry cobbler for dessert. It sure was worth a whole lot more than a dime.

The women visited in the shade while the children played and waded in a small creek that fed into the Navasota. A few older boys patrolled the creek banks to keep the little ones out of trouble.

The bugler sounded recall, and the camp fell silent. There was to be a meeting of veterans and various activities for the women and children. We elected representatives to the newly organized United Confederate Veterans. We were to be the Joseph E. Johnston Camp. I was glad about the name, as I had served under him in the defense of Atlanta. I had a deep respect for the man.

At the conclusion of the meeting, all the guests were moved out of harm's way so that Ol' Valverde could be fired. It was a rifled three inch gun of a type I had seen many times. When the lanyard was pulled, the cannon fired with a terrible blast. The rifled shell screamed through the air with a unique sound I hadn't heard since the war. The hair stood up on the back of my neck. My throat went dry, but I broke out in a cold sweat.

Many whooped and hollered. I stood silently shaking as my clothes became soaked with sweat. I turned on my heel and headed through the crowd to the tent. Ella noticed my sudden departure and joined me. "All the heat and speeches gettin' to ya?"

"Somethin' like that."

"Aaron, you look like you saw a ghost. What's wrong? Was it the cannon?"

"Ella, I've seen things I keep locked away. They're too terrible to remember or talk about."

"I understand. You hardly even mention the war. I know it must be hard for you. Do you want to go home early?"

"No. I'll be all right in a bit."

That night there were all kinds of dances taking place, folks playing games under lanterns, visiting, and children playing everywhere. I forced myself to participate and tried to put on a good front. Of course, I couldn't fool Ella. The children fell asleep outside, and I gathered them up and laid them gently in the tent. Ella had Ed S and was having a nice chat with some ladies she had met.

I leaned back against the trunk of the huge burr oak, thoughtfully packing and lighting my pipe. I became lost in memories of things I had sealed away many years ago. There are things no boy should ever have to see, things no one should ever have to endure. The single discharge of the old cannon and the whistling of its rifled shell unleashed ghosts I had thought had forever been banished from my mind.

Ella saw me smoking under the tree. I didn't even know she was there until she and Baby Ed sat down next to me. "I've had a wonderful time today. Do you want to go home, Aaron?"

"No. But I've borrowed a good horse for tomorrow to ride down to Groesbeck and then head across to the old home place at Navasota Crossing. I'll be gone before daylight, and likely won't be back before dark. Can you manage the children all day?"

"What do you think I do every day, Mr. Turner?" She slipped her arm through mine. "Leave me a little money to eat in the mess tent."

I forced a smile. "Guess I haven't been much fun tonight. I can't be around here and listen to any more speeches about how glorious the war was. They musta been in some other war than the one I saw. I need to do some ghost ridin' tomorrow."

Ella looked puzzled.

"Ghost ridin'. Visitin' the graves and places in my memory where the ghosts walk. I think it'll help."

Ella placed both my hands in hers. "Aaron, I didn't know you before the War, but the men who did thought the world of you. I think you are the best man, in every way, that I have ever known. A fine man, a fine husband, a wonderful father. I'm proud of you, and I love you with all my heart. I always have." She wiped a single tear from my cheek and left me to finish my pipe in silence.

Sleep had been a misery to me that night. Memories came flooding back. Nightmares filled my sleep, and ghosts and demons of the past haunted me relentlessly. I left on a long-legged borrowed horse before there was a twinge of purple in the eastern sky. I rode south to Groesbeck.

I reined in front of the house where my half-brother, Lucius King, had lived, and next door was Marcus King's house. They had been good to me. They had been Mother's sons from her first marriage. Close by was the two story cabin my father had built for Momma in Leon county. After the war, we had disassembled it, modified a wagon to haul the large logs, and rebuilt the cabin here. The gallery banister was hanging down, blocking the front door. The windows my father had shipped in from New Orleans were mostly broken, and the sturdy tile roof was sagging. I could see my bedroom window on the second story. I didn't get down, just circled the decaying house once and rode away.

The house where my sister, Mary Ann, and her husband Pinckney Hawkins, had lived appeared to still be occupied. An older woman was hanging up laundry.

I stepped down from the horse. "Mornin' ma'am. Can I water my horse?"

"Hep ya sef." She spoke around a lip full of snuff that had dribbled down her chin.

"I just wondered if you knew what became of the people who used to live here, the Hawkins?"

"Sure. I bought the house offen theys son after the Hawkins died. They had gone visitin' down the coast and caught yaller fever. Kilt bof of 'em." She spat a long black string of tobacco and made no effort to wipe her chin. "They kin?"

"Yes, ma'am. She was my sister. When did they die?"

"I bought the place five year ago this summer, whenever that was."

Remounting the borrowed saddle, I realized no one was left. "Ma'am!" I kicked the horse into a crisp trot for the cemetery. I didn't step down. Momma's grave was there by Lucius. Now Marcus and Mary Ann had joined her. I was the last of the line. Ella's parents were buried in the next row. There was nothing here; just ghosts. I wheeled the horse to take the country lane that was the shortest way to Navasota Crossing.

Heavy growth of trees along the Navasota River appeared on the horizon. I urged the horse into a lope. The river was down and crossing would be easy. Once there had been a ferry here, as this was on El Camino Real, The King's Highway. Now it was a seldom used wagon road with grass growing in the ruts. The horse picked his way across the knee-deep green water and vaulted up the far bank. I was back in Leon County for the first time in many years.

The foundation of our old home was visible in the weeds and grass. The other buildings of the farm had been burned down by the Klan. The fences had disappeared. No livestock grazed the lush pasture. The old church building was still there, but leaning precariously to one side. The steeple had fallen down and the pieces scattered. Every pane of glass was missing from the misshapen windows.

The cemetery was a tangle of green briar and tall weeds. I unsaddled the horse and looped the reins over his neck to rest and graze while I poked around. The largest stone lay flat, simply carved "Turner." There were some smaller stones nearby. They were unmarked, but I remembered being told they were the graves of children they had lost, the brothers and sisters who had died before I was ever born. There was nothing left here for me. I tipped my hat at my father's grave, knowing it was unlikely I would ever return.

I stopped long enough in the Navasota to let the horse drink his fill. I checked the daylight remaining, and guessed that I would return to Mexia after that damn cannon had fired.

When I returned, Ella had saved chili and cornbread for my supper. I danced with her and held her tight under the big tent until the band played the last note. I cuddled baby Ed close to my face, and held Lela and Minnie in my lap, as I had my arm around Al, who stood at my side. In the morning I would return to our life in Callahan County with my sweet wife and children. They were real; they were my life and my world. The rest had been nothing but ghosts and echoes from the past.

10

Wedding Bells at Baird; Along Came John

Fall, 1890
Turner Ranch, Callahan County, Texas

THE SPRING AND SUMMER OF 1890 had been kind to us again. The rain had fallen just right, and the grass was thick and green. For a rancher, it was as good as it gets. We just didn't have nearly enough cattle left to use it.

Keenan, Kirby, and Al helped me drive one hundred and sixty-nine head of long yearlings to Baird. They were good cattle, and brought eighteen dollars a head. Money was still very tight, but we were steadily rebuilding the herd.

Al had grown into a long-legged ten year old, and was getting to be some real help on the ranch. He could rope, brand and castrate: the basic cowboy skills. Once his feet started dragging the ground from his Welsh pony, he graduated to a full-sized horse. Kirby was teaching him how to play the guitar, fiddle and mandolin. He had a real knack for it.

The Nixon boys weren't really boys anymore. Keenan was twenty-five and Kirby was twenty-seven. Where had the years gone? There were a couple of young ladies who attracted their attention. They had started going to Baird every Sunday, and for all their singing schools and brush arbor meetings; not that they didn't need a little of the devil knocked out of them, especially Keenan.

In August of 1890, they had a double wedding at the Methodist Church in Baird. They asked Al and me to stand up with them. Keenan's bride was a beautiful girl named Lauren. Kirby married the sweet, pretty Sara. The wedding was the Callahan County social event of the summer.

Everyone knew and liked the boys and their brides; the wedding drew a crowd that flowed out the door and onto the grass. There was a big dinner and dance after the wedding with barbecued beef, wedding cake, and watermelon. We had shipped in barrels of beer from Fort Worth, and paid extra to have it packed in ice the whole way to Baird on the train. The celebration lasted until well past midnight. I didn't remember seeing Robin dance before, but that lady could raise some dust.

Matt Dawson played the guitar with Jake on the fiddle. Kirby finally was persuaded to join them on his fiddle, while Keenan played the guitar and Al picked the mandolin. Al didn't have a shy bone in his body, and played his heart out to the crowd's approval.

Keenan remodeled the bunkhouse to make it more acceptable to Lauren. Kirby built a small mail order house close to his mother in our growing unnamed crossroad community.

The Fort Worth paper was at the barber shop the next time I went to Baird for a haircut and shave. "Well this is about the stupidest thing I ever saw!"

"What's got you worked up, Aaron?"

"Prohibition."

"Never heard of it."

"Some do gooders down in Austin are tryin' to git a law passed to make it illegal to make, posses or consume alcohol."

The scissors stopped clicking. The barber shop got deathly quiet. The barber stared at me over the top of his spectacles. "You gotta be kiddin'."

"No, sir. I'm not. If a man don't want to drink, that's his business. But it's nobody's business to tell him he cain't."

"Oh, you hardly touch the stuff more than a drink or two at weddin's and such."

"It says Texas attorney General Jim Hogg is dead set against it 'cause the governments got no right to tell the common man whether or not he can have a drink."

"Well, don't you worry none. I been around a long time, and such foolishness as that will never happen."

Sweet Ella was expecting again. I had prayed for a good woman. I guess I got one a lot better than I deserved. She was as good a woman as my mother, and better than anyone else I knew. She could laugh and cut up, but didn't take sass from anyone. She knew how to handle teamsters and cowboys and kids. And I guess I loved her as much as a man could love his wife.

On December 5, 1890, her water broke. She went out on the porch and rang the bell for Robin. Hearing it, she sent Travis Dawson to ring the school bell, then sent all the kids to the Dawson's house except Al. Kirby was unloading freight at the store. As soon as he was finished, he and Sara came over to the house. Keenan had to make a run to Baird, so he left Lauren at our house and took Al with him in the wagon.

Ella's contractions were hard and the baby was slow coming. She strained against the cotton ropes, braced her feet on the footboard and pushed with all her might. The baby's head was showing but his wide shoulders wouldn't budge. With the next contraction, Robin had Sara and Lauren push down on Ella's belly. With a scream, first one shoulder, then the other forced its way into the birth canal. One more mighty push and the baby was born.

He had the broadest shoulders Robin had ever seen on a baby, but he was healthy and squalling. Ella named him John, and Lauren gave him the middle name Karr from her maiden name. Young John Karr Turner had a head full of dark auburn wavy hair and light gray-blue eyes. He nursed like a young colt.

Once they got used to having him in the house, the children doted on baby John. Ed was too young to care, but Al, Mamie and Lela hardly ever let him cry without picking him up. He was a very happy little boy. There was something about him that was hard to describe, but when people looked at him, they would break into a smile, just like they did around his oldest brother. Al and John were destined to develop a strong life-long bond.

Jim Hogg used his position as Texas Attorney General to stop Prohibition, but he also used it to promote his political career. On January 21, 1891, he became the first native-born Texan sworn in as Governor.

He campaigned against the "soulless corporations" who preyed on the common folks. He preached against the insatiable appetite of insurance companies that took a man's money, but were mighty slow paying it back. And he spoke against the ruthless abuse of loans and foreclosures. Hogg promised to rein in arbitrary and unfair practices of the railroads, establishing the Texas Railroad Commission to regulate them. First and foremost, a Texan and a Democrat, he was "anti-Republican, anti-trust, and anti-capitalist." I sure was anti-Republican, and had been since Reconstruction. I wasn't too sure about the rest, but if he was against it, so was I. Big business, Republicans and Yankees hated him. But the common folks, like me, thought the world of Jim Hogg.

In the spring of 1891, Keenan and Kirby decided to break the hinnies to ride and pull a buggy. They had grown into beautiful young animals. Their heads were more refined than a donkey or mule. Except for the somewhat longer ears and coarser mane and tails, they were more like a horse than a mule. Their build and muscling resembled a horse, and not the stockier mules, and their gait was horse-like. They possessed the stamina, if not all the strength, of a mule, along with intelligence and stubbornness.

"Boss, you know hinny sounds like a skinny chicken."

"Some people call them jennets. You like that better?"

"Heck, yeah! Jennet. A matched pair of dun jennets. That sounds better."

"How do you tell 'em apart? I know Al calls 'em 'Honey and Punkin'."

"You can't unless you look real close. Punkin has a few little white hairs on her forehead."

"They follow Al around like puppies."

The Nixon brothers introduced them to blankets and saddles gradually, until they showed no fear. Soon they accepted saddles tightly cinched with burlap sacks of grain tied to the horn. It wasn't long until the boys were climbing on them and stepping on and off, then riding them in the round corral without a hop, skip or a buck. They were ready to leave the corral for the real world.

The morning was sunny and clear. Under saddle and rider, they performed perfectly in the pen, calm and focused on their jobs.

"Al, open the gate and let 'em out!"

The mounted riders headed out side-by-side into the green grass at a walk, trot and then a lope. When they pulled up on the lead ropes, they stopped perfectly. Gentle use of spurs set the pretty jennets into forward motion, and right into an unseen covey of quail, which exploded into flight right under their feet. Both jennets blew up like a powder keg.

Keenan got a deep seat, grabbed the horn in his right hand, and tried to pull Honey into a tight left circle. She wasn't buying what he was selling. She bucked harder. He used his left spur to try to get her into a circle, but she squalled like a stuck hog and took her bucking up a notch. Finally, she took off at a dead gallop for Pecan Bayou, flowing clear and deep a hundred yards away. Keenan tried every trick in the book, but she was going like a runaway train. She galloped headlong, taking thirty feet a jump, until she landed knee deep in soft mud, launching Keenan head-first into the cold water.

Meanwhile, Kirby had all he could handle with Punkin. She jumped straight up with her feet collected and fish-tailed her rump. He was barely holding his own until he lost his right stirrup. With each jump, he came higher out of the saddle, finally slamming into the hard ground.

Honey walked out into the water and nuzzled Keenan. He called her some ungentlemanly names as he grabbed the lead ropes. Al was waiting on the bank to take the rope from Keenan. Before I could stop him, Al swung up into the saddle, patting her gently on the neck.

"Those ol' quail scared my girl, didn't they, Honey. They's noisy, but won't hurt ya none." She stopped shaking, calming down quickly. He rode her back to the corral, dismounted and closed the gate. He walked over to Kirby, who lay face down in the dirt.

"Kirby, I know you ain't dead! I see you breathin'." He reached down and rolled the dirt-covered freckle-faced cowboy onto his back. "Kirby, wake up!" The only response he got was a groan. That was enough to convince Al that Kirby was going to make it. He tightened the jennet's cinch, mounted, repeated his calming routine with her, and rode her quietly into the corral.

He rode each of them around in the corral, taking them one at a time out into the pasture, across the creek and back again. "Pa, they just got spooked. They're all right now."

We stood speechless. I had never seen an eleven year old do what Al had just done. He finished training the jennets over the next several weeks under our watchful and amazed eyes. Whatever it was that Al possessed, he would display his talent repeatedly many times in his life.

11

Dudley

Fall, 1892
Baird, Callahan County, Texas

THE SCISSORS CLICKED AWAY AT Kirby's red hair. "What did you and Sara have?"

"Girl. Named her Courtney." He had to spit out snippets of hair to talk. Our barber was nice, but not known for neatness. "She's real pretty; got red hair."

"Keenan, heard y'all had one."

"Yep. A boy. Named him Remington, after my cousin."

"Red-head?"

"Nope. Brown like his Momma. Long and lean, too."

"Aaron, don't let these boys catch up to ya."

"They won't. Got one in the oven, due in February or March." I thumbed through a well-read copy of the Fort Worth paper. "The Dalton gang finally got what they deserved. Says here they rode up to Coffeyville, Kansas and tried to rob two banks at once. The town folks caught 'em in a cross-fire and shot 'em to pieces. You know the Dalton and James bunch caught up with us once in the Nations. Fella workin' with us was back in the trees; shot Jesse James' horse dead right out from under him. We got the drop on 'em, and convinced 'em it was a good time to leave."

"You never told us that!"

"Keenan, there's a lot of stuff I don't talk about. Look here. Governor Hogg is puttin' his foot down on the railroads again. Can you imagine a woman lettin' her daughter bein' named Ima Hogg?"

"Sure. Sounds like a girl Kirby was sweet on."

"Shut up, skunk breath!"

"Maybe he oughta name the next two Ura and Weira Hogg."

About that time, a thin, frail looking, bespectacled, middle aged man walked into the barbershop. "Excuse me. I'm looking for Aaron Turner."

"You found him. How can I help ya?"

He extended a long, boney hand. "Nickolas Dudley. Nice to meet you."

"Nice to meet you, Nick."

"Oh, I prefer Nickolas if you don't mind."

"Well, what can I do for you, Slim?" The boys and the barber grinned, as they knew I was giving the little fellow a hard time.

"I understand that you own a small store on the Abilene road at Lytle's Gap."

"Yes. You need groceries?"

"No. I want to buy your store."

"It ain't for sale."

"Now, Mr. Turner, hear me out. I'm prepared to pay you a fair price and contract with you to haul the freight. I've looked at the building and wares. I'll give you a thousand dollars for the lot."

"I'd sell you the lot for a thousand dollars, but the building and wares would cost extra."

"You're making game of me, Mr. Turner."

"Well, Nickolas. Let me think on it. You movin' a family down there?"

"Yes. I have nine children."

"No wonder he's so skinny, Boss!"

"I gave fifteen hundred for the store and stock. If you'd give me that, and not object to me still buying my family's groceries wholesale, I'll do it."

"You drive a very hard bargain. But, yes, I would agree to that. I can have the money wired to the bank in the morning."

"Done. I'll meet you at the bank when it opens at nine in the morning and bring the deed with me."

The next morning the money was in my account and Mr. Nicko-las Dudley owned a store. He bought a few acres to build a house and shed, and kept a big garden on the other side of Matt Dawson's house. I got to haul the freight for a new catalogue house. We helped him put it up, and welcomed them by fixing a big dinner on the ground for the house raising.

He petitioned for the store to become an official post office and him postmaster. In about a month's time, the paperwork arrived, and the "town" was officially named "Dudley." With the store and post office combined, a blacksmith shop, a school in Robin Nixon's house, and six families counting ours, there were twenty-eight men, women and children in Dudley.

The little community church at Belle Plain moved to Dudley. We hauled the church building and preacher's house for nothing and helped put both buildings back up. Their family swelled the population to a whopping thirty-one souls. Keenan said there were thirty good folks and one preacher.

———————

Ella and I did our part adding to the population of Dudley. Feb-ruary 25, 1893, we were blessed with another boy. He had a head full of curly brown hair and hazel eyes. Ella said he reminded her of her father, so we named him George, in his honor.

Al would soon be thirteen, already six feet tall and still growing like a weed and working like a grown man. He never met a stranger and everybody liked him. His auburn hair, blue-gray eyes, infectious smile and dimples could get him just about anything he wanted. But mostly, he wanted to cowboy, and was as good as many grown men.

He loved to wander. He would take a rifle, skillet, coffee pot, a little grub in a morral, a bed roll and his guitar or mandolin, riding one jennet, and packing his goods on the other, and be gone for days at a time. He was always back when we told him to be. Ella worried he might get hurt or bitten by a snake and we wouldn't even know where he was. But the boy had the wander lust in his eyes and loved to go. Sometimes he would camp on the river and fish; at other times, he would explore the Double Mountain country. I saw a lot of myself at that age in him. I didn't have the heart to hold him back. He had come by his independent streak honestly.

Minnie was eight and Lela was seven. They were both tall for their age, slender and graceful. They loved school, reading and helping their mother in the house and outside. Ed S was five; he loved to be outside like Al, and spent a lot of his time with me.

John was three. His brothers and sisters adored him. If there was a favorite sibling, it was John, even after George was born. His red hair, pale blue eyes, big smile and dimples reminded us of Al. But the resemblance ended there. For John was tall, broad shouldered and stocky. He didn't have a shy bone in his body. He would talk to anyone just like he was as old as they were, including adults. He had no fear of anything, which did scare his mother and me. Nothing daunted him. Ella and I knew he was marked as a special child, but as yet we could not nail down just what it was that set him apart.

The return of normal seasonal weather brought growth to our pastures and herds, benefiting all of us, for almost every one kept some cattle. The Dawson Ranch north of the Divide was the largest in the county. Jake and his pretty wife ran it well. It was a show place with perfect fences and quality cattle. It was hard to tell how many children Jake had, because when we saw them on Sunday, they were crawling all over the pews and running down the aisle. Matt Dawson and his wife had two more boys and a girl besides their oldest, Travis.

Matt, you and Jake do know what's causin' all them kids, don't ya?"

"I sure as heck do. Why do you think we have so many of 'em?

It was true that we did our part to be fruitful and replenish the earth, at least southwestern Callahan County. On March 2, 1894, with some difficulty, Ella gave birth to a baby boy we named Bill. He was wide shouldered and looked a lot like his big brother, John.

12

Twister

July, 1895
Dudley, Callahan County, Texas

THUNDER RATTLED THE WINDOWS in our house. A cold wind swept down from the leading edge of a huge bank of greenish-gray towering wall of storm clouds.

"Dad, come look at this." Al sounded worried.

I joined him on the back porch to see a solid squall line of ominous clouds stretching across the horizon from north to south. The thunderheads rose up to an immense height and were rolled under the leading edge. Lightning flickered all along the line, followed almost immediately by crashing thunder.

"Son, get the milk cows, horses and mules under the shed and chain the gate. Ed, you run out and chase the chickens up into the hen house, and close it up tight. Ella, you and the girls close all the windows."

The spring house was nearly all underground with rock sides. There was a concrete trough that carried windmill water through it before leaving for a large cistern. The roof was heavy oak timbers and sheet metal, and the door was also made of heavy oak lumber. "All right, gather everybody into the spring house." I counted heads; everyone was there, including Baby Bill. "I'm gonna sit right outside the door to watch the storm and duck inside when it gets here."

Standing beside the spring house, I saw the storm bank was much closer and uglier. The wind that swept down the front of the towering clouds was cold as ice. Sheets of heavy rain were only a half mile away. Pea-sized hail and fat, cold raindrops pelted hard into my face. I felt a tug on my jeans. John was standing there next to me! As I scooped him into my arms, the bottom of the clouds began to sag toward the ground and slowly start to rotate. The shape quickly formed a distinct funnel. Dust, tree branches and earth-bound debris were being swirled into the funnel. It twitched, twisted and twirled across the countryside.

John's eyes were riveted to the storm. Without looking up, he asked "Papa, what is that?"

"A tornado, son. We gotta get in the spring house now." I pulled the heavy door closed behind us, and barred it from the inside. An artillery barrage of large hail assaulted the roof. Rain came down in a torrent. The roar of the rain and hail was deafening. Minnie and Lela screamed, and Baby Bill cried. A sound like a locomotive could be heard above all the other noise. Ella's eyes were wide as she clutched my hand. "It'll be all right, children. It'll be all right."

The rain and hail lessened and the dreadful sound of the storm diminished as it seemed to move away to the northeast, replaced by a gentle, steady rain. I pushed the door open and helped carry the littler children across the muddy yard to the house. "Ella, I need to check on things. I'll be right back. Come on, Al."

We ventured out and could see that the storm had moved north of the Callahan Divide. It looked like they were really catching heck. I could see the debris in the funnel now appeared to have boards, shingles and barn tin in it. Thunder rolled and lightning flashed to the northeast. There was just a little sprinkle on us now. The stock shed had lost a piece of barn tin, but I could see it not too far away. The chicken house had been blown over on its side, but the hardwood floor had held it together. It was too heavy for us to budge. Opening a wooden panel, I could see inside. "Them chickens ain't too happy, but they don't look hurt. They'll keep for now."

We could see two windows on the west side of the house had been shattered and a piece of roofing tin had been blown off. "Let's see what it looks like on the inside."

There was broken glass on the kitchen floor that Minnie and Lela were carefully sweeping into a dustpan. Ella was mopping in the girls' room. Watery sunlight shone through a hole in the roof. Water and hailstones littered the floor, but the bed and dresser had somehow stayed dry. Al and I climbed up on the roof and nailed the piece of tin that had come off the shed neatly over the hole above the girls' room. The livestock could wait a day or two.

We took the muddy road to the bunkhouse to check on Keenan, Lauren, and their boys, Remington and Winchester. There was a blown out fan on the windmill; other than that, things looked pretty good. Pecan Bayou raged along in a muddy torrent to the south.

"Looks like I'll be fixin' some water gaps, Boss."

We slogged along to Dudley. The late afternoon sun gave an eerie presence to the muddy post-storm scene. Fruit and pecan trees had lost most of their fruit and plenty of leaves and smaller branches, but they would survive. The store and every other building looked sound.

Dawn came early on the rain soaked scenery. We used the mules to right the hen house. We made a list of all the things needed for repairs and hitched six mules to a single freight wagon for the trip to Baird. Al and I rode the jennets, while the Nixon brothers drove the wagon. Ed perched on the wagon seat between them. John was on his pony beside me. The sucking mud gave the six strong mules all they wanted. We needed to pick up some window glass and barn tin at Baird. As we approached town, we saw a wide swath of large trees twisted and uprooted pointing straight at town.

The town was in tatters. Some buildings were completely gone; many had lost their roof. The train depot was undamaged. It was here people had gathered. A few folks had been killed, and several had been injured. The train made a special emergency run into Abilene to bring back doctors, nurses, and two box cars of wooden shingles, barn tin, kegs of nails, window glass and lumber.

I saw the barber standing on the platform. "How can we help? There's four grown men, six mules and a good wagon."

"You know the chili parlor? It's gone. Nothin' left but the foundation blocks. The man that owned it was in there cookin' when the twister hit. Nobody has seen a hair of him. That big hay barn you rented? Gone. There's some houses that are collapsed that had folks in 'em. They probably need help pullin' off the debris."

"Okay, boys. I got some extra chains and rope in the wagon. John, you and Ed stay here by the wagon with the jennets and your pony. Don't either one of ya go wanderin' off."

We started at a box and strip house that had been laid flat. Hooking a chain to a large section of the collapsed roof, I clicked for the mules to move forward. Keenan crawled under the debris. "All clear."

I slapped the reins and dragged the tangle of lumber and shingles to a large pile that had been started. Keenan had hooked onto a section of wall. When it was moved, it opened up a large area of the ruined house.

A local man yelled. "We got bodies. Ease the mules on up." People rushed in and carried out a little girl, man and woman. All three were hurt, but alive. They carried them on stretchers to the rail platform.

We moved on to a larger house. As we dragged away one damaged section after another, Al shouted: "I see feet! Hold up!" Men moved in with crow bars, poles and buggy axles to gently raise the wreckage to find a young woman and a baby. The barber carefully crawled to the bodies to feel for a pulse. Finding none, he laid his head on their chests, but couldn't hear a heartbeat. "Fellas, they're already gettin' cold. She had a husband. Let's see if we can find him."

As Kirby dragged away another section, Al yelled. "I see him. He's breathin'! You're clear, Kirby, pull away." As the tangled debris was removed, we could see a young man. He was badly injured and unconscious. One arm crooked at ninety degree angle, both bones stuck through the bruised skin. Al and the barber eased him on to a stretcher; four men carried him away.

I ran back to check on John and Ed. I shouldn't have brought them. I had never dreamed it would be this bad. Those boys didn't need to be seeing all this. Ed was sitting on John's pony, watching all the commotion. "Where's your brother?" He pointed to the rail platform.

He was in the middle of the injured, sitting next to the little girl from the first house. "Don't worry. You and your Momma and Daddy are gonna be okay. My name's John. What's your name?" He held her hand as he talked to her. "The nurse said you could have water, so I brought you some." He gently raised a blue enamel cup to her lips. "I'll be back in a little while to check on you."

We worked to past dark. Finally, there was nothing left for us to do. I gathered my supplies and the boys, pointing the mules toward home.

13

Bunkhouse Blizzard

Turner Ranch, Dudley, Callahan County, Texas
February, 1899

POOR MR. DUDLEY HAD GIVEN UP raising a large family on a big garden and the small profits from the store and post-office. He sold it back to me for moving money. I was back in the grocery business, with income now as postmaster, plus the income from my freight line and the ranch.

Keenan gave up the bunk house for a more civilized house in Dudley for Lauren and the three boys, Remington, Winchester and Colt. He had been a busy fellow. We teased him good-naturedly about the boys' names, and asked him when we could expect Henry and Spencer. Kirby had a good start with his three girls.

After such a hard time with Bill's birth, I wasn't sure Ella would have any more children. But she was expecting another in about a month. We had convinced Al he didn't need to volunteer for the war with Spain. He was likely to get to Cuba and die of yellow fever. We had stalled long enough that they weren't taking any more volunteers. He read every newspaper he could find to follow the war. He had argued that I had gone to war at age twelve. There were things about war I couldn't put into words, but those were the same things that convinced me he shouldn't go. One of us with nightmares was enough.

Our ranch had seen a modest run to prosperity with the return of seasonal rains, and the expansion of the herd. We still were not back to the carrying capacity of roughly six hundred pairs. It took two to three years before the replacement heifers started to calve, and we sure didn't have the cash to buy any mother cows. We would take our time and raise our own. Prices had gotten a little better with the war, but were still pretty weak.

Texas had elected Joseph Sayers as Governor. He was to be our last Confederate veteran in that high office. Younger men had come along who had not endured that tragedy. Things in Texas were far better than they had been during the evil days of Reconstruction under that wicked rascal, Edmund J. Davis. His name was a swear word in our house.

Calving season was approaching, but the cattle had wintered in good flesh. The last remnants of the earless and tailless survivors of the great blizzards had finally been driven to market due to old age. Al was the only one of my children who remembered how bad it had been. "Dad, I've never seen our herd look better. I think we've got the best cows in the county."

"I'm sure proud of 'em. The yearlin's kept their weight on this winter and are ready to fatten up before we sell 'em in the fall."

Ed was riding one of the pretty jennets. He came loping up behind us. "Pa, there's a strange lookin' cloud comin' up in the north. It goes all the way across the sky. You cain't see it from down here. Want to ride up the divide and have a look?"

Al and I exchanged worried glances. We turned and trotted up the divide, with Ed, George and John strung out behind. As we topped the ridge, my heart turned cold. An enormous wall cloud rose high in the winter sky, stretching across the northern horizon. "Looks like we're in for it, boys. Let's move the cattle into the bunkhouse pasture where they can shelter in the trees."

Seven year old George swung off his pony and struggled with the gate. But he soon had it open and laid back against the fence. We eased behind the cattle and spread out. We slowly pushed the four hundred gentle white-faced crossbred cows and nearly four hundred yearlings toward the cottonwood trees that flanked both sides of the presently shallow waters of Pecan Bayou.

"Al, there's plenty of grub, coffee and firewood at the bunkhouse. I'm gonna leave you over here to break ice and keep an eye on things. Some of these storms leave as fast as they blow in, and some stick around a few days. Ring the bell around daylight and dark so we'll know you're all right. Keep ringin' it if you need help."

"Sure, Pa. Would you care if John stayed over here with me? We can play a little music and some checkers to pass the time."

"John?"

"Heck, yeah! I need some stuff from the house. I can get it and be back pretty fast. Al, I'll git your mandolin and some heavier clothes for ya."

Ella sent some extra food and a few treats for them, and I sent a gallon can of lamp oil. I sure hoped they wouldn't be here long enough to use it all.

———————

The wind rose suddenly from a mild southerly breeze to a raging blue norther, rattling the window in the dugout. Within minutes, snow was falling almost horizontally in the darkening sky. "Well, little brother, it's here! Throw some more wood in the stove."

Al set a pot of coffee to boil and fried ham, potatoes, and eggs for supper. After cleaning the plates, he started picking on his mandolin, with John keeping up on the guitar. After a bit, they switched out. They could both play anything with strings, but Al was amazing. They tossed riffs back and forth from mandolin to guitar.

Finally needing a break from music, they pulled out the checker board. Here, it was an even match. They played game after game in the yellow flickering light of the coal oil lamp. "Well, I reckon we better quit, and git some sleep. Let's check on things and go to bed."

Opening the door, they found the snow had drifted head high. Al grabbed a flat bottom shovel, and finally dug through the drift. Snow was piled six feet deep out of the wind. On open ground, some places were swept clean, but in most places it was already a foot deep.

The boys scooted the bunk beds a little closer to the stove. It just had two settings, too hot and too cold. They took turns feeding the fire box on the stove through the night, as the wind continued to howl and the snow piled deeper.

Awakening to the aroma of fresh coffee and bacon, John rolled out of bed and got dressed. "I gotta pee."

"It's too cold out there. Use the slop jar."

"Pa said we gotta ring the bell mornin' and night, so I gotta go outside anyway."

John opened the door to find snow had completely refilled the exit Al had dug the night before. He began shoveling, putting the first several scoops in the drinking water bucket. The farther he dug, the deeper the snow.

He tried to tunnel to the outside, but the snow caved in on top of him, completely burying him. Al used his hands to dig him out, laughing as he pulled his brother from the snow. John realized the humor of the situation and joined Al in laughing. While Al was bent over slapping his knees in delight, John pelted him in the head with a snowball, then bulled his way through the snow until he broke into the open, leaving his big brother standing in the bunkhouse in his long drawers.

Turning his back to the howling wind, he relieved himself, writing his name in the snow. He pushed on to the shed, checked the stock and broke the ice in the tank. He put out a shock of feed for the horses and jennets, and poured oats into the wooden trough. On the way back to the bunkhouse, he pulled the frozen bell rope until he heard an answering ring from the house. He dug the rest of the drift away from the door and knocked the snow off his heavy clothes before going back inside.

Al sat in his drawers in a rocking chair by the stove, nursing a cup of coffee. He poured John a cup and passed it to him. "How many eggs?"

"'Bout four, and some of that bacon. Wish we had some of Momma's biscuits."

"How deep is the snow?"

"Shoot, it's drifted up to the roof of the shed and bunkhouse. I guess three feet on the flat ground. I'm worried the cows may have trouble pushin' through to drink."

"You reckon the creek froze over?"

"Well, the ice sure was thick in the tank. I guess it did."

They passed the long day with music and checkers. The lamp stayed lit all day long, as the only window was blocked by snow. Before dusk, they broke ice again and rang the bell. There were no signs the cattle had come to drink. It snowed all night, but the flakes were smaller and not falling so fast.

The next morning the storm was lessening. There were snow flurries and cloudy skies, but things looked better. The boys guessed that another four inches of snow had fallen during the night, but when it got that deep, it was hard to tell. They could see the cows at the foot of the slope along the creek.

Al and John hitched the jennets to the wooden sled with a plan to break a path for the cows to get to water. The snow was almost up to the jennets' bellies. They pulled hard to drag the wooden runners through the snow, never reaching the ground in spite of the boys' weight in the sled. It took an hour to reach the bottom of the slope, but the sled had knocked the top off the snow until it was only a foot or so deep. The trip back up the gentle slope was much easier. The runners broke through to the ground under the snow. The cows followed the sled up the hill where they eagerly crowded around the trough. They waited impatiently, pushing their way forward, until finally all of them had filled up with water. Of course, the few yearlings that had straggled up the slope had to wait the longest, because they couldn't push aside the grown cows. Not all the cattle came up the hill. Those dark shapes remaining near the creek were either dead, too ill to walk, or frozen in place. There was nothing else to do and no hay to feed.

By the third morning, thin clouds dropped a few flakes as they cleared. By noon, a gentle breeze was blowing from the southwest, with just a hint of warmth in its breath, and the sun returned to its rightful place in the winter sky. Water was dripping from the eaves of the shed and bunkhouse.

The boys knew that the worst was over. They saddled the jennets and rode the slushy road home. I came back with them to survey the damage. The cattle were drawn from three days without food, and it would be a few more days before the snow melted enough to reach the good, sun-cured grass hidden beneath it. We counted eighty-one dead mother cows, and expected to lose more to pneumonia. Of the three hundred and ninety-six yearlings, only forty-two were left alive. They had suffocated in the deep snow or frozen to death.

"Daddy, that's nearly all the yearlin's we had to sell in the fall. This is bad, ain't it?"

"Yes, John. It's bad; really bad."

―――――――

Robin Nixon and her daughters-in-law tended Ella when she delivered a baby girl April 4, 1899. It was easy and uncomplicated this time. It was a real comfort to Ella to have Robin and the women there to take care of her. The baby was a pretty little thing who looked a lot like Ella's mother. We named her Marjorie.

We had lost a few more yearlings to pneumonia. The surviving thirty-nine, along with only seventeen weaned calves, our entire cash crop for 1899, were driven to the rebuilt town of Baird. The check for the sale wouldn't even cover our property taxes.

The freight business and postmaster's job brought in a little extra cash. The store allowed us to get our groceries wholesale, then did just a little better than break even. That was it. I had seen tough financial times, on and off, since the war. We had always been able to gather and sell more maverick cattle, or work a little harder to get by. This time, there wasn't anything left to do. For the first time in my life, I was forced to borrow money.

The bank at Baird was sympathetic, but had no money to loan. They directed me to an insurance company in Abilene that made loans on land and cattle. I had to pay them a $10 inspection fee to look at the ranch and livestock, and a small fee to the Callahan County clerk's office to show there were no outstanding liens. I had to designate two hundred acres as my homestead. I chose the two hundred that included the house and barn, but not the bunkhouse and buildings there. They were too far to include in one tract of land. They valued the land at a realistic two dollars an acre, and the remaining blizzard scarred cattle at five dollars a head. Because the mules and wagons were "tools of the trade" for my freight business, they were excluded from the loan, along with the store and our "personal use animals" such as saddle horses, hogs and milk cows.

All things considered, they offered to loan me up to eighty percent of the total, at six percent annual interest. They would advance it to my account at the Baird bank as we needed it. The balance would be payable, in full, in ten years. If for any reason the loan was not repaid in total, they would repossess the land and the cattle. I felt like I had just stuck my head in a noose.

The state legislature passed a set of laws referred to as "colored codes" to regulate the participation of a whole race of people in Texas society, based solely on the color of their skin. They also reinstated an old "Poll Tax" to keep poor, mostly black, voters away from the ballot box. I had seen similar "special treatment" of certain sections of the population during Reconstruction, when I had been denied the right to serve on a jury, vote or hold public office. I had hated it then, and I saw it for what it was, and hated it now. Many people viewed this as just and fair retribution for those brutal days after the war. Knowing few would agree with me, I held my tongue.

As 1899 drew to a close, itinerate preachers spread over the countryside, from brush arbor to riverside, to preach of the impending "end of days." Most of us earnestly hoped for better days to come in the new century. A few even argued that the new century wouldn't start until January 1, 1901. But we all accepted that when we needed to write 1900 on our checks, letters and bills, it was a new century. As for the gloom and doom preachers, the end of time had not arrived just yet.

On New Year's Eve, 1899, we attended a special church service at Dudley. Nearly everyone in the area was there. It was a night of introspection for me. It was a period of "hard times" in many ways. But I had seen worse and survived. I realized I was forty-nine and starting to feel some of the wear and tear. But I still held my six foot four frame erect, and bent my knees to the Lord.

After the service, there was a big dance at Matt Dawson's barn with everything from sweet cider to hard liquor. Matt and Jake, Keenan and Kirby, as well as Al, Ed and John, entertained the crowd. The church bell rang out at midnight. I kissed Ella and held her tight. I hoped I could hold on to what I had with the dawning of the new century.

14

Growing Pains

Turner Ranch, Dudley, Callahan County, Texas
October, 1900

I COULDN'T AFFORD TO HOLD OUR calf crop over until next year. I had bills to pay. We saved every nickel and dime we could, but we couldn't seem to catch up and sure couldn't get ahead. I could feel the ranch we had built up from nothing slowly slipping away. We worked longer and harder, made do with what we had. But I couldn't make it rain, or stop a blizzard.

Dudley had grown a bit with the arrival of two new families. James Smith had been a drummer boy in the Union army. Now he was an old man with a flowing white beard and piercing blue eyes that could look right through a man. He had moved his family from Missouri in search of a better life. I never knew why he chose Dudley or what he hoped to find here. He took up a quarter section of bottom land along Pecan Bayou that had deep rich soil. They built a pretty yellow house with fancy white trim work all around the large front porch. The house was filled with children who were expected to work long days in the field. Mr. Smith donated a quarter of an acre of land on the southwest corner of his property for a new church.

Another family, headed by the white-headed Horace Coffman, took up another quarter section. They built a house near the Smith's. Together they built a small church building. The sign above the door read: "Dudley Church of Christ."

"Now we got nearly fifty people and two churches. Next thing you know there'll be a bank and a fancy hotel." We laughed at the idea. We found the Smith and the Coffman families to be fine people and good neighbors.

I had gone to hear the preaching a couple of times. Smith and Coffman took turns preaching and leading singing. I grouched about it to Ella. "That's the singingest bunch of people I ever heard. And they preach a stern old Gospel, too."

"Oh, you don't like it because our preacher isn't there."

"No. I don't like it because they don't allow no kinda music; no piano, no organ, no nothin'."

"Well, that's their way. Who's to say which is better?"

"I like it better with a piano to keep us on key."

They had brush arbor meetings in the summer and singing school all year long. We nearly always went, because there wasn't anything else to do around Dudley.

We finally had a full calf crop of three hundred and fifteen calves. I kept the twenty best heifers for replacements. If we were ever going to get out of the hole, I had to get the stocking rate back to the carrying capacity. Without a dime to spare, we couldn't buy cows, so we would grow out the best of ours. Even so, the long yearlings we sold weighed above average six hundred and fifty pounds, and the price was finally a little better. I didn't have to borrow any money that year, and was able to pay back a little of what we owed. It was a start.

Nature blessed us with rainfall that was a bit above average, too. The grass grew thick, lush and tall. Our farming neighbors made good crops of dry land cotton, sorghum, corn and hay. Folks had a little to spend, and the store showed a profit of ten or twenty dollars a month. My small salary as postmaster helped pay the bills, as did the modest profit from the freight business. We were paddling along, making a little progress in life financially. But I never felt poor. We were rich in family and friends. That counted for more than money in the bank.

August 2, 1902, Ella gave birth to a handsome baby boy we named Jesse. He had dark curly hair and blue eyes. All of the other children spoiled him. It's a wonder the boy every learned to walk, for someone was always holding him.

Al was now twenty-two. He took care of the ranch while I ran the freight business. He was master of the string bass, guitar, fiddle, mandolin, and banjo. If it had strings, Al could play it. But his true love was the mandolin. There were some songs that he played so sweetly that his mother and sisters cried at the beauty of his music. He was good to a fault to his brothers and sisters, and did everything I asked of him. But Al had a part of him, deep inside, that was wild and untamed, like the sandhill cranes in the fall sky, or coyotes howling on a clear night. The outdoors pulled at his soul. I believe if he had been forced to stay inside any length of time, it would have broken his heart.

Lela and Mamie were tall slender, pretty young women, with ready smiles, of fifteen and seventeen. Their personalities were very much like their mother. They helped with the house, garden and younger children.

Ed was a long legged, growing thirteen year old who loved music, horses and cows. He was already a good ranch hand and always had a smile for his mother. He never gave us much trouble.

Then there was twelve year old John. He was growing as fast as Ed, but broader and stouter. His red hair had become a more restrained auburn, but his gray-blue eyes could see right into your heart. He loved his mother and me, and his brothers and sisters. I could not say that he was my favorite, for all children are their father's favorites in their own way, but we were very close and shared a special bond. Ella felt the same way. His siblings from Al to Jesse trusted and sought out John. He responded with empathy, kindness and concern. That is not to say that he didn't have a mischievous streak, for he most certainly did, and a great sense of humor. He was especially close to Al, and very competitive with Ed and Bill. John could mend a bird's broken wing or tend a nest of abandoned rabbits. But he was not shy about hunting. He helped take care of anyone in the house who was sick. The other kids would beg their mother to "send John" when they were hurt or sick. Something about John made folks feel better just by his presence. He was good with music like Al.

Younger brother George was nine going on nineteen. He stayed up with John step for step. He loved to laugh and play pranks. Bill was built and looked much like John. Wherever John went, Bill was in his shadow or at his side.

The replacement heifers were better than any cattle we had raised. They were about seven-eighths Hereford. They still showed signs of their longhorn ancestry with spots and stripes. They had much longer horns than purebred Herefords. But they were of obvious quality. The heifers were ready to breed by the time they were two years old, and the market animals were ready to sell by the time they were eighteen months. They filled out heavier and made more beef with less waste than the old time longhorns. The breeding age cows now numbered more than four hundred for the first time in several years. But each year, we fell a few hundred dollars short of where we needed to be.

On a cold, sleet-filled day, February 15, 1905, Ella gave birth to what was to be our last child. Robin Nixon and her daughters-in-law assisted the delivery of a precious little girl who brought joy to all around her. We named her Ruth. I was soon to be fifty-five. Perhaps it was time we stopped having babies.

My prediction that Al would spread his wings and leave the nest came true. On December 11, 1908, he married a beautiful girl, Noel Mc-Farland, in Abilene. John stood up as his best man. Al and his brothers, joined by the Nixon and Dawson brothers, played at the big dance and dinner. We all danced the night away. Ella and I could still hold our own on the dance floor. Al was a happy young man.

They rented a little place outside of Dudley, where Al tried his hand on the plow. He kept cattle, a couple of work mules and a good saddle horse. I confided to Ella that I didn't think the plow would fit his hand for very long. A year after their marriage, Noel gave birth to a pretty little girl named Odessa. She was my first of many grandchildren. I was pushing fifty-nine when my first grandchild was born, and my youngest child was just four years old. Time was rapidly catching up to me. I had packed those six decades of life completely full of living.

Ella was worried about all the children and their Christian duty. She especially worried about George. He had been missing services to go fishing on Sundays. She had explained her concerns very clearly to the gangling teen. If he wasn't in the building by the time the bell quit ringing this coming Lord's Day, there would be hell to pay and no hot tar.

Being a sultry summer day, all of the church windows had been left open as well as the large double doors. As the bell slowly tolled ten times, we could hear hoof beats coming at a gallop from the direction of Pecan Bayou. Ella kept looking at the empty seat she had saved for George.

Just as the last note pealed from the bell, George rode his mule up the steps, through the door and down the aisle to the astonishment of all of those present. The only sound was the heaving breath of the hard-ridden mule. With a grand gesture, George, still mounted, swept off his hat and bowed from the waist to his mother. "Mother dear, never fear. The Prodigal son is here!"

"George Turner!"

"But you never said nothin' about stayin'!"

He rode the mule forward, past the mourner's bench, and turned him around. With a wave of his hat, he spurred the mule and galloped out of the astonished congregation. As the hysterical laughter fell away, all eyes turned to Ella who was rocking back and forth in the pew: laughing uncontrollably.

In the spring of 1910, a strange light appeared in the sky, a glowing head with a tail of lightning. The paper said it was Haley's Comet. It could be seen every night as soon as the sun went down until the next morning's brightness hid it from view again, from April 20 through April 29, then disappeared. Scientists explained that it was a natural phenomenon that occurred on a regular and predictable pattern. But those who were less scientific took it as some kind of omen; some said for good, some said for evil.

We gathered outside each night with our friends to watch it. Matt Dawson had a telescope he had salvaged from the closed college. He set it up on a tripod and carefully focused each night so that each of us could see it in its full glory. I was sad when it was gone. It was too beautiful to be a harbinger of evil. I was wrong.

I received a letter from the insurance company. Since the note had not been paid in full on the due date, the ranch and cattle were being foreclosed for the remaining balance due of two thousand two hundred dollars. I wrote for an extension. I thought in two years it could be paid off in full. The bank at Baird even sent a letter of support, explaining the likelihood that I would be able to pay it off with the extra time. The appeal was denied and I was served a summons to appear in Taylor County Court.

I couldn't afford a lawyer, so I went hat in hand, with Ella and the children at my side. The banker from Baird appealed to the court for leniency, but the judge pointed out that the loan had been quite specific. If the balance was not repaid in full, the land and cattle were forfeit. He explained this to the sullen farmers and ranchers who comprised the jury. Their sympathy for me was easy to see on their faces. But, the verdict was unanimous. The ownership of all twenty square miles of land and over four hundred head of cattle transferred to the insurance company. They would sell all of it, and remit to me any amount in excess of the debt. Ella and the girls cried.

"Dad, we'll still have our house and two hundred acres, the store, post office and freight business. We'll make it just fine."

I turned to look into John's nineteen year old gray-blue eyes and reassuring smile. Perhaps he was right. "Sure we will, son. Sure we will."

No one in that part of the state had the twenty-five thousand dollars it would take to buy the ranch and cattle. The insurance man from Abilene came out to the house. "Mr. Turner, I grew up twenty miles from here at Tuscola. The droughts and blizzards finally broke my folks. I don't feel good about the way this turned out. I'd like to make you an offer that might make this deal a little easier to swallow. I have been told by the home office to hire an experienced ranch manager at fifty dollars a month on a year to year contract until it sells. I'm offering you the job."

I stood up and pointed the stem of my pipe at the insurance man. As I opened my mouth to speak, Ella said "We would be honored. Thank you for trusting us."

The fire of anger that had been building in my heart toward the far away insurance company extinguished itself. This was better than anything I could have hoped for, short of never having gone into debt.

The ranch was gone. The high grade cattle that we had bred, now belonged to a faceless insurance company, as did the ground upon which they stood. But I was their caregiver, and had land to roam just like always. The fifty dollars a month was enough to keep our family afloat. And we were all still together. It was enough.

Part Two

Exodus

1

John and Jezebel

January, 1911
Dudley, Callahan County, Texas

SMOKE HUNG IN A FRAGRANT wreath around my head as I enjoyed my favorite pipe and tobacco. The night air on the porch was crisp and clear, but tolerable in my heavy coat. I would normally have been in bed hours ago, but John was out and had not come home yet. Had it been one of his older brothers, I wouldn't have thought much about it. But this was very much out of character for twenty year old John.

The jangle of trace chains and the sound of steel rims on gravel announced his arrival. He was whistling "Cotton-eyed Joe" as he reined up at the porch.

"Dad, is somethin' wrong?"

"That's what I want to ask you. Put the buggy in the shed and tend the mare. We need to talk when you're done."

Of all the boys, he had given us the least trouble. We hardly ever worried about him. But we didn't know the girl he was courting, and it wasn't like him to be out this late. He came humming across the yard and bounced up the steps. He was freshly shaved, had put tonic on his hair, and was wearing his best clothes and hat.

"What's her name, son?"

He looked a little surprised, and then a smile spread across his face showing his dimples. "Is it that obvious? Her name is Johnnie Lee."

"Kinda unusual name for a girl."

"There's nothin' usual about her. She's the prettiest girl I've ever seen."

"And how old is this pretty girl?"

"Sixteen, almost seventeen." His smile got wider with each answer.

"Family?"

"She and her pa live in one of the abandoned houses over at Belle Plain. They aim to fix it up. His name is Robert Lee; says he's named after General Robert E. Lee. He's a horse trader from around Limestone County. It's just him and Johnnie. Her ma died of consumption some years back, and the other kids moved off."

"Robert Lee from Limestone County. Hmm. About my age? A thin man, probably under six foot tall? Wears a patch over his left eye?"

"That sure sounds like him. He's got the eye patch and all."

"I'd like to meet both of 'em some time."

"Sure. I'm plannin' to ask her to dinner Sunday if Momma doesn't care. You want me to invite him, too?"

"Ah, no. Next time I'm by there with a load of freight, I'll just sorta stop by."

"Son, you know how your mother and I feel about certain things."

His blue-gray eyes flashed in the moonlight, as he looked me straight on. "Yes sir. I sure do. And none of that's goin' on, Dad. You raised me better than that."

One thing about John, the man didn't lie. "Go to bed, son. We got work to do in the mornin'. Good night, Romeo."

"Night. Sure sorry I worried ya."

———

Ella rose up on one elbow. "Did you talk to him?"

"Woman, you could hear me talkin' to him right through the wall."

"Sounds to me like you don't know much more now than you did, except for her name. Johnnie Lee. What kind of name is that for a girl, anyway?"

"I figured out one thing I didn't know. Remember when we was courtin' there was some horse thievin' goin' on around Groesbeck?"

"Sure I do. Daddy had some horses stolen right behind the house. They caught the guy who did it and sent him off to prison."

"Yeah. His name was Robert Lee. He's that girl's father, and they are livin' in a fallin' down abandoned house over at Belle Plain."

"Did you tell John?"

"No. I'm gonna go over to Belle Plain and see for myself. I kinda suspect it is the same man. If it is, I'll have to decide whether or not to tell him."

―――――――

Two days later, I detoured off the Baird road to the ghost town of Belle Plain. I saw smoke rising from the chimney of a dilapidated house. Makeshift corrals held horses of dubious quality. A thin, dirty man wearing worn-out bib overalls, without a shirt or shoes stepped out onto the decaying porch with a double barreled shotgun. A greasy black eye patch covered his left eye."

"What the hell do you want?"

"I want you to point that shotgun somewhere else before I take it from ya!" He pointed the gun at the ground. "You Robert Lee?"

"Who's askin'?"

"I'm Aaron Turner. I think my son has been callin' on your daughter."

A strikingly beautiful girl with raven hair and dark eyes stepped out of the sagging front door wearing a dirty, ragged flour sack dress incongruously wrapped with a fringed purple silk shawl. "Well, you must be John's sweet ol' daddy he's so proud of. I'm Johnnie Lee. Wipe the drool off your chin, Grandpa."

"Yes, I'm John's father. And I know you, Robert Lee. You stole horses from my father in law, George Fisher, around Groesbeck back in 1875."

"That was a long time ago. I served my time. Now, git off my place."

"This ain't your place. You're a squatter. I'd just as soon you move somewhere else."

"That ain't none of your business, Grandpa. As far as me seein' John, that's none of your business, neither."

Johnnie gave me a stare that would melt cold steel. I slapped the reins across the mules' backs until they reached a fast trot for home. Trouble had come to Callahan County.

On Sunday, John squirmed in the pew. As quick as the last amen was said, he was out the door and flying off in the buggy, leaving a trail of red dust. He pulled into the front yard just as Ella was setting the food on the table. He helped Johnnie down and walked to the door holding her hand and smiling like he didn't have good sense.

As she swept through the door, all eyes were on her. Ed, George and Bill stared like they had never seen a girl. They exchanged winks and elbows in the ribs.

"Mother, this is Johnnie Lee."

"I'm glad we finally got to meet, Johnnie."

"This is my father."

"We've met." Johnnie gave me the same hard look I'd seen at Belle Plain. John seemed oblivious to the tone of her voice.

"I was just settin' things on the table. Y'all come on in and take a seat."

It was fifteen year old Bill's turn to say grace. I glanced up to see Johnnie giving me a hard stare. As soon as the prayer was finished, she handed John the purple shawl. "Put that somewhere it won't get greasy or dirty." Ella cut a look at me.

"Johnnie, how long have you and your father lived at Belle Plain?"

"Honestly, Mrs. Turner, I don't see how that could be the slightest concern of yours."

That snapped everyone at the table to attention. All eyes were on our guest. "Johnnie, Mother is just bein' friendly."

"This whole visit was your idea. I don't give two cents about meetin' your raggedy ol' white trash family."

"Johnnie Lee!"

"Take me home. Now! And get my wrap."

"We ain't had dinner yet!"

"I ain't hungry. I'm just bein' checked out like some sale barn brood mare."

The kids all stared at their plates or the ceiling. Jesse shot milk through his nose. Ella slowly stood up. "Young woman, you're a six-teen year old girl. I will not have you disrespect my husband, my home or my son. John, you take her home and come straight back. We've got some serious talkin' to do."

"Yes, ma'am. I'm real sorry, Momma."

"Yes, ma'am. I'm real sorry, Momma." That girl was mocking my son right in his face!

I stood up and motioned for everyone else to get up. "Time to leave, son."

As they drove away, I could hear her giving him a good sized piece of her mind, and watched her wagging her finger at him. The poor boy was in over his head in pure trouble with that Jezebel.

Ed spoke the obvious. "Momma, John's got the best heart of any-body I know. That witch ain't fit to be in the same house with decent folks. She sure as hell ain't fit to be with John."

"But ain't she easy on the eyes." Bill muttered. Ella hit him in the back of the head.

Our attention was diverted from John's problems when Al's wife, Noel, gave birth to a baby boy February 28, 1911. Our friend, Robin, had been the midwife; she was now starting to deliver my grandchildren. I was pretty proud to have my first grandson, or as Keenan teased, "The first one you know about!"

The idiots in Austin had finally managed to bring the issue of Prohibition to a statewide referendum. The Texas Democratic Party, so firmly united since Reconstruction, was divided on the issue into two camps. There were those Texans who firmly supported making alcohol illegal. They came from the ranks of the Baptist churches of the various types, the Presbyterian Church, the Church of Christ and their piano playing cousins, the Christian Church. The old heathens like the Methodists, white and Mexican Catholics, and several others, felt it was a man's right to decide for himself about drinking.

There was a lot of ink and paper used to argue one side or the other, and a great deal of hot air expended by preachers and politi-cians who seized Prohibition as their own personal crusade. It seemed a great waste of time to me when so many more serious problems faced Texans. Our schools were a patchwork shambles. People were losing their land and homes trying to make a living growing corn, cotton or cattle. The railroads, banks and insurance companies held the common folks by the throat, yet we debated Prohibition. The referendum failed to pass by a very thin margin. For now, we could keep our alcohol.

———

The winter gave way to a glorious spring. The rains, that had so often eluded us, came in gentle abundance, falling generously on the thirsty land. Wild flowers and sweet clover covered the countryside. The native grasses broke dormancy in luxuriant shades of green.

As spring progressed, the farmers' fields came to life. Grain sorghum and corn erupted in neat rows. The mild weather and rains were ideal conditions, and if a man watched closely, he could see the corn grow. The cotton got planted early, and by June the young plants were in good solid stands.

The pastures were home to newborn calves following their mothers through the deep grass. The prices for corn, cotton and cattle were terrible. As much as I regretted the loss of my land and cows, the insurance company's checks for managing the ranch came once a month and paid the bills.

Ella's garden was really growing. She and the girls kept every weed pulled before it had a chance to grow. The fruit trees had bloomed heavily and now small fruit covered the branches. Baby chicks followed their mothers all over the yard and garden looking for bugs.

Pecan Bayou gurgled happily near the house. It was a uniquely beautiful spring. But the spring of 1911 would be remembered for less pleasant memories.

———

John, our ever loving, kind, obedient son had fallen under the spell of a modern day Jezebel, Johnnie Lee. Without a word to any of us John and Johnnie Lee eloped. Using our buggy and mare, he drove her to Baird to stand before the Justice of the Peace. She was now seventeen and didn't require her father's consent.

John had approached Jake Dawson about working on his ranch and for Johnnie Lee in the house. John spent hours cleaning the small cabin that came with the job. The day they got married, John dropped her off at the ranch, and then drove the buggy home. I met him in the shed as he was hanging up the harness.

"Son, why are you needin' the buggy on a week day?"

"Dad, let's go up to the house. I need to talk to you and Mother." John looked sad and sober, like a man preaching his own child's funeral.

He sat down at the kitchen table. Ella poured each of us a cup of fresh coffee.

"Mother. Dad. I married Johnnie Lee in front of the Justice of the Peace at Baird this morning."

I felt my face flush red, but held my peace. Ella set her coffee down with a clatter. "John Turner! Of all our sons, you're the last one I would have expected to behave like that. You never even talked to us. Is she with child?"

"No, Mother. You raised me better than that. I knew you and Dad wouldn't approve of the marriage. We both have jobs at the Dawson's place. Jake thinks you approved of the whole deal."

"You lied to him, son."

"No. He just assumed that was how things were, and I didn't correct him."

Ella's tears began to flow, speaking more clearly than any words. The look on John's face showed he was actually surprised at his mother's reaction. I don't know what he had expected. Leaving him to talk to his mother, I stepped out on the kitchen porch and lit my pipe.

Soon, John quietly eased out on the porch. His face was red and tear streaked. He sat next to me on the steps. "Pa, I'm sorry. I never stopped to think how you and Mother would feel about this. I didn't mean to hurt anybody."

"I know that, son. We're concerned that Johnnie doesn't seem like a good match for you." I was trying to be as gentle as I could.

"I love her, Pa. I know she comes across pretty rough. But she's had a really hard life. She doesn't trust people. But she's got a lot of good in her that other folks just don't see."

I had a strong premonition that he was making a mistake that he would live to regret. But he was an earnest, sincere young man who had always been able to see the deeper good in other people. Anxiety filled my heart for this son I loved so much. "I hope you made the right decision. We just want what's best for you." I reached out to shake his hand, but he grabbed me around the shoulders and hugged me tight.

The seeds of worry that sprouted that June day would grow into full-blown heartache before summer passed. She would hurt this good man to the depths of his soul.

Feeling a twinge of conscience, John told Jake the rest of the story. Jake had known him all his life. He couldn't stay mad at him, and said they would work things out.

John poured all he had into the job. He was a top-notch ranch hand. Johnnie was a different story in the house. She spoke disrespectfully to Mrs. Dawson, a thing that could not be tolerated, but for John's sake they let it go for now.

The third week at the ranch John was fixing fence on the back side of the place. Jake loped up on his horse. "What's the hurry, boss?"

"Just leave your work where it is and drive the wagon on up to your cabin. We need to talk."

"Somethin' wrong?"

"I hope not."

He slapped the reins over the mules to get them into a trot. The cabin was located in a grove of live oaks behind the Dawson's house.

"John, I need to look around in your house."

"Well, sure. It belongs to you. What's goin' on, Jake?"

"My wife says two leather suitcases, some expensive silver, nice clothes and other things are missin'. She saw Johnnie carry them in here this mornin'."

It didn't take long to search the tiny one room cabin. John found two suitcases under the bed and pulled them out. "This them?"

"Yeah." Jake opened them displaying the other missing items.

"Boss. I don't know what to tell ya. I think we better go talk to Johnnie."

As they entered the kitchen, Johnnie saw the suitcases. Rather than explain, she proceeded to cuss both the Dawsons in horrible language. She then turned her acid tongue on John. She cussed him like a drunken teamster.

He used the ranch wagon to load up Johnnie's things and drive her back to Belle Plain. They sat in silence as the wagon bounced down the road as fast as the mules could go. John set her belongings out on the porch as Mr. Lee laughed and cussed at him from the rickety porch. But it was Johnnie who had the last word. "Well, Mr. God-fearin', church-goin' John Turner, it would suit me just fine if I never saw you again."

John drove off without a word or a backward glance. Anger, embarrassment and betrayal took over his whole mind. If the mules had not turned in at the Dawson's gate on their own, he would have missed it.

John returned the wagon to the barn and gathered up the few things he had in the cabin. He rolled them up in a blanket and tied it behind the saddle on his own horse. Jake saw him, and walked out to talk. John tried to speak, but only a croaking voice emerged. After a few false starts, he finally choked out "Jake, I'm so sorry. I didn't know."

"Heck, John, I knew that. This wasn't your fault. If you want to go, I understand and won't stop you. But you've got a job here any time you want it."

"The way she cussed you and your wife... You've never been anything but good to me. I'm real sorry."

"She singed your tail feathers pretty good, rooster. There ain't a bit of that on you. You just do what you got to do. No hard feelin's."

I saw John coming down the road. The way he sat his horse, I knew something was bad wrong.

"John?"

"Dad, I guess we need to have a sit down talk at the kitchen table again. Let me put my horse up, and I'll be right in." He looked like some of the battle weary soldiers I remembered from the war.

He stumbled around some with his words, but told Ella and me what had happened. The heartache and pain radiated from his face like a fever. "Can I stay in the bunkhouse until I sort things out?"

"Sure, son. But I expect your boots under the table for supper here every night. Your father's got some chores where he needs help. I guess you're not goin' back to Jake's place."

"No. When I think of what she did and said, I don't think I could ever work there again."

Our son with a heart as good as gold now had it shattered like glass. It would be many months until we felt like the old John was back.

The Texas Pacific agent had seen Johnnie getting on a west-bound train with a whiskey salesman. She left the day after John came home. As far as we knew, she never came back.

John worked odd jobs for farmers and ranchers for the rest of 1911. Our family rarely spoke of Johnnie Lee, and never in front of John.

2

Healing a broken heart

December, 1911
Smith Farm, Dudley, Callahan County, Texas

JOHN RODE UP TO THE SMITH FARM. They had sent word that hands were needed to pick cotton, and John was out of work at the moment. His good boots were replaced by rough brogans. He wore his oldest work pants, long-sleeved shirt, and the floppy straw hat of a farmer. He hoped no one would see him dressed like this. It wasn't dignified for a cowboy to pick cotton. But Farmer Smith had invited everyone around to help get his cotton out before it got wet.

"Hello, John. Glad you could come. I guess cotton pickin' isn't your idea of fun." His blue eyes twinkled from his weathered face and long gray beard.

"How hard could it be?"

"About as hard as anythin' you've ever tried. My daughter, Effie, is the best cotton picker on the place."

John looked up, and up, to see the six foot tall curly red-headed girl dressed in her brother's old clothes with a cotton sack slung over one shoulder. He quickly pulled off his hat and extended his hand. "Hello. I'm John Turner."

"I'm Effie Smith. I've seen you at one of the singin' schools down at the church. You oughta come more often, you could use the practice." A smile brightened her face. "I heard you say you don't think there is much to this cotton pickin'."

"Well, how hard could it be?"

"I got a new silver dime says I can out-pick you any day of the week and twice on Saturday."

John was taken aback. "Oh, it wouldn't be fair to take advantage of a girl."

"Well, young Mr. Turner, how do you think I got that dime? I won it off a fella yesterday. You scared of losin' a dime?"

"You're on. What are the rules?"

"My father weighs ever sack we bring in before he dumps it in the wagon. He pays pickers a penny a pound. At the end of the day, we'll total up who wins, unless you get tired and go home early. No green bolls, rocks or dirt clods, just cotton."

"Sounds fair enough. When do we start?"

"As soon as he says the dew has dried off the field, we'll go."

"Listen up all you pickers. There's a water barrel and dipper here in the shade. My wife is gonna set out some lunch. You can grab some when you want it. You work fast or slow. I pay by the pound, not the day. No pullin' whole bolls or green bolls, no trash. If I see it, I'll pull it out of your sack. If you do it too often, I won't need you. It's dry enough. Get to pickin'."

John was nobody's fool. It didn't take him long to figure out that this was the sorriest job he had ever been roped into. The burrs that held the boll were hard and rough. They dug into his fingers constantly until they were oozing blood. There was no way for a tall man to get to the cotton except on his hands and knees. The cotton sack got heavier with every handful added to the long cloth bag. The strap pulled relentlessly on his broad shoulders. The ground was hard, and the clods were misery to his knees. But Effie, one row over, picked like she was born to it. Her long fingers pulled the soft locks out of the burrs effortlessly until her hand could hold no more, and then deposited them into the sack. He silently watched her technique, secretly learning as he went down the long, long rows.

Each time she got up to empty her sack, he was just steps behind her. Mr. Smith called out the weights as each bag was dumped into the wagons. Sometimes, he would be a bit ahead of her. Sometimes she would be ahead. But she worked like a steam locomotive, unlike any frail woman he had ever seen. He grudgingly gave her his respect, although he would be reluctant to ever admit it.

If Effie stopped for water, he did, too. He politely drew a dipper for her each time. When she made a sandwich and ate while continuing to work, he did the same. There was no stopping her, but he wouldn't give up.

The December sun rose in the sky, feebly managing to make the job just that much harder. The heat reflected from the dark soil and the cotton plants blocked any hint of a breeze. It must have been the hottest December day he could remember. When he reached for a bandana to wipe the sweat from his eyes, he could hear her quietly humming a hymn. What kind of woman was this?

The sun finally eased down toward the western horizon as they reached the last rows of cotton in the field. Effie suddenly seemed filled with a new burst of energy and pulled ahead of all the other pickers. John summoned all the strength his aching body had to give and drew closer to her down the row.

"John, if you're tired, I can finish that row for you."

"That'll be the day!" But the human cotton picking machine pulled steadily farther ahead.

The last sack was hung on the scale and dumped into the wagon to haul to the cotton gin at Baird. "That's the last of it! Oh, you did a fine job. We got it all out before the rain, and the field looks to have made better than a bale and a half to the acre. Gather round and I'll count out your wages."

Effie and John waited until the last minute to collect their pay. "John, that's four hundred and eight pounds! That must be a record for someone who has never picked cotton. Here are four silver dollars and eight copper pennies."

Effie straightened up to her considerable height. "Daughter, you picked the most I can ever remember you pickin' in one day, a solid four hundred and twenty pounds. Here are four silver dollars and two dimes."

Effie walked to John and held out her palm. "I ain't got a dime on me, just these eight pennies and some silver dollars."

"You still think pickin' cotton is easy?"

He looked at the worn knees on his pants and his bloody fingers. His shoulders screamed with pain, as did his back. "I guess it's harder than it looks. You sure you didn't throw a few dirt clods and green bolls in your sack?"

"John Turner, do you want me to whip you right here on the turn row? I don't cheat!"

"I'm sorry, Effie. I didn't mean it like that. Well, I guess I really did. I apologize. You beat me fair and square."

"Since you don't have a dime on you, why don't you get some change at your daddy's store and bring it to our house Sunday about lunch time?"

"I believe I'd like that. See ya Sunday."

It would be the first time John put his feet under the Smith's table, but far from the last. Effie took to doing the cooking on Sundays herself, and John was a permanent guest. Soon, he would join her at singing schools and for buggy rides in the cool of the evening.

Everyone in Dudley and most of Callahan County knew what had happened between John and Johnnie Lee. No one faulted him for anything except for being naïve to the ways of the world. John and Effie courted through all of 1912. He finally asked Mr. Smith for permission to marry her, obviously with Effie's full knowledge and consent. The answer he got was not what he expected.

"John, you're a good man, and I think you'd be a good husband for Effie. Her mother and I know all about Johnnie Lee and don't blame you a bit. The trouble is you're still legally married to her. Let me talk to Brother Coffman and the county judge about it, and I'll give you an answer in a week."

John was as nervous as a long-tailed tom cat in a room full of rocking chairs. The days dragged slowly until Saturday. He and Effie met formally with both Mr. and Mrs. Smith and Brother Horace Coffman. He and Mr. Smith were elders at the Church of Christ. Mr. Coffman was the spokesman.

"John and Effie, this is a serious matter. While we like you very much, John, it presents a problem that you are still legally married to Johnnie Lee. I have discussed this with the county judge at Baird and at Abilene. They both agreed that you are not at fault for the dissolution of your marriage because she deserted you. They also noted that no one has seen her, or her father, since she left and it may well be impossible to find her. They suggested that you might very well have a church wedding, and if you ever locate Johnnie Lee, sue for divorce because of abandonment. Brother Smith and I agree that this is an acceptable solution for us as Christians."

"So it's okay?"

"Yes, son. It's permissible to marry Effie. You both have our blessing."

John let out a war whoop and grabbed Effie around the waist and swung her around the room.

"There will be plenty of time for that later, young man." Brother Coffman admonished.

John put her down with a flush of embarrassment. "I beg your pardon."

On February 28th, 1913, John and Effie were married at the Church of Christ in Dudley. Brother Coffman presided over the ceremony, and Mr. Smith proudly gave away the bride to a young man he had come to admire. Al was best man, and Effie's sister was matron of honor.

Folks from as far away as Baird, Clyde and Abilene came to the wedding, for both the bride and groom were well known and well loved. There was a huge barbeque at the Smith's barn after the ceremony. Since the Smith's didn't hold with alcohol, it was "a cold water doin's." But they had no problem with music or dancing out of the church house. Matt and Jake Dawson, Kirby and Keenan Nixon, and the Turner brothers all brought their instruments and each tried to outdo the others. Ella and I swept across the dance floor several times. The bride and groom were obviously in love. This was what we wanted for John. His broken heart was healed, and the real, true love of his life had become his wife.

3

Exodus

April, 1913
Dudley, Callahan County, Texas

A LETTER CAME ADDRESSED TO ME from the United States Department of the Post Office. After sifting through legal language, I found that the post office at Dudley had too little mail to justify remaining open, and would be closed in thirty days. This would mean the loss of the small stipend I earned as postmaster. The store had not been earning enough to even pay Robin Nixon's small salary. I decided to close the store when the post office closed.

About the same time, a letter arrived from the insurance company. They had a buyer for the ranch and cattle and would no longer need my services. I had come to count on the check from them every month to pay our bills, and they had allowed me to hire the boys for spring and fall round ups. That was all going away. We couldn't survive on our two hundred acre homestead and the meager earnings of the freight business.

The Nixon brothers and my boys had gone into Baird on a freight run and stayed for haircuts. They found a recent Abilene newspaper to read. The headlines announced that the Texas and Pacific Railroad had reached Lubbock on the south plains. The state was opening up land for homesteading. A man could claim one hundred and sixty acres of land suitable for farming, or four sections of grazing just for the surveying expense.

After talking to Ella, Al, John and I took the train to Lubbock along with the Nixon brothers. After sizing up the situation, we rented horses and took the advice from a land agent where good prospects might be. Keenan and Kirby rode off to the northeast to check out some prime range land just below the "Caprock," as we called the drop off below the plains, in Floyd County. The boys and I rode on to the small community of Brownfield in Lynn County, and explored farther west into the edge of Yoakum County.

Brownfield was nice and clean, and lacked a freight service to bring goods from the railhead at Lubbock to the surrounding area. We liked the land farther west just on the Yoakum County line. Testing with a shovel revealed rich sandy loam and good range country close at hand.

On returning to Dudley, the decision was made to pull up stakes and move. Al and Noel didn't want to leave the land he was renting. He had been doing well with it. I agreed to rent our house and the two hundred acres on Pecan Bayou to them. The Nixon brothers planned to file for pasture land for themselves, their wives and Robin, a total of twenty sections, of pretty rolling grass land in Floyd County.

To my disappointment, John and Effie had their own ideas, too. John had a job offer in Big Spring. He had come to love anything with a motor on it. He would be an apprentice boilermaker for the railroad. The Texas Pacific left Abilene and ran through Big Spring on the way to El Paso, and from there all the way across the desert to the Pacific Ocean. For the first time in our lives, our family would not be together.

John and Effie loaded what few things they owned into the spring wagon to catch the train. I rode along beside them. We unloaded a bed, small table, two ladder-back chairs, a chest containing their clothes and bedding, and a crate of kitchen goods on the rail platform. Their freight costs and tickets were provided by the railroad.

It didn't seem so long ago that we had been on this same spot after the Baird tornado. It was then I knew that this son of mine was different from my other children. He had grown into a fine man. I was proud of him. Only Ella realized how deeply I would miss him.

I gave Effie a fatherly hug and a kiss. I started to shake John's hand, but he pulled me into his arms and we hugged each other tightly.

"Work hard. Save your money. Take good care of Effie. I'm proud of you, son." I turned away before he could see the tears in my eyes.

Big Spring was a rough railroad town, bustling with business activities off all kinds, including those specializing in drinking, gambling and prostitution. Neither Effie nor John was terribly impressed. Housing was at a premium. Whole families would live in one room of a house shared with other families. John found a ten acre tract of land outside town with a dugout for rent at a reasonable rate. The little underground home had a wool blanket for a door, no windows and a tin roof. A grove of hackberry and cottonwood trees sheltered it from the sun and wind. It had a windmill, chicken house and a large garden plot. There was little else to commend it, except it was away from the taverns and bawdy houses of Big Spring.

"This isn't what I had in mind for our first home, but I guess it'll have to do for now."

"It'll do, John. It needs some cleanin', but hard work never killed anybody. Will you spade the garden and get me some chickens?"

"You're pretty easy to please."

"I didn't say that was all I wanted. We'll do a little negotiatin' as you start makin' some money."

John learned fast at the Texas Pacific roundhouse. He was soon released from his apprenticeship and made a full-blown boilermaker. His status at work increased, as did his paycheck. Effie got a dozen laying hens, a young hog to fatten and a milk goat. There wasn't enough pasture to support a milk cow, and they could never drink that much milk, anyway. The quart a day from the goat was just right, especially since they didn't have an icebox.

John got her garden tools and seed. She wasted no time in planting potatoes, onions, cabbage and greens. As spring warmed, she added black-eyed peas, beans, squash, sweet and field corn, watermelons, cantaloupe and pumpkins. A weed didn't stand a chance in her garden. And what moisture nature failed to provide, she supplemented a bucket at a time.

There was always coffee, cornbread, bacon and eggs on the table for breakfast, and cornbread and pinto beans for supper. Sometimes a jackrabbit or cottontail found its way to the skillet. They had to buy corn meal, bacon, salt and coffee, but if there was a little extra money, they might buy some flour for biscuits or a wedge of cheese. Anything from the garden was a welcome addition to their tiny table on the dirt floor. Effie cooked outside in Dutch ovens.

As if her day was not long enough, she took in washing for some of the single men with the railroad. John would carry the clothes back and forth on his way to work. Clotheslines were strung between the trees around the dugout. A coffee can under the bed held all the extra money they were able to put together. One day they would be able to move up to something a little better.

———

I had plans for a freight service from the end of the railroad in Lubbock to Brownfield. We already had the wagons and top quality draft mules. Kirby, Keenan, and my sons helped me go over the wagons with a fine-toothed comb. The Nixon brothers had two wagons that were making the trip west, and Robin owned a light spring wagon. All the spokes were tightened on each wheel and each axle was carefully greased. All of the tack and harness was checked and oiled. The wagons were pulled into the creek to soak all the wheels. We made sure each of the six wagons had two fresh, clean water barrels mounted along the sideboards. Finally, the wagon bows were attached and the canvas stretched into place.

We planned our routes, for the Nixon family would branch off at Clairemont to travel north to Floyd County while we trekked on west to Brownfield. There were difficult decisions to make about what to take and what to leave behind.

Ella did a good job of sorting through just what she had to move for housekeeping. The rest she gave away. She dug up some of her roses and made cuttings of her fruit trees. They were carefully packed in wet sawdust wrapped with burlap. She selected the best dozen young layers and a young rooster. We would take both milk cows, but decided that it would be simpler to buy young hogs in Brownfield. All of our horses and mules were going with us. Matt Dawson came out and put new shoes on all of them.

Finally, the house goods were loaded into the wagons along with food for the trip. We had all the things we needed for cooking on the ground along the way.

The church had a going away picnic in our honor in the pecan grove near our house after Sunday services. The ladies gave Ella and Robin friendship quilts. Each family had made one or more squares with their names embroidered on it for each quilt. There were many tears and hugs as we said good bye to our friends of the past thirty years.

Pecan Bayou gurgled happily in the gray light of dawn, as the birds greeted the morning. Ed and Bill carried the last of the bedrolls out of the empty house. We had slept inside on the floor our last night there. We had eaten the last meal Ella would cook on her fancy stove, and raked out the ashes.

The harness was taken down from the hangers I had built thirty years before, never to be returned to the place it had occupied for so long. The mules were hitched four to a wagon. We had milked the cows before dawn to have milk for breakfast, but poured out the rest. The gentle cows were haltered and tied behind two of the wagons. The chickens were crated on the tailgate of the third wagon.

I drove the lead wagon, with Ed and Bill each driving one. I helped Ella up onto the seat we had padded with folded blankets, and Jesse and the girls either rode beside the wagons or settled on the other wagon seats. With a pop of the whip, the wagons lurched forward through the gate. I didn't look back.

Keenan, Kirby, Robin and half a dozen kids showed up just as we reached the road and fell in behind us with their three wagons doubled-teamed with good mules. Two milk cows were tied behind and the kids rode and herded the horses. Robin drove her own wagon.

We followed the road west out of Callahan County. Every time my family had moved, it was farther west. I had brought Ella to our first home, the house built with my own hands from a kit hauled from Dodge City, the house where all of my children had been born, the house where two of my children and a good friend lay buried. The smoke from my pipe mixed with the red dust of the road, swirling with the melancholy mood I felt as we finally reached Buffalo Gap.

Extra wagon tarps were stretched from the sides of the wagons to provide sleeping shelter. The children got the bedrolls down from the wagons and handed down their mother's cooking gear. Ed S got a cooking fire started as Bill and I tended the mules. We curried them carefully and watered them before pouring their oats on the thick grass in the shade of the trees. We hobbled them to graze for the evening. Before we bedded down for the night, we picketed all the stock between two trees. The chickens were released to water and eat before they were returned to their crate at dark. The cows had to be milked. We used all we could, then poured out the rest. The cows were staked out on good grass after they had been watered for the night.

Keenan and Kirby played the guitar and fiddle after supper. I had first heard them play on the trail to Dodge thirty-seven years ago. They were now forty-nine and fifty-one years old. I was sixty-two myself. I was too polite to guess how old Robin was, but she was older than me. She handled the four mules on her wagon like a professional teamster. There wasn't much she couldn't do better than most men. The music slowly improved my mood. As Ella and the kids finished their chores, they gathered around to enjoy the music. I guess my home was moving with me. All I left behind was a good house and lots of memories.

We settled into a routine covering roughly twenty miles a day, stopping when we found a good place to camp along the road. Often, a farmer or rancher would let us corral our stock and camp by the windmill. Finally, we arrived at Clairemont in Kent County between the Salt Fork and the Double Mountain Fork of the Brazos.

This night the women cooked a special meal. In the morning, the Nixon clan would take the road north to Floyd County. We had become like family years ago. The parting would not be easy.

The music that night was sweet and sentimental. Kirby and Keenan played *Shall We Gather at the River* as we all sang along to close out the evening. The road dust must have irritated my eyes; they seemed to be tearing up. I sat up leaning against a wagon wheel, smoking my pipe late into the night talking with them. We had become as close as brothers. The women visited late into the night, too. We all knew it was doubtful we would meet again.

It took a little extra coffee to clear the cobwebs the next morning. After breakfast, the wagons were reloaded and the mules hitched. Three wagons rolled away to the north, taking part of our hearts. We set out faces once again to the west.

———

Building in the west, clouds rose to enormous heights. The thunder grew louder and lightning flashed near. The wagon road was on thin red rocky soil. The steel rims of the wheels cut narrow ruts, but there was plenty of rock to support the heavily loaded wagons. The mules never missed a step, although Ed, Bill and Jesse got soaked to the bone on horseback.

The country we crossed was rough, with scattered cedars, hackberry and mesquite trees. There was a modest covering of grass, but this range wouldn't run nearly the cattle we could back in Callahan County. By the time we reached the north branch of the Double Mountain Fork of the Brazos, it was rolling out of its banks with red muddy water. We made camp on a good unfenced patch of grass near the road on high ground. The storms cleared, and a dry west wind blew steadily across the unwelcoming landscape.

Ed tried the crossing on horseback the next morning. The river had gone down overnight. The crossing had a rocky bottom and was only knee deep on the horse. We crossed easily in the freight wagons.

I thought of the countless crossings we had made on the cattle drives to Missouri and Kansas. I sometimes missed those days. I was ten foot tall and bullet-proof then. Life had humbled me. Then, I was single and concerned about the safety of my drovers and herd. Now I had a wife, children and grandchildren to worry about. I had poured my life into a successful ranch only to see it slip away. Family was all I had left; the only thing that mattered.

Not long after the river crossing, we found the road had a long, long incline rising up to the edge of the caprock. The grade was steep and had washed badly from the heavy rains. I borrowed Ed's horse and scouted ahead.

"We're gonna have to double team the mules to get up this grade.

No riders in the wagon. Ella, I'm sorry, but you and the girls are gonna have to walk. You might get a head start; it's a long way. Boys, shift that team over to the lead wagon."

The eight stout mules laid into their harness and moved the wagon slowly up the bottom of the slope. A hundred yards up the road, the grade increased. The forward progress of the wagon slowly ground to a halt. It was pointless to whip or cuss the mules. They had given their all. "Chock rocks under all four wheels, boys. Set the wagon brake, Jesse."

I sent Ed and Bill to bring up the other team. Once the mules were hooked to the trace chains, I took the front left mule by the headstall. Ed and Bill did the same down the line. This time, as the twelve mules pulled together, the wagon inched forward. As the forty-eight steel shod hooves gained traction, the wagon rolled slowly and steadily up the steep grade.

I turned to hear giggling from the side of the road. "Aaron Turner, the girls and I are walkin' faster than twelve mules pullin' one wagon!" I started laughing, too. It was pretty ridiculous.

We finally gained the top, and repeated the whole process on the second and third wagons. We hadn't made many miles, but we had put in a hard day. We got the teams back where they belonged and made the short haul into Post.

Post was different than any place I had ever visited. It was a planned city, laid out according to carefully developed blueprints designed by a wealthy businessman, C. W. Post. It had a clinic, schools, a library, and public buildings built to match, with neat homes on straight, wide, tidy streets. Trees were planted on every street. A water wagon ran a route to keep them growing. We kind of hated to leave the next morning.

The wagon road headed relentlessly west. Two days travel found us in Tahoka. It was more typical of the towns I had seen in other places. We pushed on toward our new home. The series of rainstorms that had drenched us earlier had apparently soaked the flat prairie. The grass was thick and green here, interspersed with wild flowers and yellow sweet clover. Shallow bodies of water dotted the plains. They had told us they were called playa lakes, from the Spanish name for a beach. In wet years they would hold water a long time. In dry times, the southwest wind caused them to disappear.

"Ella, just look at it. This is fine country."

"It's going to make a wonderful home."

Two more days of travelling west on dusty roads, brought us to Brownfield, county seat of Terry County. Here were the gates to the Garden of Eden, but the hinges looked a little dusty.

4

Home Sweet Home

May, 1913
Brownfield, Terry County, Texas

BROWNFIELD STOOD AT THE INTER-
section of four roads. It was already developing as a trade center. A
fairly unimpressive two story wooden courthouse stood on the center
of the town square. Hill's Hotel dominated the north side of the square,
with the local newspaper, the Brownfield Herald, Brownfield State
Bank, post office and various businesses completing the central business district. There were a few automobiles here and there, but horses
and mules far out-numbered them. Each person who homesteaded in
the county was given a lot in town.

I found some land for sale at the northeast corner of the intersec-
tion of the main roads north to Littlefield, and northeast to Lubbock.
It seemed like the ideal location for a freight and livery company. Ella
and I decided we would live in town, but take up some land with the
older boys. Since our land was on the county line, they gave us the
lots anyway to keep us tied to Brownfield and not the competing community of Plains. It was a good idea.

A dirt road led straight west out of town heading for Plains, the
county seat of Yoakum County. Just inside the Yoakum County line,
we selected our homestead plots, one for each of us over eighteen. The
Plains road was the south boundary of our tracts. Directly on the other
side of the road was some rougher country that had been designated as
pasture land. Here Ed selected his homestead to run cows. His four sections would carry about eighty cow-calf pairs. It wasn't enough cattle

to support a family, so he got a job in Plains where he made his home.

On each homestead track we built the minimum house required to "prove it up" and put in a windmill for the stock that we kept there. Fences were necessary to keep them from straying.

The boys helped me build a box and strip three bedroom house on our lots in town. We didn't have the money to paint it. The inside walls were covered with old newspapers to slow down the wind that blew through the cracks. We bought a used cast iron kitchen stove, nothing like the much nicer one Ella had used at Dudley.

There was a small shed for a cow, a horse, a couple of hogs and Ella's chickens. She planted her roses, trees and garden here, rather than on the homestead. Windmill water was shallow, sweet and pure.

The land here was a rich, fertile sandy loam. The county was marked by Blackwater, Sulphur Springs and Lost Draws, all which ran, more or less, from northwest to southeast. The better grazing land was near these draws. We plowed and planted twenty acres to cotton and another twenty to corn. The rest we left in grass for now.

The country here was crisp and dry, not clinging and humid as it sometimes was back home. But there were hardly any trees as far as you could see. The presence of trees meant there was a draw, a spring or a windmill close at hand.

Since trees were so scarce, the fuel of choice was cow chips. Each home and business had a small shed to protect the dried cow manure from the rain. It made a clean-burning, odorless hot fire. The fancier places like the bank and hotels burned coal.

The native grasses here were thick and strong. Blue and sideoats grama, sprangle top, big and little blue stem and buffalo grass filled the prairies. Wheat grass and vine mesquite grass grew along the draws and playa lakes. It made good grazing in late fall and early spring. The native sod only reluctantly yielded to the plow, but we only plowed as much as we could farm and left the rest in the good native grass. The time would come when we would wish we had left the whole country in its protective covering of native sod.

Bobwhite and blue quail were plentiful, as were prairie chickens. Sandhill cranes traversed this country on their way north and south.

Coyotes and bobcats were in good supply, and wolves could still be found. Antelope dotted the plains and mule deer lived along the draws. Prairie rattlers, and their much larger cousins, western diamondback rattlesnakes, were found everywhere. And the children delighted in the horned toads that lived to catch big red ants.

We built a large set of sturdy pens and barns for our freight and livery business. The sign read: *Exchange Wagon Yard, A. L. Turner, Proprietor*. If it was a sin to be proud, then I sure was a sinner when it came to my freight business.

The Hill Hotel downtown was a little expensive for freighters or cowboys coming through, so we added an inexpensive hotel where folks could get just a clean bed for the night. Soon, we were renting out all the rooms and added more.

Our freight route made the forty mile trip to Lubbock once a week, stopping overnight between Meadow and Ropesville. We placed new orders as we picked up what had arrived that week. We made our deliveries on the way home, although the biggest part of it was for Brownfield. We also kept another wagon running to the small towns and ranches out from Brownfield, and a third lighter wagon was used for local deliveries. We offered a service that had been very much needed and the business was immediately busy. I won the contract to carry the mail to Wolfforth, Ropesville, Meadow and Brownfield. It wasn't enough to live on, but made our freight business more profitable.

Within a few months, the Lubbock to Brownfield run was carrying enough freight that it required two wagons. We simply hooked two in tandem and doubled-teamed the mules. I generally kept things running in Brownfield and had one of my sons or a hired man run the routes. Ella and the girls kept the livery hotel clean and managed our home.

Al, George and John had made lives for themselves elsewhere. Ed was nearby in Plains, although at forty miles, we didn't see him as much as we would like. The older girls were courting and would soon be gone. Bill and Jesse were still at home, and would be for a few years. Ruth, the baby, was only eight years old. We planned on her being with us a whole lot longer. Like the trees we had brought with us, we had been transplanted here and began to put down roots in our new home.

5

Special Delivery

January, 1914
Big Spring, Howard County, Texas

EFFIE AND JOHN HAD STRUGGLED
through the winter months in their tiny dugout. At least the blanket-
covered doorway opened to the south. John brought in a large cast iron
Dutch oven filled with coals after supper for heat. They had plenty of
warm blankets. It would have to do for a while longer.

"John when this baby gets here in May, it sure is gonna be
crowded."

"I know. I've been studyin' on that. We're gettin' some money set
by. When we have enough, I'd like to move on up closer to my family
around Brownfield."

Rising up on one elbow, with her long, red curls hanging down
framing her blue eyes, she grinned at her husband. "You gonna open a
shop and sell ladies hats and stockings? I believe they'd come from all
around to get a look at you."

"You are one big mess, woman. I don't know why I keep you
around."

"All those other girls were too short for you, anyway."

"I'd like to file on some homestead land and maybe start a herd
of cows. It wouldn't be enough to live off at first, but maybe we could
build it up."

"There's good land for cattle down around the family we've got
at Dudley, too."

"Well, I know your family is there, and my brother, Al. But he's got such itchy feet, I don't look for him to stay."

"Well, this baby and I are goin' where ever you go. Somebody has got to keep an eye on you."

One of our chickens came back to the roost in Brownfield. George had been gone and married for over a year, but he decided to take up homestead land right next to ours. He and his wife, Catherine, set up housekeeping on their tract of land just barely inside of the Yoakum County line. If you asked any of them where they lived, they'd tell you Tokio, twenty miles west of Brownfield, on the road to Plains.

Tokio wasn't much more than a name. There was a "sometimes" store: sometimes they were open, sometimes they were closed; sometimes they had stuff to sell, and sometimes they didn't. But, as it was twenty miles to Brownfield or twenty to Plains, folks checked there first. There was a "sometimes" church, too: Sometimes it was Baptist, sometimes it was Methodist; sometimes there was a preacher and sometimes there wasn't. Ella and I went to the Methodist Church in Brownfield and I joined the Oddfellows Lodge.

Effie had a sister that had married and moved to Paris, way up in Lamar County of northeast Texas, nearly to the Red River. But the train ran From Big Spring all the way to Paris. One of the benefits John got was free travel for himself and his family. The baby wasn't due to come for over a month, and Effie knew once the baby came, there wouldn't be much travelling anywhere for a while. She decided to take a short trip while she could.

She had gotten her garden off to a solid start and given John instructions on just how to take care of it the two weeks she would be gone. John assured her he could take care of himself for a while. He had bought a middling horse to ride to and from work that could do light plowing in the garden. He helped Effie onto the horse, and led her into town, carrying her carpet bag for her.

When they arrived at the station, they noticed that there was quite a buzz stirring as there was a private railcar right behind the last Pullman car. It was about the fanciest thing either one of them had seen. The dark wood glowed. The brass framed windows were extra large and covered with lace curtains. All the brass steps and handles had been polished until they looked like gold. An automobile drove up to the platform. A finely dressed man in top hat and coat stepped out followed by enough bags for a small army. There were three Negroes in uniform, two men and a woman, and a white nurse in a starched hat and gown.

The engine had been spruced up for the special guest. All the soot on the whole train had been cleaned, and everything that could be polished was shiny. Even the windows in the passenger and dining car had been washed. There were three passenger cars, a dining car, the one Pullman sleeper, the private car, and then a dozen freight cars before the red caboose. John surprised Effie with a Pullman ticket. It hadn't cost much extra and he wanted her to get some rest. It was going to take two days and a night to get to Paris.

The grand train received special treatment at each stop. Effie was excited to see Abilene, Clyde and Baird. Night came on and she grew tired. Her back was hurting; maybe she'd twisted it getting on the horse. She finished a cup of coffee in the dining car and found her berth on the lower row of the Pullman car. She decided these berths had not been built with six foot tall women in mind. Although the mattress was fine, her back seemed to be hurting more. Settling on her side and drawing up her knees seemed to help. She finally wiggled into her flannel night gown and brushed her hair after bumping her head a few times.

The pain in her back seemed to be getting worse and her belly was hurting, too. Then the thought struck her. This baby might be coming early! No sooner had she decided she was in labor than her water broke. She pulled the call cord to summon the conductor.

"Mrs. Turner, may I help you?"

"Mister, I'm due to have a baby next month, but it's comin' now!"

"Ma'am, are you certain?"

"Yes, my water just broke."

"Oh, my! Oh, my!" He pulled off his cap and wiped his balding head with a handkerchief. "You stay right there. I'll see what we can do. Maybe there's a doctor or midwife on the train."

Soon he returned with the nurse they had seen get on the private car in Big Spring. "Mrs. Turner, this lady is a nurse. We'll help you back to the private car. Can you walk?"

"I can walk, but I don't have any way of payin' for a nurse or a private car."

The nurse smiled at me. "Mrs. Turner, my employer heard about your situation and has offered you the entire private car and my services with his best wishes. He said he wants to play cards with some gentlemen in the dining car."

They escorted Effie into the private car and eased her into a full-sized bed. The black maid had stayed to help, but the conductor and all the other men left. Stained glass lamps lighted the red satin ceiling. They brought her cold water in a cut crystal vase with a matching glass, reassuring her they had helped at many deliveries and she and the baby would be fine.

Her labor progressed through the night, steadily becoming stronger. A little after midnight, the nurse told her to begin to push. She had rigged the silk tie-backs from the curtains to the foot of the bed to assist her labor. Effie was a tall, broad-shouldered, very strong woman. This baby was coming out. With a final mighty push, she delivered a baby boy with a head full of dark red hair, blue eyes and a loud pair of lungs.

The conductor was summoned to document the time and location. "Let's see. One thirty-four A.M. We're just a couple of miles outside of Weatherford, somewhere in Parker County. I'm afraid that's as close as we're going to get for a place of birth." The baby didn't care, he had already discovered how to nurse and was noisily smacking away.

When the train arrived in Fort Worth, the conductor sent a telegram to John in Big Spring; *Early arrival. Mother and baby boy fine. ETA Paris 4 PM.*

"Mrs. Turner, the gentleman who owns the car has insisted you continue to use it until you get to Paris. His nurse and maid will travel on with you. He'll be getting off in Dallas. He's asked about you and the baby, and wondered if he could see the baby when we reach Dallas in about an hour."

"Well, of course. I need to thank him, anyway."

On reaching Dallas, a tall, distinguished-looking gentleman was ushered into the car. He removed his hat and offered his hand.

"Madame, I understand that you and the little boy are doing well. May I see him?" The nurse wrapped the baby in a towel and handed him to his benefactor. "My, what a fine red-headed child." He handed the baby back to the nurse.

"Sir, my name is Effie Turner. Thank you so much for all your kindness. I don't know your name."

"Oh, my name is not important. I was pleased to be of some assistance, although all I did was stay out of the way. Does this boy have a name?"

"No. We never could make up our minds. You have done so much, would you do the honor of naming him for us?"

He cocked back his head in a hearty laugh. "Madame, I have never had the honor of naming a child and doubt that I ever do again. There is a man who has always been a good friend to me. Perhaps you would consider the name Earl Ronald? Oh, no. That would never do. Maybe Ronald Earl Turner would suit you? I will tell my friend and he will be delighted."

"Thank you. When Ronald is old enough, I'll make sure he knows about you."

"You are too kind. I want the namesake of my friend to have something to get his start in this world, besides his charming mother. Good bye, Mrs. Turner, baby Ronald."

He turned and walked out of the car. The conductor walked over with a look of wonder in his eyes. "My wife is never going to believe all this. He made us all swear not to tell you who he is, but I can tell you he is a very wealthy man. He asked me to give you this for the baby." He neatly stacked five twenty dollar gold pieces on the night stand.

Her odyssey completed, Effie and Ronald returned to Big Spring as scheduled. John beamed from ear to ear as he met the son who was his spitting image. He grabbed John's finger and his heart that day and never turned loose.

When the birth certificate arrived some time later, it showed place of birth: *Texas Pacific train, near Weatherford, somewhere in Parker County, Texas.* They never learned the identity of their "Good Samaritan."

6

The World at War

November, 1914
Brownfield, Terry County, Texas

THE WORLD WAS NOW CONNECTED
by railroads and telegraph wires. In the freight and livery business, I
generally got the news as fast as anyone except the telegraph operator.
The world seemed smaller, and places far away sometimes affected
our lives in this out of the way corner of the world. The newly opened
Panama Canal made it much faster for ships to travel from the Atlantic to the Pacific without the long and dangerous trip around South
America.

Mexico, our neighbor to the south, had known decades of stabil-
ity under the dictator Porfirio Diaz. He had encouraged development
of railroads, industry and mining in Mexico that had brought many
jobs and much prosperity. Sadly, those working the jobs remained
very poor, while a handful of the elite members of Mexican society and
foreign investors reaped enormous profits. He ruled unhindered by ac-
countability to almost anyone. Mexico had been brutally stable. Now in
the void left by the absence of Diaz, Mexico was plunged into a bloody
three-way civil war. And like most civil wars, it was the poorest, the
oldest and the youngest in society who suffered the most.

Mexican currency was essentially worthless; only their coins held
any value. Trade with Mexico ground to a halt. There was a saying we
repeated often: "Poor Mexico, so far from God, so close to the United
States." Travel was extremely dangerous. Lawlessness along the
border, which had always been a problem, reached new levels. Money,

horses, cattle, and materials of war were in high demand. Bandits raided deep into Texas, New Mexico and Arizona. Cowboys rode the southern ranges with repeating rifles and pistols. Isolated ranches were raided, the stock driven away, the buildings burned and the people left wounded or dead.

So far, no raiding had been reported this far north. But it was a possibility that was cussed and discussed many times. My drivers and I resumed carrying guns on the freight wagons. We had not felt the need to do so since the end of the Comanche wars thirty years ago.

———————

Farther away, an Archduke of Austria and his wife were killed by a mad-man in a place I couldn't pronounce. Within months, the Europeans and their overseas allies had chosen sides and declared war on one another. The Austrians, Hungarians, French, Russians and British had fallen into a war with Serbia, Turkey and the powerful, war-like Germans. Smaller countries were pulled into the swirling whirlwind of war.

The United States had friends on both sides of the fight. They were our partners in trade. The war disrupted trade. Commodity prices for cotton, corn and cattle dropped sharply. How could war on the far side of the world affect corn prices in Brownfield, Texas? We grew enough for our own needs, and not for export. So far, the effects had been minimal. But the long-term effect remained to be seen.

———————

We did a pretty good job of discussing the world's problems at the Odd Fellow Lodge meetings. Everybody seemed to have an opinion and didn't mind sharing it.

"So, Brother Turner, how do you like the way the election for Governor turned out?"

"Did we have an election?"

"You're a stubborn ol' coot, you know that?"

"Oh, you mean ol' 'Farmer Jim'? I reckon I like him pretty well. He's a Democrat, ain't he? I wouldn't vote for a Republican if there wasn't but one man in the race. He's against Prohibition. I like that, too."

"I don't ever remember seein' you take a snort."

"If I do, or don't, what business is that of yours, anyway, Joe? I take a drop now and then. It sure ain't the place for idiots in Austin or the crooks in Washington to tell a man what he can do."

"Yeah. We all heard your opinion on that, ain't we fellas?" Several heads nodded in agreement.

"Well, if you didn't want to know my opinion on Pa Ferguson, why are you wastin' my time?"

James E. "Pa" Ferguson was known as "the little man's hero." He had campaigned against Prohibition and for reforms to help tenant farmers and ranchers. The old rooster sure could crow. We would have to wait and see if he would do any good.

And so ran our lodge discussions on one topic or another. I guess it was just a good excuse to get away from our wives if nothing better.

———

Our own young rooster, Al, and Odessa and their wagonload of kids, gave up farming in Callahan County, and joined the rest of us on the southern plains. They took up a homestead beside George near Tokio. It didn't take us long to run them up a box and strip house. It might have kept a cat out, but it let the mice, dust and wind come right through the walls.

Only John and Effie were still out of pocket down in Big Spring, snug in their little dugout. They wrote regularly as they promised. But the pull of family was working on John. His letters indicated he was looking for a way to move closer to the rest of us. I would like that. I hadn't even seen his new son yet.

7

A Bad Penny Turns Up

January, 1915
Big Spring, Howard County, Texas

"AL? WHAT ARE YOU DOIN' HERE? I hadn't seen you since me and Effie got married." John stepped forward to greet his big brother.

"Hello, little brother. You done for the day?"

"They just blew the whistle. I'll get my jacket. How'd you get here?"

"I rode."

"From where?"

"Is there a place where a fella can get a drink and we'll talk about it?"

"All right, Al. This is kinda mysterious even for you."

"I had gone to buy cattle for Pat Ross over at Fort Sumner. That rancher and I rode into town to seal the deal with a drink. We walked into this big bar with gamblin' downstairs and workin' girls upstairs. I set down my beer and standin' there between me and the bar was Johnnie Lee. She's usin' the name 'Miss Violet'."

John looked like a fellow who had just swallowed his tobacco. "You sure?"

"You think I would have rode down here from Brownfield if I wasn't? It's her. She walked over to the table and told me to tell you to go to hell."

"I gotta get home to talk to Effie. You're comin' too. There ain't room in the dugout, but you can roll out blankets in the shed. She feeds good."

Effie looked concerned at the unexpected arrival of Al. She knew he was John's closest brother, but he had come unannounced, and had three days of hard riding in the middle of winter. This wasn't a social call, but she would give John time to tell her the story.

Al loved kids; he bounced Ronald on his bony knee while he ate.

"More coffee, Al? We got plenty." He nodded as she poured. "More milk?" She added the sweet goat milk to his cup.

"Effie, that sure was good groceries. That cabbage hit the spot, fried up with the onion in a little dab of bacon. Good beans and corn-bread, too."

"Well, it's a nice surprise to see ya. You're lookin' kinda thin, but it ain't hurt your appetite."

"I'm gonna take my coffee out to the shed, have a smoke and go to bed. I got plenty of blankets. I gotta head home early, so don't count on me for breakfast. Sure good to see y'all. Night, John. Effie."

"Well, I guess you're wonderin' why Al just turned up here." Effie cocked a blue eye over her coffee cup. "He found Johnnie Lee workin' as a saloon girl in Fort Sumner."

"I hope he wasn't one of her customers."

"Effie!"

"I'm goin' right down to the County Clerk's office and file for a divorce. I'll talk to the shop foreman in the mornin'. I'm pretty sure he'll let me off long enough to go to the courthouse."

John was at the Clerk's office when they opened for business. He paid the ten dollar filing fee and the five dollars summons server's fee out of his savings taken from the can under the bed. This was more important than leasing land or buying cattle.

"We'll send you notice of service as soon as she has been served."

A week later, a letter was at the post office. He would need to come to the Clerk's office to find out when the hearing would take place. His horse raised dust all the way to the courthouse.

"Well, the Constable took the train down to El Paso and back north to Fort Sumner. There oughta be a rail line runnin' east and west instead of goin' around the world to get there." The gray-haired clerk rattled on and on. "He said Johnnie Lee signed the summons, then threw it at him and gave him the worst cussin' he ever got in his life. Guess I can kinda see how you might want a divorce, especially seein' where she works and all. It's on the docket for two weeks. You be sure any witnesses you need are here then, too."

John turned red in the face, too embarrassed to talk. He walked to the telegraph office and asked Jake Dawson to come as a witness. He would pay his train fare and expenses. The next day he received a reply that Jake would be there.

"The Seventeenth District Court of the State of Texas is now in session, the Honorable Judge Kincaid presiding. All rise and remain standing until the judge is seated."

"In the cause of John Turner, Plaintiff, versus Johnnie Lee, Defendant, Suit for Divorce for Abandonment. Is the Plaintiff present?"

John stood and addressed the judge. "Yes sir, your Honor."

"Is the Defendant present?"

The Constable rose. "This is the signed receipt for her summons. She isn't here and nobody to represent her."

"Did the she indicate her intention?"

"She was quite clear. She told me to go to hell and made remarks about me and my horse."

The judge had to gavel down the laughter.

"Mr. Turner, is your witness, Mr. Dawson, present?"

"Yessir."

"I recommended a jury trial, as this is an unusual case. A panel of six of your peers has been seated. Tell the court what happened."

John proceeded, using exact quotes as the judge directed him. There were giggles, laughs, and gasps of shock.

The court reporter stopped. "Your Honor, do you want me to write it down like that?"

"Yes. Record the testimony exactly as presented."

"Since that day, have you ever seen her again?"

"No sir."

"How was she located?"

"My brother seen her in Fort Sumner workin' at a saloon. She cussed Al, and told him to tell me to 'Go to hell'."

"That seems to be a popular destination." The courtroom and jury rocked with laughter.

The judge questioned Jake. "Mr. Turner was an employee on your ranch as was his wife, Johnnie Lee?"

"Yes sir. John was a cowhand and she worked in the house. I've known him all his life. My wife got to missin' some things and two leather suitcases. She saw Johnnie put 'em in their cabin. He found the suitcases under their bed. The missin' stuff was in there. We opened 'em in front of my wife and Johnnie. That woman gave us the worst cussin' I ever heard in my life. I sure don't want to repeat what she said 'cause there's ladies present."

Murmuring spread across the courtroom. "Thank you, Mr. Dawson. You are excused. Mr. Turner, is there anything else?"

John looked down at the floor. "No sir. I guess not."

"There were no children?"

"No children."

"Gentlemen of the jury, it has been established by two witnesses that the Defendant abandoned her husband. Under the law, the court may grant a divorce. You will recess to consider the verdict."

The jury had not been gone ten minutes until they sent a note out to the judge. In ten more minutes, they filed back into the courtroom, their faces set hard as stone.

"Your Honor, we find that the Defendant abandoned her husband ending their marriage. We grant the divorce. Further, due to her behavior during their brief marriage, we grant an annulment of their marriage. So say we all."

"Mr. Turner, legally this marriage never occurred. Since the Defendant failed to appear in court, she is assessed sixty-five dollars in court costs." The gavel banged down, and John was now married to only one woman.

John, Effie and baby Ronald joined Jake Dawson on the first train to Abilene the next morning. They proceeded directly from the station to the Taylor County Justice of the Peace. With Jake as the witness, they were married there in the eyes of law and the church. It had taken a bite out of the money can, but it was worth every penny.

Part Three

The Promised Land

1

Goodbye, Dugout!

April, 1915
Big Spring, Howard County, Texas

FROM THE GARDEN, EFFIE HEARD Ronald scream where she had left him sitting on a dirt step into the dugout. Whatever it was terrified him. She ran to investigate, hoe in hand. What she saw made her blood run cold. A large diamondback was slithering two steps above the baby rattling angrily.

As the big snake coiled to strike, Effie struck first. The sharp hoe took his head completely off. Using the hoe to drag it onto the hard-packed ground, she retrieved Ronald and held him like she would never let him go. The snake was six feet long with thirteen rattles.

When John rode up after work, Effie was cooking supper in the Dutch ovens as Ronald played on a quilt in the thin shade of a hackberry tree. The snake was stretched completely across the top step where you couldn't help but see it. He walked over and ruffled the baby's thick red hair, gave Effie a quick peck on the cheek, unsaddled his horse, brushed and fed him, and turned him into the pen. He washed up at the basin by the windmill and headed toward the dugout.

"What's for supper? Good night! That thing is huge! What happened?"

"The baby was playin' on the steps and that critter crawled down to get out of the sun. I killed it with my hoe." She never looked up from her supper preparations. "John, I don't think raisin' a baby in a hole in the ground is such a good idea."

"Well, when we get a little set by, we'll get a better place."

Effie turned and handed him the hundred dollars in gold given to Ronald on the day he was born. "Take that, plus what's in the can, and get us started near your parents."

"That belongs to Ronald."

"That snake nearly got him today. I don't think Ronald would mind." Discussion continued through supper and on past bedtime. It was finally agreed that it was time to make a serious effort to relocate.

John sent a letter to me and one to Al asking about opportunities near us. Al had day-worked for Pat Ross, foreman of the Mallet Ranch. Pat had a ranch of his own on the upper end of Sulphur Springs Draw near Bronco in Yoakum County that he didn't have time to tend. If John wanted to lease the whole outfit, cows and all, it was his. I reminded him he could file a homestead, too, and start working on it while he took care of the cows. The place came with a box and strip house and all the necessary outbuildings. It didn't take much to convince Effie it was the thing to do.

John gave his notice to the railroad. He had enjoyed his work there, and developed a life-long interest in mechanical things. He notified the landlord that they would be leaving at the end of the month. There was such a demand, the owner already had someone waiting to rent it.

The money started coming out of the can. John bought an old solid farm wagon and a pair of decent mules. They crated up the chickens, and sold the milk goat and hog. Their few belongings rattled around in the wagon like a pumpkin in a box car. A wooden grocer's box held their food and another contained the kitchen goods. The three of them sat on folded blankets on the wagon seat and headed north.

After a hurried breakfast, they left at daylight. John pointed the wagon northwest on the dry, hard-packed road toward Ackerly. They made it in good shape and camped on a little farmstead where the owner and his wife welcomed them to the use of his corrals and water.

The ground they camped on had been grazed short, allowing the fine red dust to rise with every step of man or beast. Effie found that some of it settled into the food she prepared in Dutch ovens.

"Don't complain about the grit in the cornbread and beans. I did everythin' I could to keep it out."

"Oh, a little dirt never hurt nobody." John rigged a spare wagon tarp to form a makeshift tent, and spread another under their bedding.

The road climbed slowly northwest to Lamesa. The land was pretty good pasture, with solid stands of native grass interrupted occasionally by small farms. The town was small and sleepy. They camped beside a playa lake on the edge of town. From Lamesa, one road left town mostly to the north destined for Lubbock, with a smaller road leaving northwest that would eventually take them to Brownfield.

They passed through the hamlet of Punkin Center and camped at the drowsy little town of Welch. Another day in the wagon took them to Union, where they camped for the night. There was good grass, so John left the mules staked to graze for the night. He and Effie lay together holding Ronald and watching the stars.

"Ah, look at that fallin' star. It went all the way across the sky."

"There's another. Did you see it?"

"I remember Dad tellin' us a story. His granddad thought fallin' stars were good luck. Maybe this move here is goin' to be good luck for us."

The wind blew gently through the prairie grass that night. As it passed it caused a very slight rustling sound. What they had taken for an omen of good luck was a murmur of warning. But they were too young, too in love, too optimistic to hear the message.

———————

Sunrise on the plains can be a glorious sight. Morning dawned with an awesome display of beauty. There had been light dew, and the moisture on the native grass reflected the red and gold of the sunrise. They drank their coffee and smiled. They would be in Brownfield for supper.

This last segment of the road paralleled Sulphur Springs Draw. There had been enough rains that it held some running water. It was lined with large cottonwoods and modest hackberry trees. The grass in all directions was thick and green, ideal cattle country. They drove the wagon right to the freight yard.

"Dad, come meet your grandson!"

"God love you, John. We've been so anxious to see you. Here, Effie, let me help you down."

As I gave Effie a hand climbing down from the wagon box, Jesse and Bill came running up. "John! Effie! Show us that boy!" John handed the round little boy to his uncles.

"Gosh, he looks like you and Dad!"

"I hope that's a good thing, baby brother!" John grabbed Jesse and picked him off the ground. "You've grown since I last saw you. And how's my brother, Bill?" It was Bill's turn to get rough housed. "You're nearly fit to be seen in public."

I was holding Ronald. "He looks just like ya, son!"

Ronald reached with both hands and pulled my old hat down over my ears. "Dada." This time he grabbed the ends of my moustache and twisted it. "Dada."

"I kinda think he likes me." Holding Ronald in one arm, I turned to give Effie a hug and a peck on the cheek. "You shore done good work on this boy, Effie. And he was born in a private car on the railroad. Ain't that somethin'!"

The boys vacated their bed for them for a couple of nights. Ella was beside herself to have some of her favorite folks in the house. I took John to the courthouse and he filed the papers on a quarter section of farmland joining the rest of us.

He was off to Tokio with his family to stay a few days with George, so he could plow out enough ground to get some feed planted. George was where he could help, so with two men and four mules working, they had ten acres broke out in two days, harrowed the next, and planted the day after that. All it needed was a little rain to get started.

From there, they travelled on to Plains were they spent the night with Ed S before leaving the next morning for the short trip along the draw toward Bronco. Al met them at the ranch with Pat Ross.

"Hello, John and Effie. This here's Pat Ross, the foreman at the Mallet Ranch."

"Ma'am, John. I'm proud to meet you." He tipped his well-worn hat to Effie and shook hands with John. "This is the place. It's open range, but these cows know it's home and don't stray much. They kinda like it here close to the draw, anyway. There's eight sections here and one hundred and twenty-two cows, three bulls, and I ain't tried to count the calves. You're renting the whole outfit, cows and all for a third of what the calves bring when they sell. The windmill water is sweet; there's a garden patch and a few fruit trees. The house sure ain't much to brag about, but it's got a box stove for cookin' and heat in the winter."

"Mr. Ross, I wouldn't talk down about this place a bit. We've been livin' in a dugout since we got married. Just about anythin' has to be an improvement."

"She's right, Pat. This looks like the promised land compared to where we've been livin'."

"Well, I'm glad you like it. I will brag on the cows. The mommas are all at least half-blood Hereford, and the bulls are full-bloods. Let's quit jawin' and git your stuff in the house. It takes me half the day to git much work out of Al."

"Don't pay him much attention. He only has me come out here from my place when he's got important business to tend to. I'm probably the best help he's got."

"Pat, if he's the best you got, it must be a pretty sorry outfit."

———————

Effie set about cleaning the little unpainted box and strip house like it was on fire. She swept out the red blow dirt that covered the floor, and washed the windows. She stuffed newspaper and rags in the worst of the cracks and holes. The box stove got the best cleaning it had ever had. Finally, she pasted newspaper over all the inside of the walls to stop the wind from blowing through. The little table and two chairs and one bed seemed lost in the house, but it was nice to have some elbow room.

She had the garden worked up and planted with green and pinto beans, black-eyed peas, squash, sweet corn, tomatoes, Irish and sweet potatoes. It grew beautifully in the red sandy loam soil, irrigated with windmill water. She pruned the young fruit trees which already had tiny green fruit. There were apples, apricots, peaches and pears. She was already studying a way to come up with enough money to buy some paint for the lonely little house which was shaded by the big trees along the draw.

John bought a Milking Shorthorn that had a little heifer calf at her side. He also brought home a young sow which had half a dozen fat piglets at her side. The hen house was fixed so the chickens could roam during the day, but got shut in tight every night. As pretty as the draw was, it was home to plenty of bobcats, coyotes and raccoons.

Ed had seen George and reported that there had been a nice slow two inch rain followed by some showers to get the feed plot off to a solid start. John leased the rest of the grass on his homestead to George who was able to add five more cows to his home herd. All of the grown boys had some mix of farming and cows except Ed. He stuck with just cows and his job in town. They all seemed to be getting off to a good start.

"Well, Brother Turner, what do you think about the women gettin' to vote?"

The United States had almost passed a law to let women vote. I felt like they should be able to do so. Folks sometimes didn't realize that it was the women who had given and suffered so much for us to have what we did. They gave their sons' and husbands' lives in war, they took up men's work while they were gone, or when they never came home. They gave every bit as much as the men to build what we had. My father had died when I was a year old. I had seen my mother push on without a husband for many years. She had kept our place together during the Yankee War.

"About women votin', as long as they is Democrats, I'm all for it."

The war in Europe was very real. The newspapers reported battles that lasted for days and left hundreds of thousands of men dead and even more wounded. The Germans had used a kind of artillery shell filled with poisonous gas; one whiff could kill a man. Sometimes the gas had drifted back over their lines and killed their own soldiers. It must be nasty stuff. Everybody, especially the Germans, were using underwater boats called submarines. They fired torpedoes at ships that never even knew they were there. They had sunk an English ship, the *Lusitania*, which had carried quite a few Americans. I could tell public sentiment among my lodge brothers was slowly, but surely turning against the Germans and their allies.

As the war progressed, the prices for our crops rose sharply, especially for wheat. By the fall, a wealthy investor had built a flour mill at Bronco. I didn't know how it would do because it was a long way off the railroad. But I expected to pick up some extra business hauling wheat and flour. On all of our homesteads, we broke out varying acres to grow wheat, and by fall, the fields were green with the young shoots covering the ground. Maybe prosperity had finally smiled upon us once more.

2

Bandits on the Border and Dragons in the Dark

March 8, 1916
Brownfield, Terry County, Texas

THE KEY ON THE TELEGRAPH CHAT-
tered like an angry blue jay; whatever was coming across was burning
up the wires. The operator wrote as fast as he could, muttering "Oh, my
God!" I had stopped in the Western Union office to send a quick order
to Lubbock.

"What's goin' on, Jake?" He waved a hand and kept writing.
After several minutes the key fell silent. He sent the "Received" code.

"Aaron, I gotta get copies of this to the newspaper and the
Sheriff's office. Pancho Villa and five hundred Mexican soldiers raided
into Columbus, New Mexico. They shot up the town, and killed twelve
soldiers. The cavalry rode in and chased 'em away."

"Are they sure they went back into Mexico?"

"Nobody is sure of nothin' right now. Those Villistas on horseback could turn up about anywhere. The government is warnin' citizens
to arm themselves and puttin' out word to lawmen to be watchin' for
trouble. We ain't got nothin' around here that could stop five hundred
men."

This raid shook us down to the soles of our boots. Mexican soldiers had crossed the border and attacked and killed Americans. The
town, the whole southwestern United States, buzzed like a disturbed
wasp nest for days. The Kaiser in Germany was bad enough, but this
was way too close to home.

President Woodrow Wilson had offered every reason in the world why the United States should stay out of the war in Europe. The Mexican's had brought their civil war to our doorstep. It was still a three-way fight, but Pancho Villa controlled all of northern Mexico. Wilson shipped trainloads of troops to secure the border. Twelve thousand cavalrymen under John J. "Blackjack" Pershing were to find and fight the Villistas. General Victorio Carranza had captured Mexico City and set about forming a government, fighting the Villistas and the substantial pockets of federal troops who had remained loyal to deposed dictator Huerta. For lack of a better choice, the United State recognized the Carranza government.

In April 1917, documents were discovered that Germany had offered to assist Mexico in reclaiming all the territory they had lost in the war seventy-five years ago if they would declare war on the United States. This blew the lid off the pot. The United States declared war against Germany. By June, all the men from eighteen to thirty-five were required to register for the draft. All my boys had to register except Bill and Jesse. Local boards were set up in every county across the country to take stock of the men available. Fortunately, there were enough volunteers that few were drafted. Ella cried every time she thought about it, as did my daughters-in-law.

John and Effie had their own reasons to weep. In 1916 and again in 1917, Effie gave birth to babies that were born too early to survive. The hope and joy we had all shared with their anticipated new arrivals was dashed. John buried them near the house on the Draw.

They had worked hard on their leased ranch. The herd was increasing and John steadily made improvements to the place. Effie had the house as nice as a box and strip house could be. It certainly was much more comfortable than the "hole in the ground" they had occupied in Big Spring. The fruit trees, garden, chickens, hogs and milk cow raised their standard of living considerably.

They built a minimal structure on the quarter section of farmland to meet the requirements of "proving up" their homestead. They had found planting wheat in the red sandy loam could be profitable.

Bill married a real pretty girl, Ida Rushing. They took up a quarter section joining the rest of us just inside the Yoakum County line near Tokio. They also accepted the offer of a free lot in Brownfield right next to ours. That was one thing the city sure got right. It helped the town to grow.

Ida and Ella really hit it off. Ella had never liked mice. That woman would take on a rattlesnake without blinking, but couldn't abide a mouse. Every time she thought she heard one in the house, she would send for Ida. Ida would rustle around until she found it, grab it with her bare hands and crush its little head. Bill and I got a real laugh out of it. Every so often, a dead mouse would turn up on top of the catalogue in our outhouse. Folks at the courthouse downtown could hear Ella holler.

Bill built the required small house at Tokio and planned to plow up his grass for wheat. The rest of the time he worked for me in the freight business.

My work changed considerably when the rail line was completed from Lubbock to Seagraves. It went right through Brownfield. We switched over to short haul deliveries in and near town. I knew my days as a freighter were numbered, but would ride it out a little longer.

A man in Brownfield bought a Case steam-powered tractor. Farmers coordinated their wheat harvest so that he could thresh their wheat for them with a large belt-driven threshing machine. The tractor generated one hundred and fifty horsepower. For a man who knew what it was to handle one, two or twelve horses or mules at a time, it was hard to imagine anything that powerful. I had business coming and going hauling wheat to Bronco and sacks of flour to the railroad at Brownfield.

The price for wheat was strong. Growing wheat was easy compared to cotton and corn. All it took was some rain and snow. After wheat harvest was over, the owner of the tractor bought a twelve row breaking plow. It rolled the grass under the dark red soil in a wide swath. The tractor could do in an hour what it took four men with mules three days to do.

We broke out all the remaining grassland. All the boys broke theirs out, too, saving just enough for their milk cows and mules. Ed refrained from breaking out his four sections of pasture land. It would have been low quality farmland at best.

The great fire-breathing tractor and plow could cover an enormous amount of land. It had an insatiable appetite for coal and water. This presented another opportunity for my freight business. When that monster was running, I kept all of my wagons and teams going in shifts day and night hauling coal and water. The tractor ran around the clock, with drivers taking shifts. At night, the fire box glowed like the eyes of an evil beast across the prairie. The great stack belched black smoke that reflected the burning coal in its belly. The unique smell of freshly turned earth and coal smoke permeated the air. This process was repeated by others all across the northern and southern plains. It came to be known as "The Great Plow Out."

When the seed was sown in the late fall, the plains, normally tan with dried native grass, were cloaked in green wheat. The face of the Great Plains had been changed forever. But wheat poured into flour mills, and the flour flooded overseas to feed the troops locked in mortal combat.

The Texas and Pacific Railroad, never shy about making a profit, built shipping pens at Seagraves. This saved the ranchers from driving their cattle to Lubbock or Amarillo to market. Soon, cattle were pouring in from all over the Texas south plains and the eastern plains of New Mexico. A new boom was born.

3

Highs and Lows

March, 1918
Odd Fellows Lodge, Brownfield, Terry County, Texas

"I HEARD THEY GOT A SCHOOL OUT near your place at Tokio called Turner School."

"Yes, I've got so many grandkids livin' out there they got their own little school for them and the neighbor kids."

"Well, Brother Turner, what do you think about all this Prohibition now?"

"Joe, you know durned well what I think about it. I'm just hopin' the courts will stop it before these do-gooders get their way."

"I don't think the Supreme Court is gonna throw it out. If they don't, a fella won't be able to buy a drink startin' in January."

"Well, I'm gonna set me back a little stash for emergencies. No more than I drink, it oughta last near as long as I do. I've seen a lot of sorry things to come out of Washington in my day. But I never once thought the people of Texas would be dumb enough to go along with it. I sure wish ol' 'Pa' Ferguson hadn't a got himself in so much trouble. He wouldn't have let this happen."

"Aaron, that's a big part of what got him in so much trouble, when they caught him takin' money from the breweries."

"All the same, I think the durned ol' Republicans are behind the whole shootin' match. We oughta open season on 'em once a year and let us each shoot a few to keep 'em thinned out."

"Why don't you let us know what you really think about it?"

I lit my pipe and took a few good puffs. "Joe, I think the whole country is goin' to hell in a hand-basket. We got Mexican bandits runnin' wild on the border, war in Europe, Prohibition and now, everywhere you look, a fella sees these 'infernal combustion' engine automobiles and trucks. You know in Lubbock, they're usin' trucks to deliver freight. If they ever get started here, I'm outta business. My own son, John, thinks they're the greatest invention of all time; says he can't wait to own one."

By that summer, a plague had descended on the United States. The Spanish Influenza had first been reported the year before in Spain and quickly spread to the men of both sides embroiled in the war in Europe. It had finally come to the United States. Nearly every one caught it. No one seemed to be immune. This was no ordinary influenza. The newspapers reported that almost everywhere it hit, ten percent of the population died, but in some areas it was a high as twenty-five percent. So far, it had been rare in Texas and non-existent on the plains. In 1918, an estimated thirty million people world-wide died of the flu.

Another plague revisited the border as it had periodically done. On August 27th, eight hundred Villistas crossed the border and swept into Nogales, Arizona. Four American soldiers and two civilians were killed. American soldiers, policemen and armed citizens drove them back. The alcalde of the Mexican side of Nogales, a man respected on both sides of the border, had been shot down by the Villistas as he ordered them to leave the city.

From Brownsville, to Laredo and El Paso, police and citizens were frightened. Everyone went around armed. But what could a handful of police and armed citizens do if hundreds of armed men swept across the river in an angry tide? The fear spread across Texas like a disease. All of us kept our guns close and our families closer.

By the summer of 1918, the newspapers reported that no less than 10,000 American soldiers reached France daily along with freighters loaded with fuel and war materials.

The Germans launched a huge offensive that pushed the Allies back thirty-seven miles. They were close enough that their huge rail-mounted long-range artillery shelled Paris. But the Germans pushed beyond their supply lines. Ammunition, reinforcements, fuel and food failed to reach the new front. Strengthened by the arrival of the Americans, the Allies launched a counter-attack that steadily rolled the Germans back. By September, they had been almost completely pushed out of France.

The German's own allies began to sue for peace. First, Bulgaria, then Turkey ceased to fight. Our Italian allies drove the Austro-Hungarians into their own territory. By October, they laid down their arms. With their friends falling, and their own lines in shambles, the Germans signed an armistice on November 11, 1918. More than 100,000 American soldiers lost their lives in the war, and a quarter of a million were wounded. There was quite a celebration of Armistice Day in Brownfield, as there was in every city and town across America.

Another war had ended for us, but the seeds of a different deadly conflict had been sown by the troops passing cross-country that stopped at Fort Bliss outside El Paso. We could not see this enemy, but would feel its wrath in every home.

4

The Plague

February, 1919
John Turner lease, Pat Ross Ranch,
Sulphur Springs Draw, northwestern Yoakum County, Texas

"EFFIE, I DON'T FEEL GOOD. I'M hurtin' in my bones and all my muscles hurt."

"Think you just overdid it?" She handed me a cup of coffee and rummaged in the cabinet to find a bottle of whiskey. "Here, take a dose of that."

The hot coffee laced with whiskey soothed my throat, but did little to help my other aches and pains. "I'm gonna run out and fill the chip basket for the stove. Maybe I'll go to bed right after supper."

By bedtime, I knew I was sick. "Honey, I got fever and chills. Make me a pallet on the kitchen floor. I don't want you and Ronald gettin' sick."

Ronald helped her carry spare blankets into the kitchen. "What's wrong, Papa? Mama said you was sick."

"Thanks for helpin' your mother, boy. I guess I caught a little somethin'. I'll be all right."

But I wasn't all right, not by a long stretch. Fever and chills wracked my body through the night. By morning, I could barely move.

I filled the stove for Effie to fix breakfast. "John, this isn't like any cold I ever saw. Looks like you got the flu. You think it could be that Spanish influenza your Dad was talkin' about?"

"I've never had anythin' hit he this hard or this fast. I'm gonna get my chores done then head back inside." The two mules, horse and milk cow needed their morning hay and grain. I left the calf in with the cow instead of milking her. I refilled the chip basket and headed for the house.

The clanging of the windmill stopped me in my tracks. The wind had suddenly shifted to the north. There was a thick bank of heavy black clouds across the northern sky.

"We're in for some weather. Clouds are really buildin' back to the north. I brought in enough chips for today and the chip shed is nearly full. The herd is quite a ways up along the draw. I guess they're on their own."

"There's nothin' much you can do about it, as sick as you are. Finish that coffee and see if you can get down some of these eggs. I scrambled 'em since you got a sore throat."

The hot coffee and the warm eggs felt good going down, but I had little appetite. I was soon curled up on my pallet in the floor.

As the day wore on, the wind began to howl out of the north. A tiny amount of fine red dust sifted in through every crack in the north side of the house. The windmill clanged noisily. Sleet mixed with small dry snowflakes began to fall. By night, it had changed to large swirling flakes. At first, the wind kept the open spaces clear, piling up only where something slowed the north wind. By the last time I looked outside, heavy snow was falling almost horizontal to the ground and was accumulating everywhere.

My fever rose. Chills and sweats alternately plagued me. The muscle aches were agonizing. My mind wandered in a fevered land broken by glimpses of reality, only to dissolve again as the illness overwhelmed my senses.

I awakened some time the next day. I was in the bed, and Effie was putting a cool rag on my forehead. "Effie?"

"I'm glad you're back with us, John. You lay still. Could you eat somethin'?"

"Just water. You okay? How's Ronald?"

"We're holdin' up fine." She returned holding a cup of water to my lips. I drank it all.

The cough began to wrack my body. It came from deep inside

and hurt every rib and bone in my body. My head felt like it weighed a hundred pounds. I was getting worse. I was too weak to make it to the outhouse, so had to use the slop jar. What was going on with Effie? She seemed cross.

I realized Ronald lay beside the bed on a pallet. Stumbling, struggling through the fevered wasteland of my mind, I surfaced long enough to take stock of the situation. I turned in the bed to see Effie lying next to me, obviously ill. "You and the boy both got it?"

"Two days now."

"How long have I been sick?"

"Fifth day today. Chip shed empty. Burnin' grain. Snow stopped yesterday." She raised herself up from the bed and returned with a cup of potato soup. "Eat it."

I took the cup from her trembling hand as she helped herself back into bed. "John, I think you got pneumonia. Don't get up. I have to keep puttin' you back in bed. I'm too weak now."

"The stock?"

"Put out enough hay for a few days. Filled chicken feeder, put out extra for the hog. Stacked sacks of grain in kitchen yesterday. Too sick, too sick."

My mind plunged back into the fever-induced madness. I lost sense of day and time. Glimpses of Effie helping me and bringing food and water to Ronald mingled with the delusions and pain. In a lucid moment I woke up to see that Ronald was no longer on the floor. "Effie! Is Ronald dead?"

A harried vision of my wife entered the room and sat on the bed. "No. He got better. Do you want to see him?"

"You better?"

"Weak, but better."

A fit of coughing and pain ended my lucid moment. Effie and Ronald were alive. They were better. My mind descended again into the fever sickness. There were memories of things that I think were real. Memories of Effie helping me sit on the side of the bed to use the slop jar; glimpses of her spooning soup into my mouth; holding a cup of water to my lips. Then I returned to the great gaps of blackness and voids of time and reality.

A vile taste in my mouth and sense that I was drowning woke me. I gasped and coughed out a great wad of thick yellow sputum. As I began to cough, more seemed to break loose and arrive in my mouth. I found a damp rag beside the bed to dispose of this corruption.

Effie's face appeared next to me. "I think you're gonna make it. Keep coughin' that junk up!" She returned with an empty tin can for a spittoon. "Could you eat somethin'?"

"Are you able to cook? If you are, I believe I could eat some eggs."

I could smell coffee and heard the lid of the stove clatter. Effie returned carrying the coffee with Ronald holding the plate of eggs."

"Papa, you been gone a long time."

"How long have I been sick?"

"If I haven't lost count, you got the flu ten days ago, and this pneumonia took you about four days into that. I thought we were goin' to lose you." Tears filled her pale blue eyes. She sat down on the bed and kissed me on the forehead. "Think you can hold the plate?"

I nodded and reached out weakly to Ronald's outstretched arms. The eggs tasted good, and the coffee even better. "Effie, you think you could help me out to the outhouse? I'm mighty tired out using that durned ol' jar."

With much assistance, I made it there and back. It was a bright sunny day, but plenty cold. The weak sunshine felt good on my un-shaven face. Once I was settled back into bed, I fell deeply asleep, but not into the delirium of previous days. I woke up to Effie bringing me a plate of fried potatoes and a dab of bacon with a cup of good black coffee.

"Tell me what I missed."

"When you finally took to the bed, it was cold as rip and snowin' hard. It stayed that way three whole days before it let up. Ronald took sick two day into it. I took care of both of you the best I could. The next day, the flu got me, too; fever, aches and cough. Got the last of the cow chips into the kitchen and fed the stock. I carried in sacks of grain to burn in the stove. I was here in bed a couple of days, but was able to take care of you and Ronald. John, it was real scary for all of us."

I set aside my unfinished dishes and held her while she cried.

"You are the strongest woman I ever seen in my life. We wouldn't be alive if it wasn't for you."

Over the next few days I continued to cough up horrible corruption from my lungs, but I could tell I was stronger and breathing better. I was able to make it to the outhouse on my own and proud of the accomplishment. Effie had hitched up one of the mules to the little wooden sled and brought back enough chips to keep the house warm for a week.

"See any sign of the cattle?" She just shook her head no. "Maybe tomorrow we can hitch up the wagon and go see about them."

Effie and Ronald helped me harness both mules to the wagon, and then helped me climb up onto the seat. Once my head quit swimming, I shook the reins to start us moving. We followed along the north side of the draw, angling away to the northwest. In the shade of the banks and the trunks of the bigger trees, dirty snow lay in soiled piles. We had gone about a mile from the house when I spotted buzzards circling ahead. I slapped the mules into a brisk trot. The scene brought horror to our eyes.

Along both sides, and down into the draw, lay the thawing carcasses of every cow in the herd. They had sought shelter from the storm and frozen to death. Coyotes scattered at our approach and buzzards angrily flapped away from their rotting feast. The bodies had been pulled apart and scattered in every direction. The head of a once fine Hereford bull peered at me through eyeless holes in its skull. Death and decay surrounded us. I made a slow circle on the north bank with the wagon. After one last look, I turned the mules for home at a sobering walk. Almost all that we owned had been lost. Effie held Ronald and laid her hand silently on my arm. At least we were alive.

———

The cattle belonged to Pat Ross. I had leased them along with the ranch. I had to tell him and make things right. It was three more days before I felt up to riding a horse the three hours to the headquarters of the Mallet ranch where Pat was foreman. As I rode up to the ranch office, I noticed four fresh graves in the small cemetery. I walked into the office and asked the bookkeeper where I could find Pat.

"They got him and the others that are still sick in the front room of the big house. That flu hit hard here. You look like a fella that's been sick himself."

I wasn't in the mood to talk much. I just nodded and turned for the main house. A Mexican maid answered the door and let me in the front room. Half a dozen ranch hands were laid out on cots around the big room. Pat was sitting in a chair near the stove with a week's worth of beard. He looked worse than I did.

"Pat?"

"Hello, John. Wondered if I'd even be hearin' from you. I was afraid you might have turned toes up like some of the other folks around here. Y'all come through the flu and blizzard okay?"

"Not too perky. I got pneumonia from it. Effie and the boy took the flu, too." I wrung my hat in my hands. "Pat, all the cattle froze to death and I don't know how to make it straight with you."

"Them cattle would be just as dead if I owned 'em or leased out. There weren't a thing you or anybody else coulda done to stop it from happenin'. You don't owe me nothin'."

"Now, that's way more than fair. I gotta square up with you somehow."

"What do you know about windmills?"

"I've been workin' on 'em since I was a kid."

"My wind miller died. So did his wife. She was the house cook here for the boss. You come work for me as miller and your wife as the cook. It pays $50 a month to you and $40 for her, plus you both live in this here fine house. I need you as quick as you can get moved over here."

"Mister, you got yourself a deal." And so began our odyssey on the Mallet Ranch.

Effie liked the sound of the deal at the Mallet. "Ninety dollars a month and hardly any bills. I think I'll like that fine. We can put most of our things in the little house on the homestead place."

"That's what I thought, too. I'd kinda like to take the wagon to check on the family, see how they did with the flu. Feel like goin' with me?"

"John, if it's all the same to you, I need to pack up things here. Care if Ronald goes with ya? I could get a lot more done."

We left early the next morning. I still wasn't up to a full day in the saddle. Ronald cracked the whip over our mules with some words he hadn't learned in Sunday school. "Boy, where did you learn to cuss like that?"

"I hear you all the time, Papa."

After about two hours at a trot in the wagon, we arrived in Plains to see Ed and Minta. They had both gotten the flu and been real sick, but were both back at work.

Ed stopped me when Ronald couldn't hear. "John, it was so bad here, there wasn't enough healthy men to dig graves in the frozen ground. They had to roll the bodies up in wagon tarps and stack 'em in barns where the critters couldn't get to 'em. They still haven't got all of 'em buried."

"You heard from the folks at Tokio or Brownfield?"

"No. But a few folks who have travelled through said Brownfield was about as bad as here. We lost twenty percent of the folks in Plains to the flu."

"I'm worried about Mother and Pa. I plan to take Ronald with me to spend the night at George's or Al's place at Tokio, and then go on into Brownfield the next day. I'll send a telegram if you need to come, but if things are all right, I'll just stop by here on my way back."

I could see the four box and strip houses spaced evenly along a dirt road a mile north of the Brownfield road. Two of them had corrals with milk cows, hogs and chickens stirring around and a handful of kids playing outside in the cold. "Remember meetin' your cousins, son?"

"I think so, Pa. They're Uncle Al's and Uncle George's kids, right?"

"Yes, and Al and George are my older brothers."

"I ain't got no brothers or sisters. Just cousins."

"Hello the house!"

Noel, Al's wife, stuck her head out the front door. "John Turner! Lord, it's good to see you. Look how Ronald growed."

"Say hello to your Aunt Noel, son."

"Hi. You got any cousins I can play with?" No sooner had he asked than a swarm of kids in old clothes and coats swarmed around the wagon.

"Come on, let's go play cowboys and Injuns!" Ronald was gone in a flash.

"Y'all make it through the flu all right?"

"All of us got down real sick, but we got over it. Some of the neighbors and the folks in Brownfield weren't so lucky."

"You heard anythin' from my folks?"

"Yes. A man was by the Tokio store a day or two ago. Your Pa sent word they was kickin' but not raisin' much dust."

"Guess I'll git down. We're gonna sleep over in our little homestead house. Hope it don't crowd the mice too bad."

"Al is out gatherin' a cow that strayed. He'll be along directly. George went with him. Maybe we can throw in together and all have dinner over here tonight."

Al and George came driving a single cow of dubious heritage back to his place. "Where did you get her? They have a sale at the soap factory?"

"Brother John!" Al launched himself off his horse and came running up to the house, George trailing behind. He flogged me with his nasty old cowboy hat while George looked for an opening to shake my hand. "I tell you what boys, after dinner tonight, we're gonna have us a little coyote hunt. They're payin' two dollars for a pair of ears in Plains and Brownfield."

Noel and George's wife pooled their resources and fixed a pretty decent supper of cornbread, beans and cooked cabbage. Once the adults got their plates fixed, the kids filed through, grateful to see there was plenty of food left to go around. Once the plates were cleared, the men stepped out behind the stock shed for a smoke. Al reached in his coat and pulled out a bottle of whiskey. "I been savin' this for a special occasion. I reckon havin' you here is plenty of reason to celebrate."

He pulled the cork with his teeth and gave me the privilege of taking the first pull on the bottle. A few deep swallows and I was warming up from the inside out.

"Man, that's fire in a bottle!" Al and George both took a turn, then handed it back to me.

"Nope. I'll wait 'til we get back from huntin'. I don't want to fall off my horse!" Al shrugged and took another pull and passed the bottle back to George.

"George, I'm afraid that red-headed Church o' Christ wife is rubbin' off on our little brother. Next thing you know, he'll give up tobacco, too."

I was a little unsure how I would do back on a horse. I didn't tell either one of them I was getting over pneumonia. But the night wasn't too cold, and the wind had laid at sunset. I guessed I'd be all right. Al handed me the lead rope of a stout looking strawberry roan filly. I tightened the cinch on his spare saddle. "You didn't give me a ringer did ya, Al? I got a wife and kid to raise."

"You ol' woman. That filly is gentle as a beagle puppy." As he bragged on her, she rolled her eyes and let out a loud snort. "Well, nearly..."

I expected a bumpy ride and swung up into the saddle ready to go. I barely had my leg over the saddle when she squealed like a stuck hog and started dancing. I struggled to get my foot in the off stirrup, but once I did, I took a deep seat and thought I had her under control. Somebody forgot to tell the little horse. She gathered her four feet under her and broke straight up into the night sky. My cigarette went flying. She added some fancy moves shaking her rear like a big fish.

"You got her now, John! Hold on, brother!"

I was too busy to even cuss at Al and George who were both slapping their thighs in laughter. The roan rolled hard back to the right, then launched straight up again. She was doing some serious sky busting. I had a death grip on the horn with my right hand and was pulling her head hard to the left. I finally pulled hard enough to get her head around to the side, just close enough she took a bite out of my leg! My brothers seemed to think this was especially humorous. I used my left spur to her flank and finally got her into a tight circle. She squealed and danced, but now I had her.

I let her have her head and raked her good with both spurs sending her into a headlong gallop. We crossed a good half-section of wheat as fast as she could go. I felt her starting to flag, but I goosed her with the spurs to keep her in a gallop across the plowed ground. I finally eased her down into a lope, then a long trot. We had gone about two miles from the corral before I let her slow into a walk. Lather was flying up from her neck, chest and mouth. She was breathing in great heaves as we walked back toward the corral.

"Hope I ain't rode all the rough off of her, Al. She's got a right smooth little walk."

We spread out across the unplowed ground to the south until we got to Sulphur Springs Draw. As we rode through the thick willows and cottonwoods, George flushed a pair of coyotes. He snapped off a quick shot from his pistol as they wheeled to turn due south.

The little strawberry roan had recovered from the earlier excitement and found her wheels. She galloped hard in pursuit of the fleeing coyotes, quickly closing the gap to no more than thirty feet. I gripped the saddle tightly with my knees and shifted the reins to my left hand. I felt a split second of time when only her right front foot was on the hard ground. I squeezed off a quick shot. The coyote tumbled rump over head in the short prairie grass, sliding to a stop, dead as a hammer.

Al and George yelled encouragement as they pursued the other. I slowed the filly down and rode back to claim my prize. I eased up on the coyote, but it wasn't going anywhere. I nudged it with my boots just to be sure, then gathered it up by the legs and carried it to the little horse. She shied away from the dead critter. I tossed it on the ground in front of her to let her have a sniff. She pawed at it once to roll it over and sniffed a second time. She was content that it wasn't going to hurt her and let me tie it behind the saddle.

Shots barked in the distance. It wasn't long until my brothers came back with a bloody object behind George's saddle. I noticed something different about Al. His hat was even dirtier than before and was pushed down nearly on top of his ears. His coat had a cactus pad where the pocket used to be.

"I told George I could shoot off of this horse. Once."

———————

The day was nice as Ronald and I headed east on the sandy road to Brownfield. He held the reins as the mules moved at an even trot. As we approached town from the west, there were half a dozen wagons and ten or twelve men scattered on a slight rise north of the road. There was a new sign with hand-painted letter: Brownfield Cemetery. I could see objects wrapped in sheets filling each of the wagons as the men toiled with picks and shovels in the red sandy soil.

"Papa, what are they doin'?"

"Diggin' graves, son. Diggin' lots of new graves."

We reached the freight yard before the house. I could see Mother's buggy parked outside the rooming house. Dad was working with a big draft horse. They were all right.

"Hey, old timer! Stable these mules and I don't mean later!" Dad turned on his heel, stomping right up to the wagon, dragging the big horse behind him.

"Who do you think you are, orderin' around an old man?" Recognition spread across his face. "John! Ronald!"

"We sure fooled you, Granddad!" Ronald laughed.

"Get down son, and bring that boy with ya! Ella just rolled up here with supper for the roomin' house. We generally eat here when we got overnighters."

Mother's cornbread and beans were as good as always, washed down with strong black coffee. I didn't know the boarders and they didn't have much to say.

"Son, if I had known you were comin' I would have made an apricot cobbler. Ronald, did you get enough to eat?"

"Yes ma'am." He smiled as he stuffed another slice of buttered cornbread into his mouth.

"John, you look thin. Effie feedin' you all right?"

"I wouldn't be here at all if it weren't for her. We all took the flu, but mine ran into pneumonia. I was out of my head, on and off for ten days. Effie had the flu, but she took care of me and the boy, the animals and kept the stove goin' so we wouldn't freeze to death. The shed ran out of chips. She had to burn half of our sacked grain. She's one hell of a woman."

"Son, all of us took it. I don't remember ever bein' that sick. They say nearly two hundred folks around Brownfield died from it."

I remembered the wagons and men working at the cemetery. "I need to collect the bounty on a couple of coyotes. What time do the county offices open in the mornin'?"

"Right around eight o'clock. Say, did you hear that the politicians approved for women to vote? I'm all for it. Ella's been tellin' me what to do for years." He caught a playful swat with a big spoon across his boney knuckles.

"No, I knew they were talkin' about it. Pa, I ain't told you. I lost my whole herd while I was down sick. They froze to death, every last one of 'em."

"I sure am sorry to hear it. There's been stories comin' in from all over. Mostly folks talk about this flu. What are you gonna do now?"

"You know Pat Ross. It was his place and cattle we was leasin'. I went over to the Mallet Ranch where he is foreman. He hired me on as the wind miller and Effie for Mr. DeVitt's house cook. Between us we'll get $90 a month, plus live in the big house. You oughta see it. Pat showed me around. It's big as a courthouse. Mr. DeVitt knowed Prohibition was comin' and he had carpenters build cabinets from ceilin' to floor over every wall and around the windows and doors of his study. Those cabinets are stuffed plumb full of Scotch whiskey. Pat said two panel trucks drove out from Lubbock and delivered it right before the dead line."

5

John Turner, Wind Miller for the Mallet

June, 1920
Mallet Ranch, Yoakum County, Texas

TWO HUNDRED SECTIONS IS A LOT of land: a hundred and twenty-eight thousand acres. It was stocked with Hereford cows and the best Hereford bulls money could buy. Mr. DeVitt didn't do anything half way. The ranch was divided into four units. They covered parts of four counties, but didn't all quite join up. There was open range or leased land separating some of it.

We could drive the cattle anywhere we needed them to go with one big exception. We never, ever allowed a cow to set foot on the Lazy S, or Slaughter Ranch, which joined the Mallet in a couple of places. There had been bad blood between Mr. Slaughter and Mr. DeVitt not so long ago. I didn't know, and I guess I didn't care, who had started it. I worked for Mr. DeVitt. Any ranch hand worth his salt always rode for the brand that fed him.

I was the one sent to "rep" at the Lazy S round up. I looked through the cattle to see if any of them carried the Mallet brand. There were usually a few that had strayed. I got no help from the Slaughter men cutting them out, and I was not invited to the chuck wagon to eat.

I determined when their rep came to the Mallet to treat him better. I cleared it with Pat first. By default, I was the wagon cook at roundup and dipping times. I invited their rep to the wagon for coffee, breakfast and lunch. The hands had been told to help sort off any Lazy S stock. Slaughter's man didn't seem to know what to think. But the next time I had to rep at their place, I got a little help and plenty of food and coffee. We never did tell Mr. DeVitt, and I'll bet a dollar they never told Mr. Slaughter.

The calves were sorted off and driven the short distance to the railroad once a year. Every three years the grown cows were culled to get rid of cancer eye, cows with bad bags or that were barren. Every year all the cattle were driven to the dip pens which were about six miles north of the headquarters. Every bull, cow and calf on the place was dipped in the obnoxious smelling vats to get rid of vermin.

We had to hire extra cowhands during these times. I often cooked chicken fried steak, or thick beef steaks, stew or chili. But once each gathering I fixed son-of-a-bitch stew. This was a cowboy specialty and one I was especially good at cooking.

I would butcher a still nursing calf the night before. Just about everything but the hide and hooves went into the stew. I would cube and brown boneless meat with onions and add water to make a broth. Next came thinly sliced tongue, heart and kidneys. I liked to brown it in a skillet before I added it to the pot. A whole lot of potatoes and more onions came next, followed by a few cans of tomatoes. The long bones of the calf were added to the pot to cook out all the rich marrow, and then the bones were thrown away. The marrow gut, which is part of the stomach, sweetbreads, brains and lungs were added last. The whole thing was seasoned with garlic, salt, pepper and Louisiana hot sauce. I served it up with plenty of cornbread. If it had been a good year, Mr. DeVitt would send out a keg of beer on ice the night we had the stew. Often he would drive out in his automobile and eat with us. He may have called us Pat or John, but it was always Mr. DeVitt to him.

Effie and I lived in the big house. Pat and his wife lived in the foreman's house. Effie kept house for Mr. DeVitt and fixed all his meals. He sometimes joined the hands at the kitchen table, but often took his meals in his study. The half a dozen full-time hands lived in the bunkhouse, but took their meals in the big house, too.

A cowboy complained to Effie one night that the beans were a little too salty. She never said a word, but I knew that poor fellow was in for trouble. The next night, Effie set the plates around. As the complainer dug into his food, a horrible frown came over his face. He looked up to see all of Effie's six foot frame standing over him. "What's the matter? Your food too salty?" We all laughed at his expense, but he never complained about the food again.

Mr. DeVitt had the world market cornered on scotch in his study. As he finished a bottle, he pitched it out a window he habitually kept open year round for ventilation. After tidying up his office one afternoon, Effie heard a loud crash of breaking glass followed by a string of cussing. She ran to see what had happened. "What idiot closed that window?"

"Why, Mr. DeVitt, you closed it. You said dust was gettin' in." Effie was relieved when he finally started to laugh.

It was not the last time his habit with the bottles caused some laughter. One morning while hanging up the wash, Effie heard a small little voice cussing a blue streak. She came around the corner to find Ronald on top of the pile of empty bottles waving a stick and piece of string over an imaginary team of mules. The cussing was especially accomplished for a little boy.

"Ronald Earl Turner! Where in the world did you learn to cuss like that?"

"That's what Pa says to the mules."

From the open window of the study came a hardy laugh. "Let the boy go, Effie. That's the best job of cussin' I've heard in a long time." Mr. DeVitt saved the day.

As I made my rounds of the big ranch's windmills, I found one out of service that I had just fixed. Nothing was too obvious, so I proceeded to pull the sucker rod. The twenty foot joints of cypress wood screwed together. As each joint was raised up, it was held in place while it was unscrewed from the next in line. It was hard, back-breaking, repetitive work. I finally got to the last joint that held the ball valve. A brand new brass bolt was stuck in the mechanism holding the valve open and preventing any water from being pumped. There wasn't a brass bolt anywhere on the windmill. It would have been a lot of trouble for one of the Lazy S cowboys to come this far to sabotage a well. As I was resetting the rods, I had my answer. A large crow landed on the platform just below the fan and was angrily screeching for me to leave. I climbed up to the platform as the crow flew in wide circles around the windmill. There was a nest made of twigs, brightly colored string, shiny broken glass and two more brass bolts. Apparently one had worked its way loose and fallen down the well casing. I replaced the bolt in the nest. A piece of repair leather was cut to fit around the well shaft and over the casing. My problem was solved.

On winter evenings, one of our favorite activities was roping coyotes. Pat and the rest of the cowboys and I would saddle up our fastest cow ponies and spread out across the wide expanses of prairie. A man could ride for miles without coming to a fence. Sometimes the neighbors joined us, and sometimes one or more of my brothers would show up. I don't recall the Lazy S cowboys joining in. I guess that would push things just a little too far.

We would spread out about fifty yards apart, covering a quarter mile or more of country in a sweep. We would ride forward at a trot trying to stay in a rough line. When anyone flushed a coyote, the race was on. Sometimes three or four would flush at a time. Everyone converged on the running predators. The men on the outside would try to stay just enough ahead to keep the coyotes from turning. Some men carried hemp ropes. I liked a light four-strand braided rawhide rope. It was too light for roping a cow, but was perfect for a calf or coyote. The fast horses would gallop down on the fleeing fur-balls. A man generally just got one try. If he missed, someone else was right there to give it a go. We would often rope five or six in a good night. The best idea was to rope them by the neck. Sometimes if they got roped around the middle or by the back legs, those coyotes would climb right up a rope. The next person going into Plains would take the ears to collect the bounty which was equally shared by all the participants. One poor cowboy from New Mexico managed to rope and trip his own horse. He was really lucky it didn't kill him or the horse, but he heard about it for years.

———

One wonderful addition came to our family during our first year at the Mallet. With help from Mrs. Ross, Effie gave birth to a healthy, beautiful little girl. She had curly ginger colored hair and her mother's pale blue eyes. She was named Ella Francis in honor of both of her grandmothers. The poor child was spoiled by me, Pat and Mrs. Ross, Ronald, Mr. DeVitt and any of the ranch hands deemed clean enough by Effie to hold her. It is a wonder she ever learned to walk, for someone carried her wherever she went and she got almost anything she wanted. In spite of all this spoiling, she was a most agreeable child. She was quick to laugh and had a smile for everyone. My parents and extended family doted on her. And to the best of her ability, Ella Francis returned all the love she was given.

We stayed on the Mallet Ranch for two years. When Pat Ross took a job elsewhere, Effie and I decided it was time to get Ronald in school. There was a good job opening in Seagraves running the steam mill at a large feed mill and store. I had saved up my money and we bought our first automobile: a used Oldsmobile rag top. We arrived in Seagraves in style.

6

Hanging up the Harness

July, 1922
Oddfellows Lodge, Brownfield, Terry County, Texas

"JOE, LET ME EXPLAIN IT ONE MORE time. I'm applyin' for my Confederate Pension."

"Okay."

"I enlisted in Limestone County, in 1862. The courthouse with all the records burned down."

"I'm still with you, Brother Turner."

"The State Confederate Pension Board needs an affidavit from someone who has known me a long time that I'm not related to."

"Yes."

"That person needs to sign this here affidavit in front of a witness that I am one and the same person listed in the Confederate Service records."

"Now that's where you lose me. I've known you since right after the war. I've known you and your mother since about 1870. But this here paper says you are one and the same person as Aron Loyd Turner, son of Nancy Turner who enlisted in 1862 and served in the Texas Fifteenth Regiment, Company F. Everybody knows you spell your name AARON LLOYD."

I stoked my pipe until the tobacco was glowing cherry red. "Joe, that's exactly why I need you to sign it. Someone misspelled my name in 1862 and it got into the records that way. I just need you to sign that I'm the same man."

"And I ain't goin' to jail or nothin' for this?"

"Joe, the Terry County Attorney is the one who wrote this for you to sign. No, you ain't goin' to jail."

"Well, a fellow just can't be too careful about these things."

With Joe's affidavit signed and witnessed, my application could move forward. No one doubted I was the same fellow on the paperwork; they just needed someone to verify it. Confederate Pension Application 47373 could go ahead.

Ella and I had talked about it. I was soon going to be seventy-two years old. I was worn out. A company had moved into Brownfield using trucks for deliveries. In town I could deliver just as fast as a truck, but on the run outside of town, I couldn't compete. And trucks were pretty cheap to run and maintain. It was time to give up the business. I had sold off all the good draft animals and wagons to area farmers. A man wanted the pens and boarding house for about what they were worth.

The pension would be $108 dollars a year, paid quarterly. That's not a lot of money, but we didn't have any debt, and we had some money from selling the livestock, wagons, harness and property. We should be able to get along. Plus, I still had my paid up quarter section of farmland at Tokio that made some money from the wheat crop every year.

The letter finally arrived that my pension would begin in January. I had worked hard all my life. It was time to put my feet up, smoke my pipe and enjoy my grandkids.

7

Fly Away Home, Little Angel

July, 1923
John Turner home, Wharton Place, north of Seagraves,
Gaines County, Texas

"MOMMA, I AIN'T FEELIN' VERY good. I threw up at school and I got the scours pretty bad." Nine year old Ronald could be very descriptive. "A bunch of the other kids got it, too."

"You wash your hands good?"

"Yes ma'am."

I had gotten a good job as the boiler maker at the Seagraves Gin. Freight cars dumped huge loads of coal to feed the hungry furnaces that fired the steam-powered engines that drove the cotton gin. Two men kept shoveling coal into the open mouths of the furnaces during the peak of ginning season, but that was still months away. The welds needed checking, all the valves and fittings had to be calibrated along with a hundred other things.

I had also gotten the job of public weigher. The scales could be fitted with tall side-boards to weigh livestock, but I weighed everything from cotton to corn. It didn't pay a lot, but it all helped.

The Wharton place was not too far from town, but I still drove my Oldsmobile to work. Several folks in Seagraves and Brownfield had cars and trucks.

We grew enough corn for our livestock and to grind for our own table. We kept a big garden where we grew pinto and green beans, black-eyed peas, potatoes, squash, onions, okra, cabbage, greens and other vegetables. We also grew ten acres of cotton. It was all Effie, Ronald and I could manage. There had been a couple of good showers to help the crops. The corn was shoulder high and tasseling. The cotton was boot-top tall and covered with blooms.

I had accumulated a nice herd of Shetland ponies including mares and a good stallion. Folks bought them to pull buggies or for their kids to ride. Ronald was sure proud of his little riding mare.

The summer held promise of a good year. But I would always remember the summer of 1923 with unspeakable sadness.

I rocked Ella Francis while Effie finished the supper dishes. Ronald had gotten better in a day or two, but now his baby sister was not herself. She had not eaten supper. Effie said she had thrown up twice that afternoon. She settled gently against my shoulder as I hummed *Rock of Ages*.

Ronald tried to cheer her up without much luck. She gave him a weak smile and mumbled "Wred." She had picked up on my nickname for her brother based on his dark red hair.

Effie took her to get ready for bed. The toddler's stomach rumbled just before the slimy diarrhea hit. It had a strong odor like vinegar. It happened again during the night. By morning, it hit every twenty minutes. I dropped Ronald off at school and left Effie and Ella Francis at the doctor's office.

"The doctor says it's summer diarrhea and it's real hard on little ones. He wants me to give her rice water with a pinch of salt and sugar, as much as she'll drink."

I took them home and went back to the gin. Ronald walked over after school and played in the gin yard until I got off work. Things didn't look good when I got home.

"She drinks the rice water just fine, but she throws it all back up. Her little bottom is gettin' scalded from all the dirty diapers, and I'm down to the last two clean ones."

I rocked the poor thing while Effie stirred the kettle of diapers boiling in the yard. As they got clean, she dunked them in a pot to rinse, then hung them up to dry in the hot west Texas wind.

I took the first shift that night with Ella Francis so Effie could get some rest. I spooned the rice water into her sticky lips as she dutifully swallowed it. But without fail she vomited within a few minutes. I hadn't changed diapers much since she was a tiny baby, but tonight was different. I lost count of the dirty ones. She didn't cry, but only groaned as she clung weakly to my shoulder. Effie got up around two to relieve me. I bent down to kiss my darling girl. Her eyes fluttered open as she uttered "Papa."

I stirred up some cornmeal mush for Ronald's breakfast and got him ready for school. "We're takin' this baby back to the doctor." Effie, exhausted, only nodded her agreement.

The doctor was kind and concerned. "Folks, she's getting very dehydrated. You've done everything anyone could have asked of you to keep liquids in her. I don't have much to offer. I can give her a little paregoric to slow down the diarrhea, but if I give her enough to stop it, it will kill her. Unless things change a lot by tomorrow, I'm afraid she isn't going to make it through the night."

Effie quietly began to cry as she bundled Ella Francis into her lap. "Doctor, if we took her to Lubbock or somewhere, is there anythin' that could be done?"

"I'm so sorry, Mrs. Turner. No. I don't think there is anything else to be done anywhere." A nurse in a starched white hat brought in a small bottle with a rubber-tipped dropper. The doctor printed instructions on a white label.

I drove by the gin and explained to the manager that I wouldn't be back the rest of the day. We stopped by the store and bought a stack of diapers before we headed home.

The day dragged slowly along. The windmill whirled and clanked in the hot, dry wind. I kept the wash and rinse kettles going while Effie tended to the baby. Ella Francis wouldn't open her mouth, but Effie tenderly pried her cracked lips apart to give her more rice water. The inside of her mouth was dry. The rice water rolled out the corners of her mouth. The few drops of paregoric slowed the diarrhea considerably, but it was a losing battle. Ella Francis didn't open her eyes or speak the rest of the day. Effie clutched her gently and rocked as she quietly sang hymns.

"Effie, it's time for me to get Ronald from school. I'll be back as quick as I can."

When we pulled up at the house, Effie was sitting alone on the porch. A cold hand clutched my heart. I ran to the house. "Effie?"

Her face turned to mine with the saddest look I had ever seen. "It's over. I wrapped her up in a blanket and laid her on our bed." I reached out to hold Effie and she began to cry silently.

Poor Ronald looked lost. "Momma?"

"Son, your baby sister died this afternoon. She's gone to live with the angels." Ronald fell into his mother's arms and sobbed.

I stepped into the bedroom and unrolled the blanket just enough to look at her face. She was blue and lifeless. I unwrapped the blanket and pressed my ear to her chest. My little girl was forever gone. We buried her behind the house in the shade of a cottonwood tree, and buried our hearts with her.

8

Band of Brothers

July, 1924
Brownfield, Terry County, Texas

IF YOU ASKED ANYONE IN BROWN-
field who was the prettiest young lady for miles around, the answer
was Ruby Carson. She was one of the prettiest girls I had ever seen, and
I had been looking at them for almost seventy-four years.

The most eligible bachelor in Terry County was our youngest son,
Jesse. His brown wavy hair, bright eyes and dimples had turned many
a young girl's head. Jesse was six foot two, lean and muscular. He was
a musical wonder on anything with strings. He was not fascinated with
engines like John, and didn't own a car. He much preferred a horse.
That didn't stop him from borrowing Bill's car when he needed to be
somewhere fast.

It was only natural that the two would find each other. Jesse had
spotted her a couple of years before at church. They had managed to
be at the same singing schools and church socials. Ella and I were not
surprised when he told us he and Ruby were to be married.

The appointed Saturday arrived soon enough. Ruby's sister was
the maid of honor and Bill stood up with Jesse. A nice service at the
Methodist Church was attended by an amazing number of people.

Both families had thrown in together for a big barbecue and barn
dance. A whole steer had been roasted over coals for twenty-four hours
until the juicy meat was tender and falling off the bone. Gallons and
gallons of pinto beans and countless plates of corn bread lined groan-
ing tables. I had sprung the cost for a large keg of beer that had been

sent by railcar directly from Fort Worth to Brownfield. We set it inside a tub of ice and salt to keep it perfectly cold. Nobody asked how I came to get something so rare in Prohibition, but one of my brothers from the Oddfellow Lodge knew how to get it done.

Turner men, ca 1915, Brownfield, Texas.
Back row: Bill, Aaron, George, Jesse. Front row: John, Al.

When the band struck up *Turkey in the Straw,* it was none other than the Turner Brother's Band. All of the boys could play, and they had taught me to play the guitar well enough to keep up with them. Al could play anything, but excelled on the mandolin. John and I played our guitars. Ed S brought his booming string bass. He plucked the strings to keep the rhythm together. George and Bill both played fiddle, handing off the melody, back and forth like it was hot.

Someone had managed to get the piano from the church into the barn. I wasn't asking any questions. Our youngest, Ruth, tore up the keyboard.

They started with traditional tunes that we all knew, but they had heard a barber from Turkey, Texas, who played a new variation of the old favorites he called "Texas Swing." The boys had paid close attention to his methods of improvisation, and adapted and modified them to their own set of skills. When they started playing "Swing," ever person in the barn was on their feet. All those who were able crowded onto the dance floor. Ella and I even hobbled through a dance or two.

Ruby turned loose of Jesse's arm long enough to let him show off with the fiddle. The crowd responded by throwing silver dollars in an old hat until it was pretty nearly filled. The crowd danced until the boys in the band couldn't play anymore. It was quite a party and the talk of the county.

The Turner Brothers band was certainly well received. They got an increasing number of requests to play at wedding receptions and barn dances. Of course, these were all occasions where the use of alcohol was common and often to excess. Sometimes the boys tended to tip the jug a little more than was prudent. Al and George were especially notorious for imbibing, but the others were not immune. Sometimes, even normally reserved John would follow their footsteps. Effie, being from a more conservative, non-drinking family, didn't approve of John's use of alcohol to excess.

The band had been booked to play in Seagraves. Effie refused to go. She said she was tired of seeing John "make a fool of himself." She told John if he wasn't home sober by midnight, he'd find the doors locked.

Being a natural born Turner, John was bull-headed. He decided he would show Effie what was what. He checked his pocket watch to make darn sure he wasn't home anywhere close to midnight. And he took his turn at the beer barrel just often enough to be sure Effie could smell it.

He drove his Oldsmobile home to the Wharton Place. Just as

promised, both doors were locked, but a window was up a ways. He pulled a bucket to the window and climbed through.

Now, Effie was a very hard sleeper. It was rumored that she could sleep through a tornado. John found her asleep in their four-poster bed. Both big toes on her six foot frame protruded from beneath the covers. John had a wicked streak that sometimes came to the surface. He very gently tied both of her big toes to a bedpost with hemp twine, then yelled: "Effie, get up! The house is on fire!"

Now a thing like that would wake the dead. Effie came alive and jumped out of bed. When her toes hit the end of that twine, she crashed hard on the floor.

John was laughing and slapping his thighs, heehawing like a donkey. While he was laughing, Effie was untying her toes. She grabbed a blue-speckled wash basin and beat the living daylights out of his head.

When I saw him, he still couldn't wear his hat. But he told the whole story. "Pa, it was worth every bump on my head."

We enjoyed having all the family close together. Automobiles cut the distance from Brownfield to almost nothing. We got together often and had a lot of fun. The kids played together. There was always music and some kind of dominoes, and plenty of food.

Jesse and Ruby broke the mold. Before the year was over, they moved by wagon to Hagerman, New Mexico. They would not be the last to leave.

Part Four

The Death of Dreams

1

The Unclouded Day

March, 1928
Seagraves, Gaines County, Texas

OUR COUNTIES ELECTED A SHERIFF
for the whole county, he then appointed men in each of the communities of any size. The caliber of the men he chose had a great deal to do with his success or failure as a lawman. "Soon" Birdwell had been elected sheriff of Gaines County, with John on the ticket as the deputy sheriff for Seagraves. John was well liked and trusted. He enjoyed his job, and like everything my son did, he took it very seriously.

After the devastating loss of Ella Francis, they finally had another child, a boy named John, Junior. He was known by this name for most of his life. Junior just sort of stuck to him like a cockle burr to a sheep. But to be a junior for John, he looked very much like Effie.

On a windy March day in 1928, downtown Seagraves hummed with activity befitting a prosperous and growing town. The bank had closed for the day and was settling accounts. Both the car dealerships had several people looking at cars or getting one serviced. Folks were getting prescriptions filled at the drug store, or enjoying a sandwich or fountain drink. The early afternoon crowd was already making their way into the dining room of the Simpson Hotel, and guests lounged on the second floor gallery. The Seagraves Tailoring, Cleaning and Pressing business was busy as usual.

No one knows for sure what happened, but it was assumed that one of the hot clothing presses ignited the highly flammable cleaning fluid. Although some inside tried to use fire extinguishers, the blaze was just too intense and spreading too fast to contain. Seagraves had no fire department. In minutes, downtown was a blazing inferno.

Bells rang all over town alerting the residents of danger. They had only to step outside to see the towering flames and smell the sickening smoke of an extremely dangerous fire burning out of control. Every man and boy, and not a few women, who could carry a bucket were organized into a bucket brigade by John.

A group of older girls and young women ran into the Simpson Hotel to roll the much beloved piano to safety. The wooden structures burned with such intense, crackling heat, that those at the front of the line were changed with each bucket of water. They would run to the back of the line, their clothes smoldering. But it was too much for the hundred volunteers. Indeed, it was too much for almost any number, for the hot dry wind stoked the flames like a furnace. Finally, the fire brigade pulled back as the fire jumped the street and began burning behind them. It was too dangerous to do anything else. The fire raged into the darkness, and the embers glowed and timbers cracked in the flame lit darkness.

By morning, only the Simpson Hotel, with its tile and stucco façade still stood, scorched, but otherwise unhurt. The Ford dealership and Seagraves Motors on opposite corners of downtown stood mostly unhurt because of their brick and stone walls and metal roofs.

Seagraves was a gritty little town. Within a day and a half, the safe had been pulled from the hot rubble, and the bank was in business in the corner of the Ford dealership show room. The pharmacy had received fresh supplies from Lubbock and was operating out of Seagraves Motors. Twenty one businesses had been destroyed, but the town, booming from cattle and shipping, bounced back.

Our wheat crop had not received much moisture, but what it had received had come at just the right time. A slow two and a half inch rain had come only a few days after the seed had been buried in the sandy soil. Another three-quarters of an inch had come in time to stimulate the plants to put out tillers from the base. We were blessed with a wet eight inch snow that held moisture through to the critical time when the heads of grain filled. In June, the fire-breathing harvester had reaped forty bushels of hard red winter wheat per acre, which sold for $2.35 a bushel on the turn-row. We had cut wheat from 140 of the 160 acres.

It was the most money I had in my hands since I sold the freight business. The boys all had similar crops except Ed. He still ran cattle, but the winter moisture got the sturdy native grasses off to a solid start.

I had been a horseman all my life. I had cussed and discussed the "infernal combustion engine" for years. But it took four hours to get to Seagraves, or eight hours to Plains, by buggy. An automobile cut the time to an eighth. I wanted one; I really wanted one. I finally got up the nerve to talk to Ella about it. To my amazement, she wanted one, too. When I broke it to my sons and lodge brothers, I got the amount of ribbing I deserved.

The General Motors dealer was just starting to get in the 1929 models in September of 1928, a process that never made sense to me. But there was a fine looking, lightly used, 1928 Chevrolet four door sedan really worth the money. It was black and shiny, with "suicide doors." It looked like a box on big wheels, but it had a huge motor that would get up and gallop. I spent my money from the bumper wheat crop on the only automobile I would ever own. Ella was intensely proud of it. John taught me to drive it in an afternoon.

Ella and I finally felt a bit of prosperity. Besides the automobile, we bought a battery powered radio. We could listen to programs from Lubbock, Amarillo, Ft. Worth, Dallas, or as far away as Chicago.

A moving picture show opened up in downtown Brownfield. They had one over in Seagraves, Plains and every town of any size. We could catch a double feature with a newsreel and a cartoon for a nickel. Our Saturday routine became a trip downtown for a nickel hamburger and an afternoon at the picture show.

We even splurged and bought Ella an ice box. We could keep food fresh longer and have cold drinks all year round, as long as the ice man brought the large blocks of ice, made right there in Brownfield. Civilization had caught up with us. It was now not a cause of much excitement to see an airplane land somewhere on flat ground around town. We had come a long way from mules and muskets.

Our enjoyment of life increased even more when Jesse and Ruby and their family moved back from New Mexico. They had a place near our land and his brothers' homes at Tokio.

"Well, look here. It's Brother Turner, the owner of an automobile."

"Hello, Joe. Hello, boys."

"I didn't know if big men like you would associate with common folk like us here at the Odd Fellow Lodge."

"Ah, stick a sock in it Joe."

"Now that you got your hat and coat hung up, tell what you think about the presidential election."

"Al Smith, a Democrat from New York. You'd think we could do better than a Yankee."

"Don't forget, he's a Catholic, too."

"Well what difference does that make? You think he'd be a better president if he was a Methodist?"

"He does support gettin' rid of Prohibition."

"That's true. But that's not why I'm going to vote for him. I'm votin' for him because he ain't a dang Republican. In my house, Republican is a dirty word."

"I figured you didn't like Herbert Hoover."

"I don't know Herbert Hoover. I do know he's a Republican and I ain't givin' him a vote for dog catcher."

In November, 1928, I did cast my vote for Al Smith, the Catholic Yankee Democrat. But the folks of Texas must have lost their minds, as Herbert Hoover swept the state, just as he did the whole nation. He had run on a platform of "Prosperity and Prohibition." I didn't care too much for Prohibition, but I did like prosperity just fine.

2

Winds of Change

Fall, 1929
Brownfield, Terry County, Texas

THE SLATE GRAY SKY STRETCHED away endlessly over the tan horizon. Our children and grandchildren bent over the long leafless rows of short, stubby plants covered with fat white bolls of cotton encased in hard, prickly black burrs. Long cotton sacks trailed behind them in the red sandy rows, slowly filling with fluffy locks of seed-filled cotton. One here and there would stand and stretch, or hoist up the sack and head back to the wagons.

"Here you go, Granddad." Ronald hung a long, full bag in the hook of the scales. He returned to dump it in the wagon after stopping for a drink.

"You're doin' good, son. Keep it up."

Sandhill cranes called so high above us their gray shapes were invisible in the overcast sky. It was cotton picking season on the south plains. Schools turned out until the crop was gathered. This ritual was being repeated on countless farms across the flat, wind-swept plains.

Jesse's oldest boy struggled in with a heavy bag. His given name was James Franklin Turner, Junior. But since he was a baby, he had simply been called "June."

He wasn't quite tall enough to reach the hook, so I slipped it over for him. "June, you're makin' quite a hand at pickin' cotton. This sack weighs almost as much as you do." He just smiled and wiped the red dust from his face on a worn out handkerchief.

His, father, my youngest son, Jesse, handed me another bag and leaned on June. "He givin' you any trouble, Dad?"

"None I know about. You been slippin' rocks in the sack so I'll pay you more, son?" I smiled and tousled his dusty hair.

"No, Granddad. Pa said if I worked hard, I got to keep all the money."

"How's the crop comin', Dad?"

"I've been totin' it up. Looks like we made about three hundred and fifty pounds to the acre, on a hundred and forty acres. It's bringin' eighteen cents a pound. With my Confederate pension, your mother and I oughta be just fine for another year."

"Same on our place. I got a little set of cattle with some calves ready to sell. What's all this talk about the economy bein' in trouble?"

"There is a banker in our lodge. He said that the stock market, not the livestock market, but shares of stock, crashed somethin' fierce in October. Said it shook folks up so bad, they started callin' loans in, takin' money outta the banks. He says money is real tight, prices on a lot of things has gotten real cheap, 'cause nobody will turn loose of a dollar, factories are closin' and lots of folks are outta work, or expectin' to be outta work soon."

"What does all that mean to us?"

"I don't know, really. I guess we were already too poor to know the difference."

In the days ahead, you couldn't tell there was an economic problem in the back eddies of the country. But in the future, "The Great Crash" of October 29, 1929, would become "The Great Depression." The day would come when we would understand poverty's hardship only too well.

———

We took a break from picking cotton for a family gathering out at Jesse and Ruby's place at Tokio. Ed and Minta drove over from Plains. John, Effie, Ronald and John, Junior came from Seagraves. Al and George were there with their families. They lived so close they just walked. Ruth and her husband came out from Brownfield. Ella and I drove out in our Chevrolet.

Our grandchildren, a running horde of all ages from toddlers to teens, invaded the place. It was so good to see them having fun together. Ruby had a Brownie camera that her parents had given her. She took pictures of groups of cousins, our kids, family groups, and in as many ways as you could imagine to arrange us.

The women had outdone themselves on the potluck dinner. Fried chicken, roast beef, ham, and vegetables graced the side tables. The kitchen counter disappeared under pies and cakes.

Once the adults had eaten their fill, the children were called to eat. As their mothers filled their plates and glasses, they took their seats wherever they could find them. The adults had pulled some of the chairs outside to enjoy the unseasonably warm weather. As Ella came out onto the porch, she began to yell. "Aaron! Aaron Lloyd Turner! Aaron!"

"What's wrong?"

"The automobile! Look!"

She had given strict instruction to the children not to play in the car. But someone had not listened and had left the doors standing open. But the reason for her anger was the presence of Jesse's small flock of goats crowded inside her fine automobile!

All the men ran to chase the goats away. As they were chased out of the front seat, they reappeared in the back. There were goats everywhere. They were finally driven into full retreat, but the interior of the Chevrolet held evidence of the goat invasion. Sandy footprints and goat droppings covered the once pristine seats. Ella was so angry she was fit to be tied. But the rest of us saw the humor in the situation and couldn't control our laughter. Al was enjoying the situation more than anyone. Ella turned and punched him in the arm and fell out laughing herself. We all pitched in and soon had it almost as good as new. Of course, when the weather turned hot, we would always catch a faint odor of goats.

———

Our daughter, Marjorie, had married Ennis Ware a couple of years after we moved to Brownfield. They had been happy, but had so wanted children. In early 1929, after being married for twelve years, the doctor confirmed that Marjorie was indeed pregnant; pregnant with twins. Ella and I had shared our secret worries about her, as Marjorie was not a sturdy woman. She and Ennis fixed up their little house to accommodate two babies at once. The women from church and town held a nice baby shower for her.

After the cotton was in the gin and before the babies were due, she went into hard labor. Ennis drove her to the little hospital here in Brownfield. The doctor said the babies were both head up, both breach. The only way he could save the babies was by surgery, a "Caesarian-section" he had called it. He told Ennis that if they didn't act fast they would lose Marjorie and the babies. She begged the doctor to save those twins, no matter what.

We had gotten word there was trouble and had come to the hospital. Ennis didn't have a choice. He kissed Marjorie and told her he sure did love her and he would see her after the surgery. I believe he knew that he would never see her alive again.

Another doctor and three nurses came in. They wheeled Marjorie away after we all told her goodbye. They took her into an operating room and prepared for the surgery. It must have been something un-usual, as there were so many people there to help.

Half an hour passed; the longest half hour in Ennis Ware's life, that's for certain. I know the anguish I felt as her father was even greater for her husband. Finally, the surgery doors swung open. Two nurses I had not seen yet came out carrying two bundles. They announced Ennis had a son and a daughter. Before he even looked at the babies, he asked about Marjorie. They said the doctors were still doing surgery; there had been some complications.

Ennis, Ella and I admired the babies before they took them back to the nursery. Ennis declared the boy's name was to be Bobby LaDell, and the girl, Marjorie Latrelle. The fear in his voice was thick.

Another half an hour passed. The surgery door swung open. Both the doctors walked out. Although it appeared they had changed out of their surgery gowns, there were smatterings of blood to be seen here and there; not just a little, but far more than I had expected. Marjorie's womb had burst open as the twins were being pulled out through an incision. A large blood vessel had ruptured. Although they tried every-thing they could do to stop the bleeding, Marjorie had bled to death.

Ennis thanked the doctors in a voice choked and hoarse with emotion. He shook my hand and thanked me for being there. But when he hugged Ella, a flood of tears were released from both of them, and not a few of my own.

After three days, the twins were allowed to go home. Ella stayed at their house and my daughters-in-law took turns helping out.

The day came for the funeral. Ennis was there with both the babies, sitting with our family and many of his relatives, too. The Methodist preacher did a really fine job, but there was not a way except for this to be the saddest funeral I could remember. The piano rang out the beginning notes of *Shall we Gather at the River*. I clutched Ella's hand. We had seen much heartache together before, and we would again. But this was especially hard. That song brought back a flood of memories for me of friends and family that I had loved and lost. It was a sad, sad day.

Folks would remember 1929 mostly for "The Crash" and the beginning of what would be called "The Great Depression." I always knew it as the year Marjorie died. And I remembered it every time I saw those sweet babies growing up without a mother.

3

The Shadows Grow Longer

Spring, 1930
Brownfield, Terry, County, Texas

      "AARON, I SURE HAVE HAD A HARD time catchin' my breath. Seems like I'm always needin' to sit down and rest."

"Don't you think it's from chasin' after those twins?"

"Oh, maybe that's part of it. But I believe there is more to it. My feet and legs are swellin' a lot, too. I believe I need you to take me to the doctor."

We were in to see the doctor later that week, the same one who had delivered the twins. He seemed to take what Ella was saying seriously. He listened to her neck, heart and lungs. He poked around on her liver. Then he gently pressed in on the swollen skin of her lower legs. It left deep dents where he pressed. He asked if he had been more thirsty than usual or had to "make water" more than in the past. She said she hadn't. He even did a test to see if she was passing sugar, but it was normal.

"Mrs. Turner, you've got what has been called for a long time "dropsy." The newer name for it is heart failure. Your heart muscle is wearing out and not pumping hard enough. It lets blood back-up in your lungs, liver and legs. It explains why it's hard for you to breathe, especially when you lie down, why your liver and legs are so swollen."

"What can you do for it?"

"This is very powerful and dangerous medicine. I want you to take one single drop in water three times a day; no more, no less. If you start seeing yellow lights, let me know immediately. If this works like I feel certain it will, your heart will pump better; you will breathe better; and the swelling in your liver and feet will go down. Come back and see me in a month."

Every morning, noon and night, Ella opened the bottled labeled "tincture of digitalis" faithfully. She never saw any yellow lights, but it seemed as if she was ten years younger. She was sleeping and breathing better. The swelling in her legs was almost gone. She took it with her in her purse, but guarded where none of the grandchildren could get into it. The doctor had said just a few drops could kill a child.

It was nice to see Ella feeling so much better. I wish I could say the same. For some months I had been noticing the same symptoms she had displayed. I had kept my peace to see how she did. I finally told her the truth. When it came time for her to go back to the doctor, I planned for him to see me, too.

I almost never missed a lodge meeting. I don't know how to explain why it was important to me. I suppose since I was no longer able to work, it gave me a place to fit in with other men. The rest of the week, I was at the house with Ella. A man can only find so many chores to do outside. And sitting inside listening to the radio was not the life I had known. Every evening, I sat on the back porch as the sun went down and smoked my pipe and remembered better days. I did get out every Sunday morning we were able and went down to the Methodist church. The hymns moved me, sometimes more deeply than I cared to tell. I sang in the cracking weak voice of an old man, but I figured God didn't care. I enjoyed the sermons, even the ones that ran a little long. It was good to stop and visit a while after services. The men clustered to one side and the women the other, while a double handful of children played outside.

I had left with my brothers and a brother-in-law for the war in 1862 and seen things and done things I had never spoken of to my family. I had been up the Shawnee Trail to Sedalia, Missouri when I was just fifteen, and later the Chisholm Trail to Abilene and then the

Western Trail to Dodge. Now, my life consisted of a weekly lodge meeting and Sunday services. I felt like a ranch horse penned up in a stall.

Just as I had suspected, the doctor confirmed that I had heart failure, too. He prescribed the same medicine in the same dose as Ella. He told us we could use out of the same bottle, and to both come back in a month.

Within days, I was feeling better. I walked better because my feet and legs were not so swollen. I could breathe like I did when I was sixty. I didn't have to prop up on four pillows at night. I felt much better.

I couldn't lie and say I felt like a young man, for I was nearly eighty, but I sure was glad I had seen that doctor. Although the medicine made me feel better, it reminded me of my mortality. I had lived a long, full life. Each time I took the magical green drop in a glass of water I could feel the cold hand of death reaching closer. Now I depended on a simple bottle of medicine to stay alive. Once, I had felt there was no mountain too tall to climb, but now the "molehills" of daily life were becoming a struggle. Life's evening sun was moving lower in the sky, and the shadow I cast upon the earth was growing longer each passing day.

4

Hard Times get Harder

Fall, 1931
Brownfield, Terry County, Texas

"GRANDDAD, JUST LOOK AT IT! I never saw a cotton crop like that on your place." Ronald hung his own cotton sack on the scale, then dumped it in the wagon.

"Son, I've been figurin'. As close as I can tell, we're makin' pretty close to six hundred and twenty-five pounds to the acre, or about a bale and a quarter."

"We'll all be rich by Christmas!"

"No. I'm afraid not. I'm payin' y'all a fair price of a penny a pound to pick it, just like always. I got another two cents a pound in the crop. It'll cost a half cent to get it ginned. Grandmother and I will get about a cent and a half to the pound."

"But look how many pounds it's makin'!"

"Do the math. Six hundred and twenty-five times one and a half cents works out to just over nine dollars an acre. I got a hundred and forty acres, Ronald. That's a little over twelve hundred dollars. I need five hundred to set by for next year's crop. That leaves us seven hundred dollars to live on for a year. I'm sure glad I got my Confederate pension."

"Are you sayin' we're poor, Granddad?"

"I didn't say no such thing. We got a good house and a quarter section of land. We don't owe a dime to nobody. There's folks in this country that ain't got a pot to pee in, or a winder to throw it out of. No. We ain't poor, yet. Now get back to work. I swear you talk more than all the other grandkids combined." I tousled the red hair of the tall, lanky young man. He reminded me of myself at that age, except I swear I didn't talk that much.

My cotton wasn't the only good crop that year. John and Effie added another boy, Aaron L. Turner, named for me. So folks could tell us apart, they gave him the middle name, Lynn; which was what we all called him. He joined seventeen year old Ronald, and three year old John, Junior. Ronald had dark red hair like most of the Turner men, as did baby Lynn. But John, Junior, was a true cotton-top. I guess it takes all kinds to make the world go round.

That night after a long day weighing and hauling cotton, I took a much needed bath in the large galvanized bathtub in the house. After supper, and a late smoke of my pipe, I sat down with Ella to listen to the radio. We had tuned in to a station out of Fort Worth. Bob Wills and the Texas Playboys came on. The words to *Take me back to Tulsa* crackled through the radio: "The little man raise the cotton, the big man gets the money."

"Ain't it the truth."

———————

John had an old Model T Ford truck he had fixed up for hunting coyotes. Gaines, Terry and Yoakum Counties, as well as most of the surrounding counties, had a bounty for killing coyotes of two dollars each. A fellow had to present a pair of ears to the county to collect. John had figured out how to make some money at it.

The old truck had a set of four wire kennels on both sides of the truck. Each kennel held a greyhound. He would head out to some open range country he hadn't worked in a while and drive until he saw coyotes. He would run after them as fast as that tough old Model T would go. Once he felt he was close enough, he pulled down hard on a trip rope that opened the kennels on one side of the truck, releasing the greyhounds on the run.

The dogs would chase the coyotes a long ways with John keeping them in sight. Once the dogs showed signs of getting tired, he would release the other dogs. He didn't worry about the first dogs; they would wait where they were until he came back for them. The second dogs would light out after the already tiring coyotes and run them to a standstill. Once they had them at bay, the dogs knew to keep circling to hold the coyotes in one place.

Between the two rows of kennels was a third one that opened out the back of the truck. Two huge beautiful Irish wolf hounds would be released when he yanked on the rope. These enormous, fearless dogs would close in for the kill and take down the whole pack.

Once the excitement was over, John would collect the ears, and round up the dogs. Ronald loved to go with him, as did any of my sons. Sometimes John would make ten or twelve dollars a night, which was enough to pay for two weeks groceries for most folks.

5

Reap the Whirlwind

Spring, 1932
Brownfield, Terry County, Texas

I WATCHED WITH DISTASTE, SAD-ness and sympathy, as the newsreel played to the packed crowd. In the bigger cities, people with ragged clothes, and thin, sad, dirty faces waited in long cold lines for a bowl of soup and a piece of bread. Workers lounged outside locked and rusting factories and mills. People who had been evicted from their homes lived in squalor in shacks made of wooden packing crates and cardboard. These towns had come to be called "Hoovervilles" due to the President's lack of response to the crisis. How could this be happening in our country? But the saddest, was also that which made me most angry.

When our soldiers returned from France, Congress had voted them "Bonus Pay" in honor of their meritorious service to the country and the cause of freedom. They had been issued "Bonus Certificates" to be redeemed at a later date. These veterans, mostly men in their mid-thirties, had families to feed. Most were out of work, and all of them were out of money. They had written, begged and pleaded for the certificates to be honored.

They had risen up in the country's hour of need. Now was their hour of need. It was time to fulfill the promises made to them. But Congress and President Hoover turned a blind eye and a deaf ear. Thousands of desperate veterans had descended on Washington to demand that the country live up to its promises. The newsreel showed them living in sprawling shanty towns throughout the marble and granite elegance of Washington.

They were an embarrassment to President Hoover. He ordered General McArthur to disperse the men and destroy the camps. I watched in horror as United States Cavalry charged the defenseless men and camps with drawn swords. They struck men down with the flat of their sabers, as their mounts trampled those who could not escape. They were followed by the arrival of hundreds of infantry with fixed bayonets, wearing the gas masks we had seen from the Great War. They lobbed gas grenades against American citizens, American veterans, American heroes. The ugly tanks of mechanized infantry followed and fired live rounds into the fragile shacks, setting them ablaze.

The newsreel ended with smoke and ashes swirling upwards as our country's finest men stumbled away in agony and disbelief. I stood and shook my fist at the grainy screen.

"No!"

Men and women around me did the same. Even Ella was on her feet, crying into her handkerchief. My sense of righteous indignation flamed as scalding tears streaked my face.

We did not wait to see the movie, or ask for our nickel back. Dozens of us, young and old, walked out of the theater in disgust. My old failing heart was filled with anger. And President Herbert Hoover seemed the best place to focus my rage. None of us would soon forget what we had seen.

Across the previously sleepy backwaters of America, folks became keenly aware of politics. I never saw more men reading newspapers at the lodge meetings, post office, bank and barber shop. The women organized political study groups. Hoover had poked a hornet's nest with a sharp stick and there would be hell to pay.

———————

John and Effie stopped to pick us up to drive to Plains to see Ed and Minta. We all piled into his Oldsmobile and headed west on the graded road. John drove that car like his pants were on fire. Ella was hollering for him to slow down.

"It's no use, Mother Turner. When John gets in his automobile, it only has two speeds: go and go faster. Now, hold on tight to Lynn!"

Ronald rode shotgun, with Effie in the middle. John, Junior, was on her lap squealing with delight. I've got to admit, it was the fastest I had ever travelled, and it was kind of exciting.

We had a good visit with the Plains branch of the Turner family. Minta was a mighty good cook. We said our goodbyes and John put his powerful machine back on the road. His headlights showed that the north wind was picking up a right smart of dust. We hadn't gone ten miles until it was hard to see the road. John slowed down a little, but I guess it was not quite enough.

We felt a terrible bump and the car came to a sudden halt. The engine was still running. John and Ronald stepped out.

"Dad, the rear wheels are turnin', but they ain't even touchin' the road!"

John peered into the sandy darkness under the automobile. "I'll be a double Dutchman! We're high-centered on some kinda cow!"

John grumbled as he pulled a couple of shovels out of the trunk and started digging sand from under the trapped animal. "Longhorn cross steer. Kickin' like he ain't hurt too bad."

Effie got to laughing. "Here we are, seven of us, stuck with the wheels off the ground in the middle of a dust storm, high-centered on a longhorn steer!"

John Junior must have thought that was the funniest thing he ever heard, for the little boy reared his head back and started laughing so hard, it got me and Ella to laughing, too.

Ronald and John could hear it all. John just grumbled, but Ronald got to laughing so hard he could barely shovel. Finally, a deep rumbling laugh echoed from under the car. "This is about the dang sorriest mess I ever got in my whole life."

About that time, the steer went to kicking and wiggling harder. "Look out, Ronald, he's comin' out your way!"

A yearling brindle longhorn steer emerged from his sandy trap, none too happy. He chased Ronald around the car until the lanky boy jumped into Ella's lap, right on top of his baby brother. John saw what was coming and jumped in the front seat just before the steer hit the closing door a hard swipe with his foot long horns. He stood in front of the Oldsmobile, bellowing and slinging snot and slobber. He charged the heavy front bumper hard enough to rock the car.

"Come on Dad, let get outta here!"

"Those shovels cost three dollars apiece, and I don't aim to leave 'em. You climb over Granddad and get out on that side while I distract him over here."

Ronald climbed out unnoticed while John waved his hat out the open window at the angry steer. He came around to butt the door a few times pretty hard.

"Got 'em, Dad."

"Oh, you're not gonna believe this! See his brand? That's one of Ed's steers!"

In a final act of defiance and revenge, the steer raised his tail and flopped a good green load right on the front grill of the John's Oldsmobile. It made the whole car stink all the way back to Brownfield. I can't remember a time when we all laughed so hard.

———

"Well, look who hit the door! Welcome, Brother Turner!"

"Hello, Joe; fellas."

"Aaron, Ma's runnin' again."

"Are you kiddin' me? That's great news. She's just what Texas needs."

"Not everybody thinks so."

"Well, they can go butt a stump."

"What do you think about this Roosevelt feller runnin' against your buddy, Hoover?"

"I think Roosevelt oughta be worth somethin', just because he's supposed to be some kinda kin to Teddy Roosevelt."

"It don't bother you that he's a rich Yankee?"

"Sure it does. Be he's got one iron-clad thing goin' for him. He ain't Herbert Hoover. He ain't worth a bucket o' warm spit."

"We can count on ol' Brother Turner to tell us just how he feels."

"You was there when they showed the newsreel of the Bonus Army, weren't you, Joe?"

My friend of many years sat silently in his chair, staring at the open firebox on the stove. "Yes. I was there. I was plumb ashamed to be an American the way Hoover treated our veterans. I walked out right behind ya."

"I know you did, Joe. I know you did."

"I'm sorry if it seemed like I was takin' it out on you, on any of you brothers. I lived through Reconstruction. I've seen what out of control government can do. It gets me kinda worked up."

"I ain't quite as old as you, but I'm old enough to remember. Those were the worst days my family ever knew. I'm scared of President Hoover. We gotta vote him out."

"That's just what I plan to do. Vote for this rich damn Yankee Democrat and Ma Ferguson, too."

"Hoover can go to hell, for all I care."

I shifted in my seat and pulled out my pipe. I took my time to fill it, light it, and get it drawing real well. "Joe, that's somethin' I won't say about any man, even Edmund J. Davis. I think Hoover is a right sorry fella. I hope God lets him live long enough to be forgiven for the sorry things he's done. I seen hell up close and personal in the war. I wouldn't wish it on any man."

You could have heard a pin drop in the lodge hall. Joe shifted and turned to look me right in the face. "Aaron, I guess I didn't mean it like that."

"I know you didn't, Joe. You ain't that kinda man. Sometimes a fella gets worked up and says things he don't mean. But we all knew you didn't mean it like that, brother."

When the election arrived, Ma Ferguson was elected governor of Texas once again, and Herbert Hoover would need to find a new house. I didn't know a lot about this Roosevelt, but I had my hopes pinned on him, as did much of the nation.

———

The few rains we got after planting our cotton was just enough to sprout it and let it burn up. The wind began to blow relentlessly from the west and southwest. What plants survived made a single tiny boll on the top of the plant like a surrender flag. There was no crop.

Lela had married a man from California and was living in Los Angeles. We only heard from her at Christmas and other scarce letters. Marjorie lay in the Brownfield cemetery.

The drought ran my boys off their land. George took his family and moved to Sweetwater. Jesse, Ruby and the kids moved to Barstow, Texas. Al had wandered off to Mexico, while his family was in Arizona. Bill moved to Dunn, a small community not far from Snyder and owned a store and gas station.

All of them lived too far away to visit easily. And travelling just wasn't easy for Ella or me anymore. And they all had families to support.

Ed was forty miles west at Plains with Minta and one son. John was twenty-two miles south at Seagraves. And sweet Ruth lived not too far from our house right here in Brownfield. The family I had gathered around me had scattered when they could no longer eke out a living on the south plains. I didn't blame them. I didn't like it much up here either, but we were too poor to move away.

There was a saying: "If a man ever stays long enough to wear out a pair of boots in the south plains, he won't ever leave." What they didn't tell you, was that he would be too poor to go anywhere better.

6

Alphabet Soup

Spring, 1933
Brownfield, Terry County, Texas

THE RAINS ABANDONED US. THE failure of the past years' crops left the light sandy loam soil without any protection from the relentless dry wind. In this country, it was common for the wind to get up in the heat of the day, but then calm down at night. Now it blew morning, noon, and night. Spring was an especially bad time for windstorms. The winds carried away the fine rich red topsoil that had been built for countless years beneath the protective blanket of prairie grass.

The grass was long gone over much of the Great Plains of the United States. And the bare fields had nothing to slow the howling wind. As the dust-filled wind blew from west to east, it picked up more and larger particles of soil. It filled in the empty furrows, it buried the bottom wire of fences, and it covered the roads, only to be blown clear by the next wind to deposit in great heaps along the roads. It filtered into every crack and crevice in our home. It accumulated in the attics, and then sifted down to foul our beds and food.

We needed rain to get something growing on the barren land to hold the fragile soil. But the skies withheld the rain and sent only wind and scattered thunder storms that washed gullies in fields, only to be dried out and blowing away before it could be used. It was as if the hand of nature had turned against us. I had lived long enough to know that this country had cycles of wet and dry periods. But this time, the grass, the guardian of the soil in dry times, was gone. We had made a fatal mistake when we tore away that protective soil. Although this country could produce adequate crops in wet years, it was not intended for farming. It should have never been poisoned with the steel of a plow. But now the damage was done. I wasn't any smarter than anyone else. I had plowed my grass under like everyone else. I shared in the guilt for the ruin of this once great grassland. We had been smarter than God, and imposed our will upon the land to its everlasting destruction.

———————

President Roosevelt wasted no time in addressing the sickness that had spread across the face of American. Over all the other "alphabet" programs towered the NRA, or National Recovery Act. It spelled out Mr. Roosevelt's plan to save the country. Signs proclaiming "I support the NRA" showed in nearly every home and business in town.

He gave us the Civilian Conservation Corps, or CCC. It was to put men back to work building roads, bridges, and dams. They began to plant wide shelter belts of trees and water them with swarms of men and buckets to keep the struggling plants alive in hopes that one day they might slow the destructive wind. Ronald joined almost immediately. He made enough money to pay all his own bills and bring a little home to John and Effie.

He gave us the CWA, or Civil Works Administration, to also build roads, airfields and public utilities. The Federal Housing Authority and the Home Owners Loan Corporation set about providing very low interest loans so that folks could keep their homes. In the big cities, they tore down dilapidated tenements and replaced them with modern apartment buildings with running hot and cold water and electricity, renting them out at rates people could afford.

The Public Works Administration was aimed at putting men to work rebuilding the decaying infrastructure of cities. They built modern sewer and water plants to eliminate the squalor of some cities. They built reservoirs to catch clean run-off water and plants to treat the waste water to make it safe to drink.

Mr. Roosevelt gave us the Social Security Administration. Everyone who worked contributed a small percentage to provide a little income for those who were too old to work and something for their own eventual retirement.

I cannot underestimate how much my Confederate Pension helped, for we were not eligible for Social Security. The meager savings we had were eroded by our lack of any income from our small farm. Some months it kept us in groceries.

The government regulated the stock market through the Securities and Exchange Commission. But of most importance to us were the Farm Security Administration and the broader Agriculture Administration Act. These programs paid us not to plant crops if we would agree to conservation measures to stop soil loss, and to regulate commodity prices and supplies.

Due to the extreme drought over much of the country, there was little of nothing to feed livestock. The government instituted a livestock herd buyout. It paid seven dollars for every adult cow, and a dollar a head for calves, sheep, goats and hogs. Millions of animals were bought and slaughtered. About half of the meat was distributed to those who needed it and the rest was destroyed. We sold everything we owned except what hogs we could feed scraps, our chickens and a milk cow. I staked her out on vacant lots throughout town to keep her fed. It gave me a reason to get out of the house.

Ed had said that a plow didn't fit his hand. He had four square miles of pasture land that had never known a plow. The fine red dust and tumble weeds from neighboring farms settled along his fences. But he had enough grass to keep a part of his herd. Plus, he and Minta both had jobs in town to keep the wolf from the door.

Joe Plaice was standing on my front porch with a look of deep panic in his eyes. "Aaron, they done it. They sure gone and done it. Ma Ferguson ordered every bank in the state closed."

"Why, Joe, come in. Would you like a glass of cold water or some coffee?"

"Aren't you worried?"

"Joe, you and I are two of the oldest men in town. How many times have you seen a run on the banks?"

"A few. But some of them never reopened."

"Did you ever lose any money that way?"

"I was too poor to have money in a bank. You know that. But I got over three hundred dollars in First State Bank of Brownfield. I want to get my money out."

"Yes, and I reckon that is why they closed 'em. Everybody was takin' money out faster than the banks could call in loans. You think they keep it all sittin' in the vault? They got that money loaned out to people like you and me on a house or a farm. It will take a while to pull it all in; but if they do, there won't be any to loan to folks like us."

"You think they'll open them back up pretty soon?"

"Don't you trust Ma Ferguson?"

"I never met her, but I voted for her every time she or Pa was runnin'. But she's a woman. What does she know about bankin'?"

"I don't know. How much do you know about it? Joe, I think it'll be all right before you know it."

Mr. Roosevelt took what Ma Ferguson had started and extended the bank "holiday." Folks calmed down after a few days, and the banks were allowed to reopen. But to tell you the truth, I took out what money I had saved a little at a time. In six months, I had it hidden in coffee cans buried in Ella's rose garden. I didn't tell Joe.

Mr. Roosevelt also had Congress take up the repeal of Prohibition. He argued that putting people back to work in the distilleries and breweries would be good for the country. I sure wasn't going to argue with him. I was down to my last bottle of whiskey I had stashed away before prohibition for our own occasional personal use. I didn't hold with drunkenness, but I believed a man had a right to a drink if he wanted it and could pay for it.

Texas had a Constitutional Convention to consider the Twenty-first Amendment to repeal Prohibition. There was the usual speech making by all the "do right" preachers. A few states didn't adopt it, but enough did that it became the law of the land. Texas sure as heck passed it. The repeal would be effective December 5th, 1933.

―――――――

John and Effie had sure had poor luck with their kids. Besides Ella Francis, they had buried four babies too little to survive. But they had their first born, Ronald, who was now gone away with the Civilian Conservation Corps. John, Junior, was a skinny tow headed little fellow of five and Aaron Lynn, was now two. That poor child had so many freckles you couldn't tell where one stopped and the next one began. But he had gray-blue eyes like mine and a big smile to break through the freckles. In October, Effie gave birth to Howard Eugene Turner. That was a lot of name for a little boy. We just called him Gene.

———

It was a time of hope. The first hope we had felt in several years. Mr. Roosevelt was going to save us all. And yet in spite of the President and all of the alphabet programs, he could not make it rain. The hot dry wind still rolled in day after day from the west or southwest. It blew through the dusty days and howled through the nights. It carried no rain clouds but took tons of fertile soil away. There were some things even Mr. Roosevelt could not do.

7

Horse Thief

Spring, 1934
Seagraves, Gaines County, Texas

"EFFIE, BOYS, I'M HOME."

"Well, hello, tall, red and handsome. Did you keep Seagraves safe from crime today?"

"Not much goin' on around there. I read through a new set of wanted posters, finished up a little paper work and made my rounds."

"Like hangin' out at the barber shop?"

"Well, I walked through both banks a couple of times, stopped in and said hello at all the downtown businesses, drove out to the gin to see my old friends, came back by the banks, and then managed to show up at the barbershop. They've got the best free coffee."

"Best gossip, too, I bet, John Turner."

"What did you and them good for nothin' boys do today?"

"Today was Lady's Home Demonstration meeting. Madame President has to keep up appearances. We had a lady talk about cannin' food."

"I'm gonna go check the horses before I wash up for supper. What's on the menu?"

"Chicken fried steak, green beans, mashed potatoes and gravy."

"I'll hurry!"

"The horses are gone! There's tire tracks at the corral. Somebody stole 'em right out of the back yard!"

"You sure one of the boys didn't leave the gate open and they strayed?"

"Nope, the gate been chained back. The hoof tracks stopped just past the gate. Looks like they had a trailer. The boys' ponies are still there."

"You got time to eat?"

"Let me think. I came by here to pick up some cigarettes at about ten o'clock, right before I drove to the gin. I saw the horses then. What time did you get back?"

"Three. There hasn't been a soul in here since then."

"So they've been gone since sometime between ten and three. It's nearly six now and comin' on dark. No. I'll eat, then load up a few things. I'll get the trailer hooked up to the Oldsmobile and head to Big Spring tonight. They got their horse sale in the mornin'"

"Papa, can we go with ya to catch that good for nothin' horse thief?"

I reached down and tousled John, Junior's, blond hair. "No son. I may be gone a few days."

"Me and Lynn could be your deputies in case there's a gun fight!" He and three year old Lynn held up their toy guns menacingly. "Gene's just a baby, he can't go."

"I need you and Lynn to stay here and guard the home place. What if them horse thieves come back to steal the Shetland ponies?"

"You mean like we could be your deputies here?"

"Sure. I'll swear you in. You boys hold up your right hands. Show Lynn which one to hold up."

The blond-headed string bean and his red-haired, freckle-faced sidekick stood with their hands raised with as much dignity as they could muster for almost six and almost three. "Do you swear to uphold the laws of the state of Texas and Gaines County, to protect your Momma and baby brother from horse thieves, cattle rustlers, bandits, and Injuns? Do you swear to eat your dinner without complainin' and take your bath when Momma says to do it?"

"We do."

Nudging Lynn, he said "Yup."

"I declare you temporary junior deputies of Gaines County until I get home." They holstered their guns and began to walk the perimeter of the property looking for trouble.

I didn't find the horses at Big Spring, Snyder or Sweetwater, but I cut the trail in Abilene. I had just missed the end of the sale as I drove up and showed my badge to the sale manager.

"Deputy, I seen those horses come through here today. Let me pull the ticket. 'Set of three head. One bay thoroughbred stallion, one good brood mare, bay, with one white sock right front foot. One weaned bay colt, four socks. All three branded JK Slant on the left cheek. Four hundred and fifty dollars. Sold by John Karnes, Seminole, Texas, to Jeff Settle, Trent, Texas."

I showed him my peace officer's license: John Karr Turner. And my Gaines County brand registry of JK Slant on the left cheek for horses, and JK Bar on the left hip for cattle.

"I'll be. Pretty brazen thing to do, steal a lawman's stock. I don't know nothin' about Karnes, but I can tell you where to catch up with Settle. He's down the road gettin' some feed."

I drove to the feed store. The smell of sweet feed and alfalfa hung in the air like perfume to a horseman like me. I showed my badge and asked for Jeff Settle. He was out back getting his order loaded.

There in the trailer were my horses. All three nickered and stamped their feet as I approached. A small man with a wiry build, red hair and weathered blue eyes was watching them load his truck.

"Mr. Settle?"

"That's me. What can I do for ya?"

I showed him my badge and brand registry and the registration papers on the stud horse that included a detailed description. Jeff looked me over, looked at the papers and walked back to the trailer. It was obvious to anyone who understood horses that they knew me. All three craned their necks to get a pat on the nose.

"Well, I guess I bought some stolen horses. Here's my bill of sale."

"I wasn't thinkin' you was the feller who stole 'em. You know anythin' about him?"

"I can tell you what hole that polecat crawled in. He said he's stayin' at the ol' Fremont Hotel off the square. He invited me to come by for a drink."

"You mind if I buy my own horses?"

"You ain't just gonna confiscate 'em for evidence?"

"You bought 'em fair enough. Here's a check for the whole amount on the Seagraves Bank. I promise it's good."

"That's plenty fair. Thanks. Just so anybody asks, I'll sign the bill of sale over to you."

I parked my car, trailer and horses down the street, and slid a sixth cartridge in my Colt. I walked quietly into the lobby of the hotel. It might have been fine in its day, but the scarlet curtains had faded, the plastered walls were peeling and there was a strong smell of stale cigarettes. The desk clerk looked up from a newspaper.

"Can I help you?"

I touched my finger to my lips and whispered. "I'm Deputy Sheriff John Turner from Gaines County. I need to look at your registration book." As he looked at my badge, I ran my finger down the grimy page. *John Karnes, Seminole.* I tapped the entry. "Which room?"

"Number two, first one to the left of the stairs."

"Alone?" He nodded yes. "You keep real quiet and let me borry the spare key. You're comin' with me. Knock on the door and tell 'em he's got a fella in the lobby wants to see him about a drink." He nodded again.

We walked up the stairs just like he was showing a customer to a room. We stopped at the door and he knocked. "Mr. Karnes, there's a fella in the lobby says he wants to see you about a drink."

There was a hoarse cough from behind the door. "Little feller with red hair?" I nodded yes.

"That's the one."

"I'll be down in just a minute. I gotta get dressed."

I motioned the clerk to step aside as I slipped the key in the lock. My pistol was in my hand.

"Hey, I told you I was gettin' dressed!"

I burst into the room with my gun leveled. When he started to protest, I stuck the barrel in his mouth.

"You owe me four hundred and fifty dollars for horses, and fifty dollars in travellin' expenses." He hesitated, sitting on the side of the dilapidated bed looking at his wallet on the night stand.

I slowly pulled back the hammer on the pistol. It cleanly rotated the cylinder and cocked with a distinct click. "This is a .41 Long Colt. I never shot a man in the head with it, but it blows punkins all to hell."

He slowly reached for the wallet and counted out the money. I took the gun out of his mouth and eased down the hammer. "Pleasure doin' business with ya. But don't let it happen twice."

I backed out of the room and met the astonished clerk. "You had that barrel shoved right into his mouth! Lord, I never seen the like. But why ain't you arrestin' him?"

"Long story. Have a drink on me." I handed the clerk a silver dollar and waltzed out of the hotel. It was a long drive back to Seagraves.

———————

Author's note: There was in fact, a good bit more to the story. The man in question was a friend and neighbor of my grandfather. The man had a wife and children to support, but he had a drinking and gambling problem that often left them short of cash. The thief waited until Granddad left for the office to steal the horses.

Growing up, there was an unpainted, unkempt house on the corner we were never allowed to cut across the yard or approach. After the man of that house died, Grandmother took food, as was neighborly, and resumed friendly relations with the widow. Granddad didn't allow Grandmother or Uncle Ronald to tell the rest of the story until after his death. He figured the neighbor's family had endured enough shame with an alcoholic father without folks knowing he was also a horse thief.

8

Black Sunday

Spring, 1935
Brownfield, Lynn County, Texas

"WELL, BROTHER TURNER. HOW have you been? Is your heart doin' all right?"

"Joe, I'm pretty good as long as I take my digitalis. Doctor says if I quit takin' it, I'm a goner."

"At least you got it to take. I bet you're missin' Ma Ferguson."

"You know, she said she was done with politics for good. I guess dealin' with all this mess would sour the sweet milk for anybody. I don't know much about this new governor, James Allred, except he's a Democrat."

"You got electricity at your house?"

"Yes, I do. Got a light in every room of the house and got a radio that runs off electricity instead of batteries. John is real interested in all this stuff. He took me out to the new generating plant by the gin. They got coal piled up like mountains outside and men shuttlin' it into a big ol' furnace that runs the steam generator. I been watchin' 'em puttin' up poles. You know they hauled 'em in all the way from east Texas by train? I guess we coulda strung up the lines on tumble weeds."

"I seen that big truck that digs the holes and sets the posts. Nearly all of Brownfield has got lines up. This Rural Electrification Act is just the ticket."

"My grandson, Ronald, is workin' for REA. He sure likes it."

"Y'all had any rain out on your land at Tokio?"

"Not enough for nothin'. My land, and sons', is just blowin' away. I paid a feller to do the conservation tillage on all of it. You knew the boys and their families starved out here and moved off. Not a one of 'em is still farmin'. Ed is holdin' on to his pasture land, but it's hardly got a cow on it. He's got a town job in Plains. So does his wife. He got a little money the other day from a company wantin' the right to look for oil out there. I'd be glad if they found some water."

The sun shone clear and warm April 14, 1935, across the Great Plains from Nebraska to Texas. Those who had been stuck inside for days by dust storms opened their windows and aired out their houses. Children went out to play. Laundry could be hung outside on the line.

Far to the north, a mighty cold front swept down from Canada. Winds reached sixty miles an hour. The dry, drought scorched land lay barren and vulnerable. The wind scoured the red clay soils of the plains, picking up tons of earth with each passing mile.

For those who looked, there was a towering wall of dirt hundreds of feet high racing south. The lucky ones reached cover before it hit. Some were not so lucky. When the storm hit, the newly installed street lights in small towns all across the plains came on, as daylight was turned to darkness. Their electric output couldn't penetrate the blanket of darkness that closed over the earth.

The air was filled with fine dust that burned the eyes and nose, and choked the lungs, making breathing nearly impossible. The power of the wind picked up small clods and pebbles and these clattered against the windows that were closed against the storm. But the dust was so fine that it found its way around every crevasse and crack and slowly, relentlessly filled the houses with dust.

Red soil filled the attics and sifted down through the ceilings into houses. Tables and beds were covered with a fine red dust. Mothers gave their children damp rags to tie across their faces to filter out some of the dust.

The people of the plains were a hardy lot. They had to be tough to live where they did, even in good years. They had endured four years of the worst drought anyone could remember. They had shouldered through more dust storms than could be counted. But this was the grandfather of all dust storms. People couldn't see their hand in front of their face inside their homes. Electricity was out and kerosene lamps were lit. But the light couldn't penetrate the darkness.

Some believed this was the end of time, and sat holding hands and praying together. Some of those unfortunate enough to be caught outside suffocated from the dust, or were buried beneath the dunes. Livestock suffered from the choking dust. And it was not just the dust, but the wind. It howled like a demon released from hell, screaming across the prostrate land.

The wind finally died down, and people began to dig out of their homes, through dunes that buried some houses to the rafters. The red dust filled the skies for days. The cloud was moved by the currents of the wind gradually eastward. Finally, the red skies reached the Atlantic shores, leaving the sun a ghostly red, and a fine film of dust settled into homes which had never been violated in this way.

A great cry went up for the plight of the plains. New programs were started and old ones were strengthened. But it was as if God Himself had turned His back on the helpless plains. And only God Himself could undo the damage to the land that men had done.

The people prayed. They raised their voices from houses of all faiths for God's mercy on the land. They prayed for relief. They prayed for rain. They prayed for a healing of the land. They prayed in desperation for salvation from the ravages of nature.

"Good night, what's that smell? Dad, your leg! Quick; step away from the stove!"

It was too late. I had gradually lost the feeling in my feet and legs. I was forever cold and never could seem to get warm. John had come to visit and I had moved my chair near the stove to warm my feet. My pants leg was smoking, but the skin beneath it was charred. I couldn't feel a thing.

"Mother, I've got to get Dad to the hospital."

The doctor did what he could to save my foot for several days, but I remembered the sight and smell of gangrene from long ago.

"Comin' off, ain't it, Doc."

"Aaron, I don't have any choice. We'll do the best we can."

They took my foot and ankle off, but the gangrene had spread.

The next surgery took it off below the knee. But the infection was relentless. The final surgery took my leg off below my hip and stopped the infection from killing me.

The pain was bad, but the morphine made me lose my mind. I would rather have the pain than feel insane. It felt as if ants were biting the leg that was no longer there. The doctor called it "ghost pain." I called it something less polite. Gradually I regained my strength.

The nurse brought in a cane-backed wheelchair, with big wheels in the front. My Confederate pension had paid for it. They taught me how to get myself in and out of the contraption, and soon I was rolling the hallways. It was time to go home to a life of more confinement and less freedom than I had ever known.

———

The windbreak trees had taken root and started to grow. Enough rain had fallen to establish cover crops in many places, but not enough to farm. The major roads in the area had been paved, although I had sold my Chevrolet since I could no longer drive.

I couldn't go out to see about the cropland. I sold my land for whatever it would bring. Each of the boys did the same. All except Ed, who still owned his pasture.

Power lines followed the roads from town to town. The success of some of the government programs was evident even here in the dusty wasteland. But even Mr. Roosevelt could not make it rain.

Part Five

Will the Circle be Unbroken?

1

Year of Jubilee

Spring, 1937
Brownfield, Lynn County, Texas

THUNDER WOKE ME FROM A DEEP sleep, followed quickly by the sound of rain splattering against the windows and pouring of the eaves. But this wasn't a normal thunderstorm that blew up and blew away in half an hour. This rain came and stayed.

It rained, on and off, light to heavy showers for four days. Mr. Roosevelt had been to Amarillo the day the rain started, and they called it Mr. Roosevelt's rain. We got over six and a half inches at Brownfield, more than the whole last year.

John came by in his deputy's car to show me the countryside. The playa lakes were full for the first time in years. Water stood at the lower end of fields, even in this sandy soil. The wheat that had been planted as a cover crop had been struggling to stay alive. Now it jumped out of the ground in glorious new green growth.

The windbreak trees, which had been kept alive with buckets of water for years, broke out in heavy swollen green buds. This rain brought with it a hope that it would not be the last.

And it was not the last rain. The pattern had been broken. Rain came in semi-regular intervals all spring. Teams and tractors that had not gotten much use carefully plowed up the moist soil according to conservation guidelines. Wide strips of wheat were left between the rows of cotton to stop wind erosion. By mid-June, cotton was popping up in healthy green rows.

Government workers and farmers cleared the sand dunes from fence lines and farm buildings. Gardens were planted again. Baby chicks, bought at local feed stores, scurried about farmsteads and yards in every direction. Milk cows were unloaded from boxcars at the rail station. A sense of hope was rising up within us again, tempered by the fear that it might only be a temporary respite.

The summer of 1937 hope returned with the rains that continued in an abundance of blessing. Wheat made thirty-five bushels across the south plains. The price was enough a fellow could make a little money. The coal-eating fire-breathing dragons rolled across the level land spewing out wagon loads of hard red wheat.

Cotton and grain sorghum looked better than I had seen them in many years. When the first winds of fall arrived, the grain was ready to cut. Men told of yields over fifteen hundred pounds to the acre, a fine crop for this area.

November brought the first hard freeze of the fall, followed by clear skies and steady dry winds to open any closed bolls and blow away the clinging leaves. John and Effie had a few acres on the rented Wharton Place. The short plants were loaded with fat white bolls. Yields across the area were about a bale and three-quarters to the acre at twelve cents a pound.

The ranchers, including Ed, weren't selling any heifers or cows. But there was a strong market for the mature steers they drove or had trucked into Seagraves.

Folks had a spring in their step and a glimmer of hope in their eyes. It was good to see. The country seemed to have survived the worst of it and was heading in the right direction.

Every week, Joe Plaice took a grocery list and enough money to do our shopping. He got around in an old buggy with a decent mare. It was all he needed. He usually picked up our mail for us, too. He and I would enjoy a smoke and catch up on local news whenever he came by.

We heard how news reels showed factories reopening and workers flooding in the gates. The food lines, the Hoovervilles of earlier days, were gone. Wages started to rise. America was slowly getting her feet back under her.

The government programs had been placed under an umbrella program called the Works Progress Administration. The projects of the WPA continued to slowly alter the face of the blemished land.

A time of healing had finally come, a year of jubilee, a celebration of life itself. But the Great Depression had left scars on the heart and mind of the country. Generations of Americans were marked by its effects.

And the land bore scars that could not be hidden. Wounds inflicted by man upon the earth would remain. Nothing could improve the looks of the land faster than a few good rains. But the home of the buffalo and cow had been mortally wounded by the plow. It had not been created to be plowed, but man had tried to shape it to his own will.

The Great Depression and blowing dust had left a mark on me and my family. We held each penny dear, and none of us would ever take for granted food and shelter.

I found myself confined to a wheelchair. It was difficult to get to the store, lodge meetings or church. What little independence I had left had been taken from me. Ella and I both were fragile shells of the people we had been, but age robs all of us of these things.

I was not a man to show much emotion. I held my own counsel. But in my heart of hearts, I wept. I wept for the great cattle trails that had been fenced over and plowed under. I wept for the life I had known during the days of the cattle kingdom. In those days, I answered to no one but God, and knew no limit of my abilities. I wept for the land that had been spoiled by good intentions. I wept that my children were scattered far and wide. But these were the silent tears of an old man facing the end of his life.

Ella was at my side as she had been for almost sixty years. We had seen the best and worst of life in our years together. I couldn't imagine life without her. But we no longer sat and watched the sunset together. While our love endured, we both retreated within ourselves to cope with life's troubles. Those troubles had slowly eroded the joy of life. We recognized that our race was just about ended. It had been a good run.

2

Healing Amid the Graves

April, 1938
Brownfield, Lynn County, Texas

I WAS ENJOYING MY PIPE ON THE front porch on a crisp April morning. I heard a horse approaching and looked to see Joe Plaice in his buggy coming at a trot. He wheeled in by the front gate, set the brake and headed for the porch as fast as a seventy-five year old man can move.

"Why are you burnin' up good horse flesh? I ain't seen you move that fast since that politician was givin' away free dimes at the bank. Sherman and a whole regiment right behind ya?"

"This is important, Brother Turner. Mighty important. Look there. *Official United States Postage. No stamp required. Gettysburg, Pennsylvania.*" And look how they got your name spelled: *Aron Loyd Turner.* That's how it's spelled on your war records, ain't it?"

It was an engraved invitation to the Seventy-fifth Reunion of the Battle of Gettysburg for all surviving veterans, both Union and Confederate, from all fields of service, whether they fought at Gettysburg or not. They would pay for my train tickets, including a Pullman berth, for me and an "Attendant." Accommodations and all meals would be provided there. There would be speeches, parades, and a special visit from President Roosevelt.

"Well, I'll be." I handed it to Joe to read.

"You gonna go?"

"I'm stuck in this wheelchair and I got a bad heart. But if somebody went with me to help out, I think I might could do it. I'll have to talk to Ella and John."

"Aaron, do you feel well enough to go?"

"I think so. As long as John is there, I'll be fine."

"Dad, I'll talk to Sheriff Birdwell. There is a Texas Ranger living in Seagraves that could help if there was any trouble. I believe we could get it done. They would pay all my expenses, too?"

"Yes, everything."

"I don't see what we got to lose. I think you'd like it."

Sheriff Soon Birdwell was as tough a lawman as carried a gun, but he had a soft spot for the handful of old soldiers left around. He said since John would be escorting a Texas hero, he could still draw his pay during the trip. It was a done deal.

Ella helped me buy a new suit of clothes and a new hat. I got them tailored to fit just right, especially allowing for my missing left leg. We borrowed a good set of leather suitcases.

"Aaron, I've never seen you look more handsome. I've got someone from the paper to take your picture before you leave."

"You aren't gonna take up with some young fella while I'm gone are, you?" I grinned mischievously.

"I reckon not. Nobody would have a worn out old woman like me except a worn out old man like you."

"We've seen some times, ain't we Ma."

"I should say so. I still remember the first time I saw you. It was that Christmas day you got baptized. I set my bonnet for you right then. I've never been sorry about it."

"Me neither, ol' gal. We've made a pretty good team."

"Would you do it the same way if you had it to do all over again?"

Her question took me by surprise. I stopped, relit me pipe and looked at the woman with whom I had spent sixty years.

"We'll, I know I married the right woman. I reckon we had about all the kids we could stand. I wished we had lived where it rained more, where the weather wasn't so blame hot and dry in the summer, and there weren't no blizzards in the winter time. But if we had, we might not like Heaven so much. Yes. There is one thing I would for sure do different. I wish we had homesteaded pasture land on the plains, like Ed done. I guess that's about all I would change. How about you?"

"I wish I had spent more time laughin', singin' and dancin' than workin'. But I guess we made out all right. I wouldn't trade our life for a tub full of gold."

"There was times we'd a been doin' good to put together a pocket full of pennies!"

John's car roared up to the house. I had finished breakfast and was waiting on the front porch.

He put my bags in the back seat. "You ready, Dad?"

"Yep. Took my little green drops. Been to the outhouse and done my duty. Let me tell your Ma goodbye."

"You know who to holler for if you need anythin'. John said the Sheriff's office here would call over to Seagraves to get Effie if you need her. Ruth is comin' by and Joe said he'd be here every day to check on you."

"I'll be fine. We used to be apart months at a time when you was drivin' cattle to Dodge. I guess I can manage eight days. John, make sure he remembers he's not out on the trail. Make him wash up, shave and look presentable. And takes his drops three times a day."

We went ripping and snorting down the road like Pancho Villa was behind us, raising a fine cloud of dust. When we arrived at the station, the place was done up in red, white and blue bunting. The high school band played *Yellow Rose of Texas* and the *Bonnie Blue Flag.*

The man from the newspaper was there to take pictures, and nearly the whole Odd Fellows Lodge was on the platform, with Joe right in the middle of them.

"Folks here just wanted to let you know we was proud of you, Brother Turner."

The conductor took us to our seats and said there was a Pullman berth made up for me if I got tired. Who could get tired with all the excitement going on everywhere? The train pulled out blowing the whistle and clanging the bell, as the band played another song. John just sat there looking at me and smiling like he didn't have good sense. A single tear rolled down my cheek, but I wiped it away before anyone but John saw it.

"Folks around here do think a lot of you, Dad. I guess I never met anybody who didn't."

I made some feeble effort to reply, but my throat was too tight and my mouth too dry to talk. My cheeks were flushed. I finally turned and waved my new hat to the crowd. I felt such a range of emotions that I couldn't pick out the strongest one. I had always kept my emotions under a tight rein. But my control over them felt like one was on a green broke filly in a flock of guineas. I must be getting old.

We moved to the lounge car and drank coffee and smoked as we watched the familiar countryside roll by. Huge dunes of red sand lined the roads and fences, but windbreaks were green and growing at regular intervals, and the farm land between them was green with crops. The pastures were looking better after the years of rough treatment, and the hardy native grasses were growing.

The train took on water and coal in Lubbock, and they attached three more cattle cars to the five that had originated at Seagraves. Soon after leaving Lubbock we moved into the dining car for lunch. I had a hamburger steak smothered in onions, with mashed potatoes and gravy and some real good rolls. John and I drank a whole pot of coffee as we enjoyed chocolate cake for dessert. The dining room steward explained that all of our meals and other expenses were covered for the entire trip.

At Abilene, I knew we were getting back to my old stomping grounds. I didn't realize how much I had missed this good cattle country. Another Confederate veteran joined the train here with much the same fanfare I had been shown.

He had also fought in the Army of Tennessee, Ector's Texas Brigade. "You boys are the ones who kept the Yankees from runnin' over us at Nashville."

His eyes brightened. "Yes. We formed up a rear guard unit. We slowed 'em down until Forrest's cavalry gave us some breathin' room.

Lord, I believe the army ran the whole way back to Franklin. What outfit was you in?"

"Cleburne's Division, Granbury's Brigade, Texas 15th, Dismounted."

"You boys gave 'em hell at Franklin. Right there where the turnpike ran into town. Broke the line and stayed there all night."

"Not near as many came out as went in. The Devil owned the ground that day."

We both grew quiet. Franklin had been a bloody slaughter that broke the back of the Army of Tennessee. He was accompanied by his grandson, a boy about fifteen. "I was fourteen at Franklin, son. I hope you never have to see nothin' like it."

We talked for a long time about the places we had been and the things we had seen. There was a lot we didn't say, too.

At Fort Worth, we had a short lay over as they unloaded the cattle cars at the stockyards. John rolled me off and I stomped around the board walk on my crutches. I didn't use them too often or too long as they wore me out.

"John, we raised cattle as good as anythin' I see out there today."

"Better, I'd say, Dad. You kept fine stock."

"These are better than those ol' brush poppers I started with after the war. Those ol' longhorns would flat git in a man's back pocket. We drove 'em to Sedalia just the one year in '66. Missouri closed their borders to Texas cattle in '67 because of Tick Fever. It didn't hurt the longhorns, but would kill those farmers' cows dead as a hammer."

A couple of more old veterans got on in Fort Worth and four in Dallas. Three of them had stayed west of the Mississippi, but one had been with Sul Ross' Cavalry Brigade. About half of us were in wheelchairs, one on crutches, one on a cane, and one old man was straight as a rod.

"I heard you say you were in Sul Ross' outfit. First time I ever saw them was in the fall of '64 in Tennessee."

"I was there. I wasn't but sixteen. Sure did like ol' General Ross and that old fire-eater General Forrest. There in Tennessee we'd ride to the fight, but about half the time we'd fight dismounted. What unit was you in?"

"Cleburne's Division, Granbury's Brigade, Texas 15th Cavalry, Dismounted. They took our horses away in Arkansas and gave us a voucher for fifty dollars."

"How'd that work out for ya?" We both laughed until we were wheezing.

The train rolled eastward. The dining room stewards pulled some tables together in a special dining car that had been made to accommodate folks in wheelchairs. The tables were a little higher and wider, and the aisles were made wider, too. There were a dozen of us old Confederate vets that ate together with our attendants. The cooks outdid themselves again. I was so busy visiting, John had to remind me to take my green drops. When I got them out and started measuring them into a glass of water, half the old men at the table did the same thing. A fellow who had been an officer tapped his glass to get our attention, then raised his glass. "Gentlemen, a toast to tincture of digitalis, our little green friend!" We laughed and drank off a toast with green tinted water.

As the train wheezed and rattled through the night across Arkansas, we moved into the smoking car. I lit my pipe and visited with one and then another of the men. John, never shy, made the rounds talking, too.

Around midnight, the train stopped in Little Rock. Another handful of vets joined here. I asked John to take me outside so I could see the Arkansas River as the train crossed the enormous railroad bridge there.

"Son, the first time I saw this river was in the summer of '62. We were still cavalry. I was a courier in Company F. That was the day they took all our horses away, good home-raised horses. We were at a big earthwork called Fort Hindman at Arkansas Post. In January, the Yankees came with a fleet of ironclads and wooden gunboats, and over thirty thousand men. The hundred pound shot from the huge cannon on the fort bounced off of those ironclads like marbles. There were only four thousand of us. They had us hemmed in from every side. The swamp covered us from two sides, the river from another, and the Union army had us bottled up."

"We held out over night, but surrendered in the morning. They loaded us on steamships and took us down the Arkansas, up the Mississippi, into the Illinois River, right to the wharves in downtown Chicago. They marched us across town to Camp Stephen Douglas. It was pretty awful there. We all took sick, but my brother David got pneumonia and died."

"You never talked about it before, Dad."

"That wasn't the last time I saw the Arkansas River. No sir. Not by a long shot. I can't count how many times we crossed the Arkansas drivin' cattle. It brings back a lot of memories; most of 'em are good. We'll talk more later. I'm kinda tired."

He and the steward got me into the berth we would share. Before John was even back from cleaning up, the length of the day and the rhythmic motion of the train rocked me into a restful night's sleep.

Morning found us halfway across Tennessee. We had picked up another whole car load of veterans and their attendants in Memphis, and more Pullman, dining and lounge cars. The train was now being pulled by two locomotives belching steam and black smoke as we rolled steadily northeast.

John walked through the new cars and met the folks there. "Dad, there is someone I'd like you meet about two cars back. The conductor got this here steward to help me roll you back there if you want to go."

The steward was a big strong black man who wheeled me expertly across the linkage between cars like that train was sitting still. The best I could tell, we were a long ways from standing still. I could see the gravel and cross-ties going by lickety-split. But he got me there safe and sound. I saw John slip him some coins for the extra service.

Sitting in a wheelchair by the window was another old vet, just like the rest of us. "Dad, I'd like to introduce you to a man says he remembers you."

"You're that hellfire courier from Texas Generals Granbury and Cleburne liked so much; that skinny red-headed kid that was all time bringin' the generals fresh meat. I was one of the aides, Lieutenant Barrett."

"You was that young officer with the extra nice homemade uniform that was always hangin' around the General. I doubted you ever paid me any mind."

"I caught that pretty sorrel mare the General gave you at Pickett's Mill when your horse got shot. Granbury said if you hadn't found General Johnston to send reinforcements, we'd have all been killed. Ever after that, I had a new respect for you. You've aged some."

We had a pretty good laugh about that. "I guess we all have the last seventy-five years. How'd you keep from gettin' killed at Franklin?"

"Some Yankee sniper shot me plumb off my horse as we were formin' into line of battle at Franklin. They had to take my leg off."

"Hmmph. I had seen plenty of fightin' before Franklin. I never wanted any more after that."

"Where did you join up with Granbury?"

"I got assigned to him just before the Battle of Chickamauga. We were together right up to Franklin. You lose your leg in the war?"

"No. That didn't happen until a couple of years ago. Gangrene from gettin' burned warmin' at my own stove. Guess you've been ridin' them wheels a damn sight longer than me."

They brought us coffee and we talked the morning away until the train pulled into Nashville. We agreed to meet again soon. I got to where I could see the town. A big band was playing and a small parade of old veterans rolled and limped up to the platform. Several more dining, Pullman, lounge and baggage cars joined the train. They added a third locomotive. There was some speech making, and a great deal more talking than I cared to hear. John rolled me to the side of the platform where I could look out across the town I had seen so long ago.

"We got beat lots of times in the war. We were nearly always out-numbered and out-gunned. Sometimes we got out-officered, but not very often. We retreated lots of times, sometimes in a big damn hurry. But we never ran away; not once in the war, except here. We ran like rabbits from a fox; sheddin' anythin' that was slowin' us down. We didn't stop until we got to Franklin. Franklin. The place stunk like death. The trenches had split open from all the bodies there. If Ector's men hadn't formed a rear guard, the Yankees would have been stabbin' bayonets in our backs; then the cavalry got 'em off of us. You mind rollin' me back in now? I seen all I want to see."

John brought me a sandwich. I didn't feel like socializing after seeing Nashville. How could something that long ago disturb me so much?

I got over my Nashville blues by supper. The train ride gave me a wonderful opportunity to meet other vets and share stories. It was a good time for me to be with John, too. He seemed to be enjoying himself as much as I was. At each stop we picked up more veterans. Once we got into Kentucky we were getting both Union and Confederate vets, and just Yankees in Pennsylvania. We mixed and mingled and enjoyed swapping stories from both sides of the lines.

On Thursday, June 30th, the triple engines slowed as the conductors announced our approach to Gettysburg. A military band played as they assembled a wheelchair brigade to roll us to our accommodations. A cavalry squad formed up at attention and escorted us along the way.

A tent city came into view. Row after row of large, floored canvas campaign tents were drawn up as only military engineers could do and arranged into wide streets, punctuated with enormous dining halls and numerous latrines and bath halls.

They rolled me to the camp for the Confederate Army of Tennessee. Rosters detailed exactly where each man and his attendant were to bunk, and to help seek out any old friends who might be there. There wasn't another man from my company. I was the last one left alive. But there was one man from my regiment, a few from Granbury's brigade and several from Cleburne's division. We were all billeted close together. In my almost eighty-eight years, I don't think I had ever seen anything like it.

―――――――――

There were boards detailing daily schedules. Thursday afternoon, right before supper, a boy scout on a bicycle brought me a registration packet, including a complete schedule of events and the menu at the mess tent. There was a neatly written heavy cardboard badge with my name, home town and service unit and dates printed on it.

A soldier from the "wheelchair brigade" came by to escort us to supper at six o'clock. It was about a block or so to the mess hall. It was a huge military field tent with a wooden floor. It was specially fixed with ramps and tall tables to accommodate wheelchairs, and there was plenty of seating for our attendants. The big tent had electric lights and large fans to help keep it cool. The food was top notch, just like it was a hotel or an officers' mess.

In my days as a soldier, food was pretty plain: beef or salt pork, beans, and corn bread. But it wasn't often that we had even that. Sometimes it had been hard tack and a little bacon or jerky. But often, it was only parched corn three times a day if we were lucky.

"Son, my brother Noah and I were the company scavengers. We rustled around to see what we could find, especially after a battle. We went through the pockets and field packs of dead soldiers from both sides and put what we found in burlap sacks. We was always glad to find cartridges, percussion caps, extra clothes, shoes or blankets. Sometimes we'd find a little coffee, sugar, food or tobacco. One fella had three cans of peaches in his gear. Why would a man go into battle carryin' peaches?" I laughed with John.

"We butchered dead horses or mules we found; it dang sure was better than starvin' to death."

"Once, near Tuscumbia, Alabama, right near the Tennessee River, some of us Texas boys kinda 'found' some hogs. We butchered 'em out and the whole company ate good for three days."

Friday, July 1 was "Reunion Day." We had the whole day to visit. Tours of the battlefield were offered throughout the day. John and I took one of these. As I sat and listened to the guides describe what had happened, I realized that what these men experienced here was so similar to the war I had seen hundreds of miles away. I could hear the Rebel yell as we crashed forward, the rattle of muskets and the roar of artillery, both the booming Napoleon twelve pound cannons and the shrill scream of the rifled three inch guns. The sour sulphur smell of gunpowder washed over me again as it had seventy-five years ago.

I realized I had tears streaming down my face as did the Union and Confederate vets around me. We shook hands and even embraced. We had all been through the same horrible ordeal. We had all stood at the open gates of hell and survived. We had been divided by war then, but we were united as survivors now. A new bond formed, a bond forged on the red-hot anvil of war, hammered by violence, but tempered by the passage of seventy-five years.

"John, I'm kinda glad you're here, and I don't mean just to push my wheelchair."

"I know, Dad. I'm glad I'm here, too."

Saturday, July 2nd, was designated Veterans' and Governors' Day. Speakers from the Grand Army of the Republic, which represented Union vets, took the stand. I had expected something quite different than what I heard.

An elderly man was helped to the podium. The microphone amplified a voice as weak as water. Instead of listing off the Union victories and our defeats, he spoke in a cracking voice of the lives that had been lost, the countless cripples and widows and orphans that had been created because politicians couldn't find a solution to a political problem. The soil of America had been stained with the blood of her finest young men to resolve with violence what they would not resolve with compromise. I was too far back to see the tears, but I could see him wiping them away with a handkerchief and hear them in his voice.

The United Confederate Veterans speaker next took the stand. His remarks were dead on center. We had fought and killed our own brothers. No one had won the war, but all had lost. He spoke of reconciliation and the desperate need to make sure that brother never rose up to strike brother again. I was deeply stirred by the thoughts they expressed. Silent tears rolled down my face without shame.

I hardly listened to the various governors who spoke. My heart was too full to listen or to talk. John sensed my mood and sat silently. As the crowd dispersed, many handshakes and embraces were exchanged between men who had worn the blue and the gray.

After lunch was a great parade that lasted two and a half hours. We were under canvas covers to protect us from the sun. Instead of regular bleachers, the tiers were built specifically to accommodate wheelchairs with folding chairs for our attendants.

Sharp, well-drilled infantry units paraded past the reviewing stands. Once they filled the field in perfect formation, their commanding officer ordered them to attention. He read a brief statement recognizing the heroism of all the veterans present. The hundreds and hundreds of neatly formed soldiers then fired a salute in our honor.

Cavalry units followed the infantry and demonstrated intricate field maneuvers. They charged the bleachers in line abreast formation, skidded to a perfect stop and presented their sabers in salute.

The artillery took the field next, drawn not by mules or horses, but by trucks. Their crews swarmed from under the canvas-covered trucks, and manhandled their 75 and 105 mm guns pointing away from the stands. They began firing from their left to right down the whole line until each gun had fired seven rounds. It was grand. I noticed I didn't break out into a sweat or begin shaking as I had done the last time I heard a cannon fire.

Mechanized artillery took the field next, the ugly tanks menacing with cannon and machine guns. I had never seen one before, and knew I was grateful they didn't exist during the war. The smoking tanks fell into a perfect line stretching completely across the reviewing field. On command, the turrets rotated until they were all pointing away from the bleachers. They fired seven rounds in perfect uniformity, rotated their cannon back toward the bleachers and exited the field. It sent a chill down my spine.

On cue, as the last tank wheezed off the field, the air was filled with nimble fighters and lumbering bombers. The bombers flew high in precise formation, circling back over the field. The fighters broke off into squadrons that flew above, below and between the bombers. They then swept across the field from right to left at full throttle not twenty feet above the ground. As quickly as they had appeared, they were gone.

Finally, boy scouts marched onto the parade ground carrying replicas of the regimental colors of every unit represented at the Reunion. I rose to cheer as our blue and white banner was announced. John held me by the waistband to steady me. The field was filled with flags of every color, but mostly variations of red, white and blue.

Sunday, July 3rd, was President's Day. It began with memorial services for those who had died at Gettysburg and on other battlefields. It was very moving. After a wonderful lunch and a nap, the wheelchair brigade took us to the main assembly area again to listen to an address by President Franklin Roosevelt just before dark. I don't remember being more excited. Even John, who was as unflappable as any man on God's green earth, was excited.

Roosevelt's Yankee accent was quite distinct, but familiar from his "fireside chats." I had seen his aides moving him near the speakers' platform in a wheelchair, but he had sturdy braces that allowed him to stand for his speech. He spoke of many things, of the Great Depression and the Dust Bowl, as tremendous obstacles that the country had overcome. "The Great American Civil War" was the worst tragedy ever to afflict this country. The need to heal those wounds had been our country's greatest obstacle to overcome. But our presence here gave proof of the success of that healing.

The sun sank below the mountains that the Union forces had defended so long ago, and it soon was dark. The lights did not come on. We sat in darkness as a man led us in prayer, then asked us to direct our eyes toward the hill known as Big Round Top. He explained that a memorial tower had been erected and an eternal flame was to burn at its peak. In the silence, a lone bugler on the hilltop played *Taps.* The haunting melody rang over the enraptured crowd. As the last note lingered in the still air, a flame burst forth on the top of the monument. The valley below erupted with our cheers. It echoed with the shouts of those old men scarred by the war who had found healing in reunion. I would never forget that moment.

Monday was the Fourth of July, the last day of the reunion. I spent the day visiting with Union and Confederate vets from all over the country. One fellow from Maine had a very well preserved uniform that he could still wear.

"Brother, turn around and let me get a good look at the front of that blue jacket." He grandly turned to show off the front of it with a couple of medals.

"Sure is pretty. Durin' the war we mostly saw 'em from the back side!" We all laughed, including the gentleman from Maine.

That night there was a steak dinner with all the trimmings, chocolate cake and ice cream. Just after dark, the sky came alive with a glorious fireworks display, by far the biggest I had ever seen. When it was over, we gathered in clusters here and there to talk until we couldn't talk any more. This had been the trip of a lifetime.

3

Last Trail West

July 5, 1938
Gettysburg, Pennsylvania

AFTER AN EARLY BREAKFAST, THE wheelchair brigade took me to the station and helped me get on the train. John and I sat looking at the rich farmland of Pennsylvania. I felt the need to talk to John about all the things I had never gotten around to telling the family or those things that I had not been able to talk about.

I felt a very strong sense of inner peace, of a great release from burdens. The ghosts who had haunted my memory for so long were gone.

Aaron Lloyd Turner, Brownfield,
Texas, 1938, dressed up for
the trip to Gettysburg.

My time at the reunion had starkly made a point to me. My time on this earth was short, very short. There were some things I had left undone. There were stories that needed to be told. Things hidden for seventy-five years needed to see the light of day. The only way I knew to approach the task was to start at the beginning.

Since John was a little boy, I had known that he was different in some intangible way from my other sons. His presence had a peaceful calming effect on others. It still did. It made him an especially good law man, a good husband and good father. He was a good son and brother, too. It must have been intended for John to be the one with me as I unfolded these parts of my life story that had been too difficult to put into words, even to Ella.

I talked and John listened. He nodded his head or asked questions to show he was paying attention, but from Gettysburg to Brownfield, from breakfast to bedtime for three days, I poured out my soul.

I told him of those days when I had endured an alcoholic, abusive step-father. I told him of the war. Chickamauga, Chattanooga, Ringgold Gap, Resaca, Picket's Mill and all the battles leading up to the fall of Atlanta tumbled out. I told him of the horrors I had experienced at Picket's Mill. I had never spoken of these things. I told him of the Tennessee Campaign of 1864 and the field of slaughter at Franklin. Even Ella had never known what had happened there. I told him of the cattle drives to Sedalia, Abilene and Dodge. I told him of the glory of my youth and the friends I lost along the way.

When I finally reached a conclusion, in peaceful, emotional exhaustion and completeness, a few tears rolled silently down my weathered old face. The job was done. The stories told. The need fulfilled. And in its place was peace; a peace I had never known.

"Thanks for lettin' me bend your ear for three days straight, son. I don't know what I would have done if you hadn't been here to listen to an old man's stories."

John sat quietly for a moment. "Thanks for tellin' me all these things, Dad. I'm really glad that I could be with you. This has been the trip of a lifetime for me."

"My family always pushed farther west as they settled. I moved farther west all my life. This trip from Gettysburg back to Brownfield is my last trail west. I've finally got the loose ends in my life wrapped up. I'm ready to cross the last river."

4

Goodbye

Summer, 1938
Brownfield, Texas

IT WAS GOOD TO BE HOME. I TOOK to sitting on the back porch on warm evenings with Ella while I smoked my pipe like we used to do. The pressure to tell all of my stories had ended before the train returned to Brownfield, but I gradually rolled out a little at a time to Ella and any of the kids or grandchildren I could get still long enough to listen.

After supper each night, we listened to the radio. Pappy O'Daniel was running for governor. He had sponsored a band called "The Light Crust Doughboys" in honor of the flour company that was one of his major supporters. It helped us pass the time.

Ella was getting very short of breath and her legs were swelling. The doctor said her heart had finally worn out. He increased her tincture of digitalis and gave her a "water pill" without much improvement.

In November, I didn't hear her rattling around in the kitchen. I picked up my crutches and stumped into her bedroom. My sweet Ella lay pale and cold in the bed.

Her services at the Methodist church found all of my living sons and daughters in attendance except Lela from California. At my request, the congregation sang *Shall We Gather at the River*. I bought a six unit family plot in the Brownfield Cemetery within sight of Marjorie's grave and laid the love of my life to rest.

My birthday in December marked my eighty-eighth year on

this earth. John had hired a man to sit with me most of the day and a dependable lady stayed all night. I was confined to the bed in the last stages of heart failure.

Christmas and New Year's Day passed unmarked by me. John, Effie and their boys came by, as did Ed and Minta, and Ruth and her family. There were letters and cards from the kids which I read and set aside to read again. The little green drops had lost their magic. I struggled to breathe, drowning in my own blood.

They finally placed me in the Brownfield Hospital. I knew I would not leave there alive.

But I felt a peace that filled my failing heart. I looked back on a long life filled to the brim. I had no regrets. I had no debts of money or deeds to repay. I was ready to depart this life for whatever lay ahead, for it held no fear for me.

―――――――

Dad finally slipped away in his sleep at the hospital with a smile on his old face. He had told all of us that he was eager to cross over to that land where there is no night, no suffering, pain or sorrow.

His funeral at the Methodist church was packed to the point of standing room only. He would have been pleased to know so many thought so much of him. Of course we sang *Shall We Gather at the River* at his services. All of the kids were there except my sister in California.

Dad, as a life-long member of the Odd Fellow Lodge, had a paid up burial policy that covered most of his funeral and burial expenses. What they didn't cover was paid by a fund for Confederate Veterans.

We laid him to rest with his pipe in his pocket next to Mother in the Brownfield Cemetery. As the brief graveside services were held, a flock of slate gray sandhill cranes called out as they circled slowly overhead. It was as if they had been sent as a special honor guard for this fine old man and veteran.

―――――――

I was executor of his estate. By the time the house and few belonging were sold and the few accounts had been paid, he left behind two hundred dollars.

This was a man who had been raised on a league and a labor of fine crop and pasture land. As a teenager and young man, he had tens of thousands of dollars in his hands from driving maverick cattle to the northern markets. As a grown man he owned a debt-free twenty square mile ranch of the best cattle country around, stocked with six hundred head of the finest mother cows in Texas, a freight business and a small store. Relentless drought, coupled with blizzards and poor prices finally drove him from the land he loved. The "Great Depression" and "Dust Bowl" chipped away until there wasn't much left but two hundred dollars.

As the world counts wealth, he died a poor man. But the legacy my father left was priceless. He taught us the worth of hard work and family. He taught us values based on a belief in God, honesty, decency, loyalty, trust, fairness and forgiveness. He left this life a very rich man.

Author's Note

              WHAT BEGAN AS A CHALLENGE TO write historical fiction blossomed into a work of love. Aaron Lloyd Turner died before I was born. My father has limited memories of him. As I learned more and more about his life, I came to see what a truly remarkable man he was and what a uniquely American experience that was his life.

He survived the horrors of the American Civil War. The trauma of battle, of killing in close combat, the loss of family and friends to the violence of war, and the depravations of being a prisoner of war were seared into his memory. And yet, he survived the furnace of war and was hammered on the anvil of life to become a man of great strength and depth of character.

He learned first-hand the brutal unfairness of Reconstruction in Texas, seeing all the liberties we hold so dear stripped away. And yet, he persevered and saw freedom restored.

He was a first-hand participant in the American phenomena of the great Texas cattle culture that rose like a phoenix from the ashes of war. He drove cattle north to market. He was there for stampedes, raging rivers, Indian attacks and all the things that have tantalized the American mind for a hundred and fifty years.

He was also there to see the coming of the railroad, barb wire and windmills that forever changed the cattle industry, brought about the transformation of the cattle kingdom into ranching as we know it today.

He was there to see forces beyond his control relentlessly hammer away at all he had put together. Droughts, blizzards and market forces finally robbed him of his land and cattle, but not his dignity.

Aaron saw the world change from muskets to machine guns,

from horses to automobiles, and the arrival of airplanes, electricity and telephones. He saw America change from a rural agricultural society to one driven by industrial forces. He didn't always like the changes, but he adapted and survived.

Seeing this through his eyes has given me much insight and understanding of events of which I knew little, and a great appreciation of the legacy left for me. In knowing him vicariously, I came to love the great-grandfather I never met, and yet came to know and appreciate.

He had been the hub around which his family turned. When he died, the family scattered, only to reunite for funerals.

My relatives will know and notice that I tinkered with dates and locations, but the stories in this book are true to character, if not always to content. As J. Frank Dobie mentions, a story teller has the right and duty to "salt and pepper the truth to make it more enjoyable to the reader." Some parts are saltier than others.

When I retired in 2012, I drove to Seagraves to visit the graves of my grandparents, John and Effie Turner, and my uncle, Ronald Turner. I came back through Brownfield so that I could pay my respects at the graves of Aaron Lloyd and Ella Turner, as I had been doing since I was a child. For the first time, it struck me that there were only five occupied graves in the plot. I had never noticed there was an empty grave by Aaron and Ella. A cell phone call to the cemetery association revealed that grave was left for any descendant of Aaron who chose to claim it.

As I stood at the foot of his grave, a small flock of sand hill cranes circled slowly overhead and landed only feet away in the unusual cold mist that shrouded the cemetery. At that moment, I felt as if the grave had been left by him for me, the great-grandson he had never met, that had come to love him. I have asked my son, Aaron Lyles Turner, to bury my ashes there.

Aaron Lloyd Turner died a man with few earthly possessions. But my life has been greatly enriched by the legacy he passed to John Turner, and to my father, Aaron Lynn Turner. It is a legacy that has influenced my life and that I have consciously tried to pass on to my children and grandchildren. The 'Circle' has not been broken. Aaron lives on through us. We *shall* gather at the river.

www.ingramcontent.com/pod-product-compliance
Lightning Source LLC
Chambersburg PA
CBHW031946010726
47493CB00007B/2101